A Brush with Murder

A WATERCOLOR MYSTERY

Gail Langer Karwoski

www.blackrosewriting.com

The author grants the final approval for this literary material.

First printing

This is a work of fiction. Names, characters, businesses, places, events, and incidents are either the products of the author's imagination or used in a fictitious manner. Any resemblance to actual persons, living or dead, or actual events is purely coincidental.

ISBN: 978-1-68433-974-7
Library of Congress Control Number: 2022900051
PUBLISHED BY BLACK ROSE WRITING
www.blackrosewriting.com

Printed in the United States of America
Suggested Retail Price (SRP) $19.95

A Brush with Murder is printed in EB Garamond

*As a planet-friendly publisher, Black Rose Writing does its best to eliminate unnecessary waste to reduce paper usage and energy costs, while never compromising the reading experience. As a result, the final word count vs. page count may not meet common expectations.

Praise for

A Brush with Murder

"Noted children's author Gail Langer Karwoski gives us her first adult mystery novel, a tale of feisty, modern women friends who find themselves on an art retreat in a dreamy southern locale featuring azalea gardens and thoroughbred horses—where every moment unexpectedly drips with new dangers, and cadmium-red herrings appear, then blur into obscurity, like drops of wet pigment on watercolor paper. Keeping us guessing until the very last moment, Karwoski paints a story of intrigue and drama that will delight—and tickle—every reader, until the murderer's portrait is finally revealed."
–Allan Forrest Small, award-winning Watercolor Artist

"A fun, clean, easy read with lots of intrigue. Peek into the world of thoroughbred horses. Visit a painters' retreat, and follow clues to solve a murder. I would love to see Jane and her fellow watercolor artists return for another mystery to solve. A must-read for those who love cozy mysteries."
–Muriel Ellis Pritchett, author of *Rotten Bananas and the Emerald Dream*

"This cozy is like curling up in an armchair with a mug of hot tea and listening in on a group of friends as they talk about painting and unexpected intrigue. In this fast-paced and entertaining book, delightful characters stumble onto a murder scene while at a painters' retreat. Join in their adventures as they solve the mystery!"
–Debra Harden, Board of Directors, Oconee Cultural Arts Foundation

For Patricia A. Adams,
who began the Tuesday Watercolor Group,
Women of Watercolor, aka, WOW!

Class Roster
Alexander Robert Treville
Plein Air Watercolor Workshop
Gardens & Horses Retreat Center

Sheryl Calhoun. *"Golden Girls." Capri pant set. Came with Catherine Manfred. Worked with Margaret Culpepper. Rupert Horne's aunt.*

Margaret Culpepper *Slim, stiff, snobby, salt & pepper hair. Lives in St. Simons, formerly Gilbertville. Granddaughter - Maggie.*

Amanda Golden *Art teacher - middle school. Lives in Charlotte. Came with Rachel Sanchez. Shirley Temple curls, dimples.*

Arthur King *Accountant. Lives in Gilbertville. Widower. Owns horses at Gardens & Horses.*

Catherine Manfred *"Golden Girls." Capri pant set. Came with Sheryl Calhoun. Worked for Stauntons. Has asthma.*

Judy McAndrew *Short blonde hair. Nickname Dee Dee. Maiden name Thaxton - Harry's sister. Went to SCAD. Lives in Columbia SC.*

Donna Norton

Alicia Pickridge *Younger than husband. Dropped out of SCAD. Loves horses.*

Teddy Pickridge *Alicia is his second wife. Grew up in Gilbertville.*

Maggie Ramsey *Margaret's granddaughter. Age 15. Rides horses. Lives in Gilbertville.*

Jane Roland

Rachel Sanchez *Art teacher – elementary school. Lives in Charlotte. Came with Amanda Golden. Hates gambling, horse racing.*

Saundra Staunton *Black hair. Husband Walter (expensive suit). Lancelot's owners. Has stable. Knows Catherine & Sheryl.*

Grace Tanner

Harriet Warren *Redhead. Nickname Harry. Maiden name Thaxton – Dee Dee's sister. Went to SCAD. Lives in Columbia SC.*

Pam Gerald

A Brush with Murder

CHAPTER ONE

As soon as Jane's car turned into the gated entrance, Donna said, "Well, look at Grace sitting there. She looks like a painting, doesn't she?"

Jane giggled. It was true. Their friend and fellow painter, Grace Tanner, was seated on a black wrought iron bench beside the brick stairway that led up to her front door. Her luggage was piled in a neat stack at her feet. Her platinum hair gleamed in the morning sunshine. Framed by the deep green of the camellia bushes on either side of the entrance to her house, Grace looked like she'd been posed by an artist. Even her sundress, awash in misty strokes of lilac and pink, contributed to the impression: She was the Portrait of an Elegant Woman Waiting to Travel.

"Good Morning," Grace called. A smile brushed across her face, altering the placement of the highlights and shadows on her perfectly-proportioned facial features.

"Have you been waiting long?" Jane said. 'I had to stop for gas."

"Oh, no, I think I probably got out here early. I was just too excited to sleep."

Jane picked up one of Grace's bags. "Donna says you look like a painting, sitting there so composed. Rather appropriate since we're going to an artist retreat."

If truth be told, Grace did not feel nearly as composed as she looked. She had worried through the night and slept fitfully. It was ridiculous, she knew. She was 62 years old, and painting had been her joy for as long as she could remember. Ever since she'd retired from teaching, she'd devoted her afternoons to painting landscapes and florals in watercolor. Blossoming trees bending over bubbling streams, pastel-colored bouquets in shimmering glass vases. But this was her first artist retreat. Although she was going to the Gardens and Horses Retreat with friends from her Tuesday painting group, she could feel the butterflies flapping around her insides. What if everyone else at the retreat was a better painter than she was? After all, she'd never painted outdoors - "en plein air" - before. What if she couldn't manage to keep the pigments wet enough to work with? When she was a teacher, Grace had often reminded her fourth graders that mistakes are how we learn. But in spite of that sage-old advice, she knew she'd simply die of embarrassment if she was the worst painter at the retreat.

Donna called out the window, "Okay if I keep the front for now?" she called. "It's a long drive. We can swap partway if you want."

"That's fine with me," Grace said. "I thought we might want to stop after an hour or so and take turns with the driving. So Jane doesn't have to drive all the way to South Carolina."

All three of them had brought portable painting easels as well as packs of paper and bags of gear for the retreat. They each had rolling suitcases holding a week's worth of clothing and toiletries. Although Jane's sporty red SUV was the largest of their cars, its luggage compartment was already crammed full, and they hadn't even started to load any of Grace's bags.

Pushing and shoving at the heap of baggage, Jane managed to stand their three suitcases in a row with the other bags around them. But some of the bags were full of tubes of watercolor paint. Jane worried that they'd have a mess if the tubes got crushed. Plus, the zippered bags holding their easels were awkward shapes, and there seemed to be no way to pile them in without sacrificing the driver's view of the road.

Frowning, Jane finally said, Maybe we better take everything out and start again." So she and Grace took out all the bags, laid them on the lawn, and repacked.

"Do you need my help?" Donna called.

"Now she asks!" Jane moaned as she shut the rear door.

Jane was backing down the driveway when Grace said, "Thank you so much for volunteering to drive, Jane. I just don't see how we'd have managed to fit all that stuff in my compact. I guess we could have packed lighter, but still. Between all that painting gear and a week's worth of clothing."

"I never have understood how your mother knew," Donna said. She swiveled around to face Grace in the back seat. Donna's sparkly beaded earrings swished against her shoulders as she moved. But her turquoise beret - the one that she loved to wear when the group went to gallery openings - perched firmly on the marshmallow of white hair that framed her face.

Grace blinked. "My mother? Knew what?"

"That you'd live up to your name. Grace. How'd she knew that you'd turn out to be so gracious?" Donna said. "We've hardly even started to drive, and you've already thanked Jane for taking her car. Plus, you offered to drive, and you've been as helpful as you could with the luggage. You have the best manners of anyone I've ever met, you're gracious like your name. So how did she know?"

Grace smiled, but she felt a bit flustered by the praise and not at all sure if this required an answer. "Well, I guess I never thought about it before. I suppose she just liked the sound of the name."

Jane glanced at Donna and shook her head. "I had no idea where you were going with that question."

This wasn't the first time that Donna's remarks had struck Jane as peculiar. The newest addition to their painting group, Donna Norton had moved to the area with her husband just four years ago, and she d come to the art center in search of friends. Like Grace, Donna had been an elementary school teacher before retiring. But there the similarity ended. Donna had taught in a very small, very rural community out West; in the same community where she was born. The other women in their Tuesday painting group were from upscale, suburban backgrounds, but Donna's childhood stood out - just like her palette and paintings. As a child, Donna had ridden horses through the hills. She'd milked cows and slopped pigs. Her paintings were full of livestock, old barns, and rusted trucks. Like her art, her clothes and her conversation were a mix of practical, knock-around-the-yard work-wear and bold, unexpected flashes of color.

The drive to the retreat would take nearly four hours, but it seemed much shorter once they were on the highway. So much to chat about - updates on the doings of children and grandchildren, husbands and sisters, summer travel plans and art exhibits that they'd viewed in galleries and online. The three exchanged news about the other members of their Tuesday painting group who weren't able to join them for the retreat: Pam Gerald had decided not to come because she was up to her ears in boxes as she emptied out her house in preparation for down-sizing. Maisie O'Rourke's husband had just retired, and they were off visiting another of the exotic locations on their bucket list. And Betsy Winkle was transitioning between work and retirement; she still had deadlines to meet on the latest manual that she was editing. Mixed in between the swirls of conversation, the three stopped and swapped drivers, got a quick sandwich at a picturesque cafe, and filled Jane's car with gas.

Just past three in the afternoon, they pulled into Gardens and Horses, where the retreat would take place. Following the hand-lettered wooden signs, they located the resort hotel with its imposing facade of mahogany and stone.

"Let's bring our things up to our rooms," Jane suggested as she parked under the portico. For this retreat, they had decided to splurge and get themselves separate rooms. "Then meet down here in the lobby at quarter of four and take a walk around the grounds before dinner."

"Always the organizer," chuckled Donna.

"And aren't we lucky that she is!" Grace added, with a wink at Jane.

Jane Roland blushed. In addition to being the group's unofficial organizer, she was also its quietest member. Her short, neat brown hair and trim figure matched her personality. She was a woman who didn't want to be the center of attention or appear bossy, but she was secretly proud that she knew how to take charge of every situation. Jane had always lived on her own, even when it wasn't "done" for a woman to choose to not marry. Since she'd never relied on a partner to make decisions or help with any task, she exuded competence and confidence.

Thirty minutes later, Jane was waiting in the lobby when the elevator discharged Grace and Donna.

"Oh my, look at this place. It looks more like a greenhouse than a hotel lobby," Donna said. "I bet we could find enough flowers to paint right here without going out to the gardens."

"You know, that's not a bad idea - painting in here," Grace said. "I wonder if we could come in here if it gets hot in the afternoons and set up our easels around those sofas. There's plenty of room. Do you think the hotel staff would mind?"

"We'd need to get permission," Jane said. "But they probably wouldn't mind. The place is spacious - we certainly wouldn't be in anybody's way. And the other guests might enjoy watching painters at work. I'll ask the manager when we get back from our walk."

On the counter, there were stacks of glossy brochures that opened to a map of the sprawling grounds. Jane opened one and chose their walking route. "Let's follow this Live Oak Path. It leads to the center of the grounds, where the Horse Museum is."

"Oh, yes, let's go see the gardens around that museum," Grace said. "My guess is they're spectacular."

"Unless the horses have trampled the plantings to death," Donna said. "I never could keep any flowers around my barns when I had horses."

They set out walking and found themselves on a soft, dappled trail under thick, twisty limbs of live oaks. Passing signs for a greenhouse, a groundskeeper's residence, and a rose garden, they walked toward the center of the gardens where the Thoroughbred Horse Museum was housed in a stately brick building. Surrounding the museum were life-sized bronze statues of horses in various poses - running, jumping, and standing at attention. Underneath each statue, on square marble pedestals, were bronze plaques about the award-winning thoroughbreds that each statue represented. Jane and Grace paused to read the plaques, but Donna grew restless with the lengthy histories and walked ahead.

"Which way is north?" Donna called from the other side of a spectacular rhododendron planting. The bushes formed an umbrella above her head and were covered in lavender blooms. "I think we'll get the most shade on the north side. That's where we should stake out a spot for our easels. Do you know how many people are going to be at this retreat? Maybe we should pick our spot and get out here before the others, tomorrow morn."

Jane and Grace finished reading the horse plaques and ambled in the direction of Donna's voice. They heard her exclaim, "Oh, my, there's a reflecting pool over here. Now this is where we could get some great paintings. Oh, my, this is pretty!" Donna continued. "Wait 'til you see the way these trees reflect in the water! I bet everyone's going to want to ...."

When Donna's voice trailed off, Jane and Grace looked at each other. Donna was 75, the oldest member of the group, and they knew she had a weak heart. It wouldn't be the first time that she'd gotten dizzy in the heat.

"Donna?" Jane called. "Everything alright?"

"Oh, my. Oh, my. Oh, my," Donna babbled. "I think I need a place to sit down."

Jane and Grace hurried along the path to catch up with her.

The rhododendron path opened onto a walkway surrounding a pool with raised cement sides. The pool was rectangular, about 20 feet long and 8 foot wide. Irises lined the brick walkway, and giant oaks formed a living ceiling above their heads. The pool was cluttered with dark leaves, and the branches of the trees cast shadows on its surface. In the afternoon sun, the water was a mix of rich colors - sparkly gold highlights, murky black shadows, and blood-red depths.

Jane and Grace found Donna sitting, head in her hands, on a large cement bench shaped like a Victorian sofa. Rushing to her side, Jane grabbed her friend's wrist to check her pulse.

Grace slipped her arm around Donna's neck and sat down beside her. "Do you feel faint?"

"No. Well, yes, I guess I do," Donna blurted. "But it's not my heart, it's ...." She waved her hand in the direction of the reflecting pool. "It's that."

Both Jane and Grace looked where Donna had gestured.

"Go over to the pool," Donna said. "You can't see it from here. It's at the bottom."

Jane and Grace glanced at each other, then cautiously approached the pool. Shadows and leaves obscured their view until they stood by the very edge of the water. And there it was, sprawled in the bottom of the shallow pool - a magnificent horse. Not a bronze statue, but a real animal, with its feathery mane suspended in the water, mouth open as if to breathe, and legs splayed out as if to kick in protest. One of the horse's eyes was clearly visible in the murk. Large, brown, and luminescent, the eye reflected one piercing glint of sunlight. That highlight, often the painter's last stroke - the touch that brought the portrait to life - was the feature that Jane would see in the nightmares to come.

CHAPTER TWO

When her alarm went off at 7 am, Jane opened her eyes. Where was she? The room was quiet and dim as a cathedral, any hints of sunlight subdued by heaps and drapes of flowered fabric. She was lying in a bed so soft and so squishy that it bubbled up to her cheeks and practically swallowed her. It was an effort to merely shift the position of her head to examine her unfamiliar surroundings.

On most mornings, Jane was the early-to-rise type; eager to dart from her bed, determined to tackle the day's agenda. But last night, she'd slept deep and long. Maybe that's why her thoughts were fuzzy? Or maybe it was the wine? It had looked like a very expensive bottle of wine. Vintage, with plenty of dust and cursive letters adorning the label. Did expensive wine pack more of a punch?

Finally, from the depths of this valley of pillow-topped amnesia, snatches began to emerge. The luxury hotel at the Gardens and Horses Retreat. The drive to South Carolina. The walk along a sun-dappled path. Once Jane managed to block in the backdrop, a portrait of yesterday began to emerge.

There was the reflecting pool. The dead horse. The shock of it. Frantic attempts to call the lobby on their cell phones, which did not get service at the reflecting pool. The panicked conversation about whether to leave a light-headed Donna alone on the bench - and possibly in danger, who knew? - while she and Grace hurried back to the hotel to get help. Finally, all three decided to return to the lobby together. Their frightening walk along the twilight path, arm in arm - not another person in sight. The breathless wait for the clerk in the lobby to finish checking in another guest. Would the young woman never give the guest the key and turn her attention to them? Until the moment when Donna could not contain herself for a single second longer and blurted out: "We saw a horse! A dead horse!"

The clerk's puzzled expression as she looked up. "Oh, the museum is open today? It's usually closed on Sundays, you know. So the stuffed horse upset you? It does bother some people." Her enforced calm, her practiced smile as she orated to all three of them as well as the guest that was checking in. "You see, that horse was our most famous thoroughbred. A champion. A legend, really, among the South Carolina horse community - Home On The Range. We called him Homer for short. He brought us national and international medals. It seemed a shame to bury him; such a magnificent animal. The decision was made to stuff...."

"No, no, no," Donna wailed. "This horse was dead."

By then, other guests and some staff members had caught pieces of the peculiar conversation. They turned to stare at Donna and the clerk.

"Well, yes," the clerk said. "of course, the horse was dead. When he was retired from racing in 1952, he lived out his life - comfortably - in our stables. After his death, which was from natural causes...."

"No, no, no," Donna wailed again. "The horse was drowned. Or I think he drowned. In the reflecting pool. Nothing natural about it. Horses are natural swimmers."

They never did learn how the manager got wind of the commotion. Perhaps the clerk had discreetly pushed a button on her phone to summon help. When Rupert Horne materialized, he was a wonder of efficiency, as courteous as a British butler in an Agatha Christie mystery. Somehow, he whisked them away from the hubbub of the lobby and into his quiet, wood-paneled office. A pitcher of sweetened ice tea and a plate of scones awaited them on his cherry-wood desk. He poured each of them generous glasses before leaving them seated on leather-cushioned chairs while he hurried off to attend to unpleasant matters involving a horse carcass and police. Evidently, the horse was somehow fished out and removed from sight before Mr. Horne rejoined them, followed by a policeman.

The policeman asked them to repeat their story. He held a nifty little notepad and wrote his notes with a mechanical pencil, just like a detective on TV's "Law and Order".

While Jane described how they'd discovered the horse - all the horrid, graphic details - Mr. Horne avoided looking in her eyes. Instead, he stared at his slender, manicured fingertips, which he held together as if he was about to sing "The Itsy Bitsy Spider" to an unruly toddler.

Finally - and by then, it was pretty late - Mr. Horne led them to the hotel's restaurant where a five-course dinner awaited them, complements of the house. And then the hotel owner, himself - a Mr. Edmondson - visited their table and brought them a bottle of wine "from our cellars."

Donna hadn't managed to put together a coherent sentence since she confronted the desk clerk. And the bit about wine cellars had sent Jane's mind wandering off to Edgar Allan Poe. But Grace - thank goodness - had saved the dinner conversation with her polite questions about the greenhouse on the grounds. The owner promised them a personal tour of the greenhouse as he poured the dark-as-blood wine into cut-glass stems. Then he suggested that it might be best to be "discreet regarding their unusual - or should I say, horrifying - discovery." After all, there was no need to cast shadows over what promised to be an exceptional painter's retreat. "And in such a lovely setting," he added with a satisfied smile.

Grace did manage to slip in a request about painting in the lobby if the afternoons should get too hot. Yes, that would be fine, Mr. Edmonson agreed. In fact, the man was so eager to make this ugly incident disappear, he might have agreed to providing an extra night's stay for free - if only Jane had thought of asking.

Jane sighed. Her mind was operational again. Time to get her body mobile. She waded through the bed's luxury linens and dived off the plush mattress onto the plush carpet. Their plan was to meet for breakfast in the hotel dining room at eight. That would give them plenty of time before the retreat began at nine in the hotel's lobby.

Although Jane tried to think about painting as she dressed, she simply couldn't concentrate on colors or compositions. Details about the dead horse kept distracting her. How did a horse manage to stumble into a reflecting pool with raised sides? Why would it drown in water so shallow that a foal could easily stand up? It really didn't make sense. If the horse didn't drown - if it died of other causes - why was it lying in the bottom of that pool? And where did it come from? Jane assumed it was a horse stabled on the grounds, but perhaps not. There were several equine events that took place here. In the garden's glossy brochures, Jane had seen information about people bringing their horses for trail rides. And when they'd arrived yesterday, she'd noticed at least three horse trailers in the parking lot. All the questions buzzing around her head were as pesky as yellow jackets. Jane was halfway out the door before she realized that her room key was still sitting on the night table. She dashed back to grab it.

The aromas wafting from the breakfast area were a welcome salve for Jane's harried mind. To her delight, she found that the buffet was as bountiful as the bedding. Donna and Grace reported that they'd slept very comfortably, too. All agreed their rooms were wonderfully luxurious. By unspoken agreement, none of them mentioned the dead horse. As they lingered over a second cup of tea and one more of those yummy little pastries - after all, they were on vacation! - the three grew quiet. They watched the other guests browsing the buffet. Which of the guests were other painters attending their retreat? There was a very attractive black-haired woman wearing a flame red scarf. She looked like an artist. But she was with an older man who wore a custom-made suit. Surely he was a business executive, not an artist?

At quarter to nine, Jane glanced at her phone. "We better go get our supplies. The opening session starts in fifteen minutes."

Jane brushed her teeth and applied sunscreen to her face before hefting her easel bag over her shoulder. Using her hip to hold the door open, she tried to maneuver her roller bag of painting supplies out of her room, but the bag got stuck on the thick rug. Grace who was in the hall, rushed over to help.

Donna emerged from her room. "Oh, wait a minute," she called as she dropped her easel on the carpet and darted back into her room. She came out holding her turquoise beret. "You know, I was thinking: Thank goodness they gave us rooms next to each other."

"That was thoughtful, wasn't it," Grace said. "It seems like this hotel prides itself on attention to detail."

"Well, we're certainly paying for it," Jane said. "I guess that's what you get for five-star accommodations."

"I feel much safer knowing your rooms are next to mine," Donna said as they got into the elevator. "Even though we all have cell phones, I'm still glad we're in shouting distance."

"I agree," Grace said. "Modern technology is terrific, until it isn't. And it seems like cell phones never work when you really need them."

"I'll say," Donna said. "Remember how none of our phones worked by the reflecting pool?" But she said no more because they were leaving the elevator and entering the flowery lobby.

In the lobby, Jane spotted the striking, black-haired woman from breakfast. The woman held a wooden portable easel strapped over her shoulder, so she must be one of the artists in the retreat. The woman's eyes met Jane's, and they both nodded.

Two silver-haired women were sitting on the couch. Each wore an embroidered top in soft pastel shades with matching capri pants and Keds. They looked like extras from the TV series, "Golden Girls." Each had a rolling bag of painting supplies by her knees.

A few awkward moments of silence passed as the artists assembled. The retreat had been limited to fifteen painters, and by ten minutes past nine, Jane counted thirteen people in the lobby with bags or rolling carts of art supplies. Most were older women, although there was one man chatting with the black-haired woman. There was also one teenage girl standing beside a tall, slim woman with salt-and-pepper hair. Perhaps a grandmother and granddaughter attending the retreat together? Jane gave a silent thanks that the teen had not been the one to discover the dead horse - what a terrible impression that would have left on a young artist!

Finally, a middle-aged man in a tie-dyed tee and paint-stained jeans bustled into the lobby. He was wearing a stuffed-full backpack with a pad of watercolor paper sticking out of the large front pocket. Trailing him was a bald man and a woman who looked like she was in her forties. Both of the trailers carried bags, so they were almost certainly artists in the retreat. That would complete the roster of fifteen class members.

Donna poked Jane and Grace and indicated the man with the backpack. "He must be our instructor. He looks a lot older in person than the picture on his website, doesn't he?"

Jane thought the instructor seemed flustered, as if he'd overslept and needed a cup of coffee.

"Let's move to the patio, so we can talk," the instructor suggested and led the group out the French doors and onto a flagstone patio bordered with brick half-walls.

"Welcome to Gardens and Horses, one of my favorite places for plein air painting," he announced.

One of the painters sat down on a white metal chair by a matching round table.

"Yes, do sit down. I don't know if there are enough chairs for all of you. Maybe some of you can perch on the brick walls? Don't worry. I don't go in for long intros. I'm Alexander Robert Treville, your instructor, as you've probably figured out. I'm sure that by now, you've browsed my website to familiarize yourself with my work. So you know that I specialize in landscapes, particularly Southern landscapes. I'm a signature member of the American Watercolor Society, as well as...."

One of the women raised her hand, "Mr. Treville, before you...."

Treville turned to her. "Please. Call me Alec." He scanned the faces of the group. "And don't hesitate to ask questions. No need to raise your hand. Just jump right in. Of all the items in a student's bag of supplies, I always say that questions are her most essential tools."

Alec flashed a disarming smile. "I'm sure that some of you noticed that my initials - A, R, T - stand for art. So I like to say that my parents predetermined my profession before they could assess whether I had any talent or interest in the arts. Too bad for me that our last name didn't begin with an S. Then they could have named me Ian Alexander and predetermined my career as a surgeon - get it? I'm A Surgeon. I would have been destined for much more lucrative work. On the other hand, I've never been wild about blood red as the dominant color in my work."

The students all smiled. Jane spotted a table with three empty chairs and motioned Grace and Donna to follow her as she edged through the group.

"I know that many of you have questions about painting outdoors," Alec continued. "How to keep the paper wet enough is the first concern that most of us have when we begin painting with watercolors en plein air."

Grace raised her hand. "Mr. Treville, um, Alec, I wondered if you recommend working with a lighter weight paper outdoors. If 140 lb. paper would retain moisture longer than 300?"

"Excellent question," Alec said. He zipped open his backpack. Several pencils and an eraser tumbled out, but he ignored them and held up a brush. "This is the ART brush. Capital A, capital R, capital T." Smug smile. "My name. I developed it with the Pastel Company. It's a blend of natural fibers - which hold more water than synthetics - and synthetic fibers, which retain an excellent point. It belongs in the painting bag of every watercolor artist who hopes to work outdoors. An essential tool."

"That's three," Donna whispered.

"Three what?" Grace asked.

"Three essential tools," Donna said.

Grace looked up from her notepad. "Oh, I only heard him mention one - that brush he developed."

"Well, that's the one that he didn't ignore."

"Huh?" Grace said.

"He ignored your question and that lady's question. So that's two 'essential tools' that he skipped right past."

Jane grinned at the exchange between her friends. But her attention, as well as everybody else's, was suddenly drawn to the French doors. An older man in a starched white shirt and elegant suit was holding the doors open and scanning the assembled group. "Saundra?" he said.

The black-haired woman, who was seated at the adjacent table, looked up. "Oh. Walter." She looked at the instructor, then at the man. "This is our class, dear. Our opening session," she said. "Is it important? Can it wait?"

Walter scowled. "Yes it is important, and no, it cannot wait. It's about Lance."

Saundra looked puzzled.

"Our horse, darling. Lancelot du Lac. They fished him out of the reflecting pool last night. Dead."

CHAPTER THREE

At quarter past eleven, Jane opened the door to the conference room. She was the first to arrive, but Alec had left his backpack on a chair at one end of the mahogany table. Jane took the seat directly to the left of the instructor's chair. She'd already noted that Alec was right-handed, so that would give her the best angle to watch his demonstration. She plopped her painting bag on the chair beside her and propped her easel against the chair on the other side to save seats for Grace and Donna.

The air conditioning in the conference room was, like everything else in the hotel, bountiful, and she considered running back up to her room for a sweater. But she didn't want to lose her claim to these three seats. Rubbing her arms to warm up, Jane looked around. The conference room was a larger version of the manager's office - wood-paneled, leather-chaired. There were two vases brimming with bouquets on a side table that held pitchers of iced tea, glasses, linen napkins, and plates of scones. She couldn't see the rugs, of course. To protect them from paint, they'd been covered with black plastic, the edges taped to the mahogany baseboard. But she assumed they were Oriental.

Jane glanced at her phone: Thirteen minutes until the demonstration was scheduled to start. Two of the other painters came in.

Jane smiled at the woman and bald man who took the chairs at the far end of the immense oval table. "I'm Jane Roland," she said. "From Atkinsville. A small town in Georgia."

"I know Atkinsville," said the woman. "We used to live in Savannah. I'm Alicia Pickridge. And this is my husband, Teddy."

"Glad to meet you," Jane said.

As they exchanged geographical intros, Jane noted that Teddy was quite a bit older than Alicia. Was Alicia his second marriage? Jane didn't have to wonder long about the couple's history since Alicia was evidently the type of painter who squeezes out all her colors onto her palette. In a matter of seconds, Alicia told Jane that she'd moved to Savannah right after high school to attend SCAD, the renowned art school.

"I met Teddy at the SCAD sponsors' ball in my first week of classes. And that was the end of art school for me," Alicia said. "I pretty much went from mixing pigments to mixing baby food. Our first child - not Teddy's first; he already had three from his first marriage - was born one year to a day after my freshman year began. Which I never finished, incidentally, because I skipped so many classes and didn't turn in any of the assignments. I was too busy with Teddy. You can imagine that my parents were pretty annoyed, especially since Teddy's from an old Southern family. Read: 'he's Not Jewish.'" Alicia grinned. "My maiden name is Cohen."

Teddy looked down at his lap, but Jane was pretty sure that he'd rolled his eyes.

"This retreat is the first art class I've attended in twenty years," Alicia continued. "I was so excited when I saw the ad for it in *Garden & Gun* Magazine at my dentist's office. I tore out the page and called the number that same day. I think I was the first person to sign up. When I was a kid, I loved riding horses - that was my thing, you know - so this was perfect for me. Teddy loves horses, too. That's why I was attracted to him. As soon as he told me about his thoroughbreds, I fell in love." She looked at Teddy, her smile exuberant. Jane couldn't tell if Teddy was smiling or gritting his teeth.

"We were married before I even knew I was pregnant. I guess you could say our relationship was on the fast track!" Alicia giggled at her own pun.

Jane couldn't resist countering with, "You've been married twenty years, so I'd call that a stable relationship."

Alicia's laugh was tinkly, like a string of garden lights on a breezy walkway. Glancing around the room, she leaned forward. "You know, the dead horse, Lancelot. We bred him." Her face crumpled as she added, "I loved that horse."

Jane closed her lips, deciding to honor Mr. Edmonson's request for discretion rather than explaining that she'd been one of the painters who had discovered the horse.

As they chatted, students were filling in the seats around the table. Grace and Donna slipped into the chairs that Jane had saved for them. Since Alicia was at the opposite end of the long table, Jane found herself in an awkward situation. The whole group was listening to her across-table conversation with Alicia. Jane began to feel self-conscious, like a brand new student whose first attempt at drawing had been held up for display.

"I asked the desk clerk who found Lancelot," Alicia said, her voice pinging across the table. "She said it was the three women from a little town in Georgia. I guess that was you and your friends?"

So much for discretion, Jane thought. She nodded. A short-haired blonde woman at Alicia's end of the room waved at Teddy. Jane guessed the woman was in her late forties or early fifties - around the same age as Alicia.

"I couldn't help overhearing you say that you went to SCAD," the woman said to Alicia. "At least for your freshman year. I was at SCAD, too." She looked at Teddy. "Teddy and I were good friends, weren't we? I heard he'd married someone from the college, so I guess that was you."

Jane looked at Teddy, who was shifting uncomfortably in his chair. His neck was turning red.

"My sister was at SCAD, too," the blonde added, motioning at a red-haired woman with bouncy shoulder-length hair and a face full of freckles, who was seated beside her. "This is Harry. And I'm Judy. Judy McAndrew. Everybody calls me Dee Dee. Back then, my last name was Thaxton. I wonder if we were in any of the same classes? Before you dropped out."

Although Teddy certainly seemed to be squirming during this introduction, Jane felt her own neck muscles relax. Dee Dee's interruption gave her a reason to put an end to her all-too-public conversation with Alicia. Glancing at her phone, she noted that - sure enough - their instructor was late.

Alec Treville finally bustled in, pulled out the chair next to Jane, and plunked his backpack onto it. As he fished out supplies for his demonstration, an open pack of colored pencils slipped out. The pencils rolled across the table. Jane grabbed a handful, and the rest tumbled to the floor. Grace backed her chair out and stooped to gather them.

"Thanks," Alec said as they handed the pencils to him. He began ruffling through some plastic-coated sheets in a three-ring notebook.

"Would you like us to help you find something?" Grace offered.

"So kind of you," Alec said. "Yes, see if you can find the sheet of sample photos of a landscape. I think it says, 'stages of watercolor landscape painted outdoors' or something like that." He slid the notebook to Grace.

Grace began leafing through it, and Jane leaned over to help. There were tabs separating the plastic pouches holding the pages, and each page was numbered. But several of the pages seemed to have been replaced in a hurry, in defiance of the organizational system. Jane guessed that Alec had shoved his lessons back into his notebook without bothering to look at the page numbers or tabs. Clearly, he had neglected to go over his materials before this demonstration. The abrupt end of his introductory session on the patio might have accounted for his late entrance and sloppy preparation, but Jane guessed that he was perennially late and sloppy. She sighed, thinking of the hefty fee that she'd paid for this workshop, then reminded herself that you can no more judge an instructor by his organization than you can judge a book by its cover. What some teachers lacked in organizational skills, they make up for in communication skills or technical expertise.

And really, how could Alec be blamed for the helter-skelter start of this workshop? The morning introductory session on the patio had completely fallen apart after Walter's interruption. In a matter of seconds, the hotel manager, Mr. Horne, had rushed out to the patio in a vain effort to prevent Walter from blurting out the news about the dead horse. Too late, of course. The cat was out of the bag. Or, as Alicia might have put it, the horse was out of the stall.

After Walter had announced that his horse, Lancelot, was dead, Saundra stood up. She gripped the edge of the table to steady herself. Walter rushed to her side. As he guided her back through the French doors into the lobby, he kept his arm around her as if to support her.

Looking resigned, Mr. Horne had shut the French doors and turned to face the group of painters. Wearing a strained smile, he had briefly sketched the whole incident. He chose his words carefully. It seemed to Jane that he was trying to say as little as possible about the dead horse, and he wanted to whisk himself back to the safety of his office. But the painters had barraged him with questions, and he was too well-trained in guest-relations to refuse to answer.

"No, we don't know who was responsible for this shocking incident," he had said. "But the police are investigating. I assure you that all the other horses in our stables are safe. We have called in extra security."

"No, I really don't know how the horse got into the reflecting pool. Yes, it's true, that's where it was found. And yes," he said, eyeballing Jane, Donna, and Grace, "it was discovered by some of our guests. We are not sure of the cause of death. A necropsy was performed first thing this morning."

Noticing that several of the painters seemed puzzled by the term "necropsy," he explained that it was basically an autopsy performed on animals. It had revealed almost no water in the horse's lungs. "So we believe that the unfortunate animal did not drown. I really can't say more. Police matter, you understand."

As soon as the questions had slowed, Mr. Horne excused himself and scurried away. After he left, vigorous conversations sprouted at each table. Amidst the general hubbub, Jane heard one voice crack into sobs. The voice belonged to one of the Golden Girls, who were seated at the adjacent table - the same table where Saundra had been sitting. Because the three were sitting together, Jane had guessed that the Golden Girls and Saundra knew one another prior to the retreat, and her guess was soon confirmed.

"So awful!" the upset Golden Girl wailed. Tears streamed down her cheeks. "I can't stand it when animals are abused."

The other Golden Girl said, "Catherine, dear, we really don't know what happened. You've seen the stables here - they're immaculate. This was an accident."

"Sheryl, I don't believe this was an accident." Catherine sniffed. "Lance wouldn't have broken out of his stall. He was the sweetest animal. From the day he arrived at the Staunton's stable, I noticed what an unusually calm personality he had. Gentle. Much easier to handle than the other stallions. I tell you there's something going on. Something evil. Horses don t drown in a shallow pool."

Donna called over from their table. "You know, I said the same thing. My family had horses when I was a girl. They're natural swimmers. All of them are."

Catherine wiped her eyes. Looking at Donna, she said, "Yes, natural swimmers. And prized thoroughbreds - particularly stallions like Lance who bring a fortune as breeders - aren't allowed to go wandering off by themselves. Anyway, why would a full-grown horse stumble into a reflecting pool?"

Sheryl pursed her lips as she peered around the patio and spoke to her friend in a hushed tone. "Maybe the horse jumped a pasture fence because he was thirsty. Or maybe a dog spooked him. Look, Catherine, we really don't know anything yet, do we? Maybe the horse had a heart attack. They're mammals - I'm sure they can have heart attacks. Or strokes. For all we know, that horse could have burst an artery and fallen into the water. Sometimes these things happen with no warning. You remember my cat? - the vet said it died of natural causes. But what does that really mean? Something had to go wrong or Puffy would still be alive."

"Well, I agree with you," Donna said to Catherine. "If you ask me, there's something fishy about this whole thing."

Catherine took a tissue out of her pocket and mopped her forehead. Jane watched her as she wobbled to a standing position. Catherine's face looked paper white. "Excuse me," Catherine said. "I'm feeling light-headed all of a sudden."

"Oh, that happens to me, too," Donna said.

Catherine said, "I think I need to go up to the room. Excuse me."

Sheryl hurried to her feet. "Here, let me carry your supplies." And the two Golden Girls left.

Alec had finally managed to quiet down the group. But it was clear that all the enthusiasm for painting had bled out of the opening session. When he resumed his introduction, none of the students took notes or smiled at his jokes. After fifteen minutes of discouraging attempts to refocus the group's attention, Alec suggested that they take a break and convene in the conference room at eleven-thirty for a demonstration.

Donna announced that she was going up to call her husband, Bill. She didn't want him worrying about her, but she'd been way too tired to phone him when they'd gotten back to their rooms last night. Grace said she wanted to take some photos of the flowers around the hotel to use as references for future floral paintings. Jane decided to go up to her room. Her head was spinning, and she needed to be alone with her thoughts.

Upstairs, the first thing Jane did was find the thermostat and figure out how to adjust the temperature from meat-locker-frigid to spring-breeze cool. Then she sat down on the overstuffed chair by the honey-colored desk. She took out the class roster that Alec had sent to each student, and read over the names. At workshops, she liked to review the roster and take notes on it to help her remember the students that she met.

The first name she looked for was "Saundra Staunton". Under it, she wrote: *Black hair. Husband, Walter (expensive suit). Lancelot's owners. Has stable. Knows Catherine and Sheryl.*

The only Catherine on the list was Catherine Manfred. Under that name, Jane wrote: *"Golden Girls". Capri pant set. Came with Sheryl Calhoun. Worked for Stauntons.*

Sheryl was Sheryl Calhoun. Jane made a mental note to ask where all of them lived.

She found Alicia and Teddy Pickridge on the roster. By Alicia's name, she wrote: *Younger than husband. Dropped out of SCAD. Loves horses.*

The Judy who went to SCAD must be Judy McAndrew. By her name, Jane wrote, *Short blonde hair. Nickname Dee Dee. Maiden name Thaxton - Harry's sister.* There was no Harry listed on the roster, so Dee Dee's sister must be Harriet Warren.

The note-taking calmed Jane, as it always did. She took out a pad of paper and jotted down what she remembered about finding the dead horse yesterday. She'd already told all this to the policeman, but maybe she'd remember something else as she wrote, and it might prove important. Besides, writing helped her organize her thoughts. The pen in her hand gave her the illusion of controlling events, and she could feel the tension in her back muscles begin to ease.

An hour later, Jane emerged from her room feeling refreshed. She put a blank notepad into her pocketbook but left her other art supplies in the room. Alec had said that he'd do his demonstration when they reconvened in the conference room. After the demonstration, they'd have lunch on the patio at 1 PM. A local restaurant was bringing in sandwiches.

As she waited for the elevator, Jane heard voices from a room down the long hallway - near the exit sign over the emergency stairs. Glancing in that direction, Jane saw a man leave a room, shutting the door behind him. It looked like Mr. Horne, but she couldn't be sure because he turned in the opposite direction. Just then, the elevator pinged and the metal doors yawned apart. As the elevator transported her down to the lobby floor, Jane wondered: What was the hotel manager doing in a guest's room?

CHAPTER FOUR

When the demonstration in the conference room was over, Jane, Donna, and Grace dropped off their supplies in their rooms and washed up for lunch. They ambled through the lobby and out the French doors at five minutes 'til one. On the patio, extra chairs had been arranged around the three round metal tables. Each table was covered with an emerald green tablecloth. Red-checked cardboard boxes, bottles of water, and cellophane-wrapped utensils were placed in front of each chair. The three friends picked the center table, which had been set for five people, and sat down.

"Well, I guess we're gonna slum it for lunch," Donna said. She ripped open her cellophane wrapper and pulled out a plastic fork, folded paper napkin, and tiny paper salt and pepper packets. "Plastic forks. Paper napkins. My, my. How teddibly crude!"

Grace giggled. "But notice that the water bottles are glass, not plastic," she said. "And see - this isn't plain old water. This is the sparkling kind - Evian."

"Well, that's a relief!" Donna said. She twisted open the cap on her water bottle and took a sip, her pinkie raised in an exaggerated gesture of elegance. "Notice that I'm keeping my pinkie up. You're not gonna see me sinking to the level of a stall-mucker."

A teenage girl approached their table. "Are these two chairs taken?" she asked.

"No, dear. They're empty. And you're welcome to join us," Grace said.

"Over here, Gram," the teenager called. "There are two empty places."

A tall woman with salt-and-pepper hair marched to the table. "I'm Margaret Culpepper," she said in a robust voice. "And this is Maggie, my granddaughter." Margaret sat down. "Thank you for allowing us to join you."

Grace introduced Donna, Jane, and herself. "So glad to meet you, Margaret and Maggie. All three of us are in the same group of watercolor painters," Grace explained. "We drove up from Georgia together. Our small town - Atkinsville - has a very active arts center. How about you? Where are y'all from?"

"I live in St. Simons, now," Margaret said. "But I'm from this area, originally. And Maggie still lives nearby. About twenty miles from here, in Gilbertville. Maggie used to keep her horse here at these stables."

"Oh, you're a rider?" Grace asked.

Blushing, Maggie nodded.

"You know, I didn't realize that so many people at this retreat would be horse people," Grace said. "I guess it makes sense, since there's a stable on the grounds. As well as the thoroughbred museum."

"In our painting group, I'm the only horsey person," Donna said. "All the other women are suburbanites. But I was raised with horses. Rode bareback, rode barefoot. Up the hills, down the valleys. I come from farm folks. We grew our own vegetables. Raised all kinds of livestock. Milked cows. Slopped pigs."

Margaret, her lips pursed, glanced at Donna as she unfolded her napkin and straightened out the creases on her lap.

When Jane had worked as a reporter fresh out of college, she'd learned to listen with her eyes as well as her ears. Observing people's facial expressions and the tension in their muscles had become a habit. And Margaret's face spoke volumes. The woman seemed terribly uncomfortable as Donna talked about her rural background. Margaret s nostrils had even flared while Donna spoke - like a horse alarmed by a frightful odor.

"We Culpeppers have always been horse people," Margaret said. She avoided looking in Donna's direction and addressed her words to Grace. "But I would not describe our horses as livestock. We have always taken pleasure in riding, of course. And improving our horses' lineage through precise, selective breeding."

This lofty explanation was followed by a moment of awkward silence. Grace turned toward the teen. "And do you still have a horse of your own, Maggie?"

Maggie nodded. She looked at her lap as she replied. "Gwenny. That's her name. Short for Guinevere."

"Ma'am," Margaret said. "Remember your manners, Maggie. When you speak to an adult, you say Ma'am or Sir."

"Ma'am," Maggie repeated, her eyes darting around the patio as if in search of a safe place to perch.

"And look at the speaker when you answer, Maggie."

Another awkward silence. Jane marveled at the color that Maggie's cheeks had turned - a vivid shade of pink. As Jane studied Maggie, she decided the girl would make a wonderful subject for a portrait. Maggie seemed to be hovering between girlhood and womanhood. Her cheeks were round, almost childishly plump, and dotted with freckles. In contrast, her arms and torso were wiry - the body of an athletic teen. Even Maggie's hair seemed unsure of itself. At shoulder-length, it could not be portrayed as definitely short or long, and the color was not exactly brown but rather a backdrop of dark with red-gold highlights. Like her cheeks and hair, the teen's eyes danced with indecision. Green and blue flecks swam in her irises, reflecting the green of the earth and the blue of the sky.

In addition to Maggie's appearance, something else caught Jane's attention. Maggie said her horse - which was once stabled here - was called Guinevere. That was the name of the queen in the King Arthur legends, the Sir Lancelot story. That couldn't be a coincidence - could it? Lancelot was the name of the horse that they'd found dead in the reflecting pool. What was the relationship between the two horses? Jane bit her lip. She didn't think this was the moment to bring up the subject of the dead horse. Not over lunch. And not around poor Maggie, who had enough problems with that overbearing grandmother of hers.

Grace managed to jump back in the saddle and keep the conversation trotting along: "Maggie, your grandmother said that you used to keep Gwenny here at these stables. But not any more?"

"That's right, Ma'am. Father built a stable last year. Behind our tennis court. That's where we keep Gwenny now."

"Oh, I suppose that's more convenient," Grace said. "You can ride whenever you like, you don't have to worry about finding a driver to take you to these stables. You're not old enough to drive yourself, are you?"

Margaret answered for her granddaughter. "Maggie will be fifteen in the fall. Her father - my son-in-law - decided that it would be wiser to keep Gwenny closer to home. But it was definitely not a question of convenience - Maggie has a governess and tutors who could drive her over to the gardens. Let's just say that my son-in-law doesn't always agree with the way things are done at other stables. He has his own view of things. When my daughter - Maggie's mother - was alive, she had a broader tolerance for differences."

"That's what makes the world go round," Donna said. She frowned at Margaret. "Everybody's different."

Jane took a bite of her sandwich - a croissant stuffed full of chicken salad. She quickly leaned over her box to prevent the contents from spilling onto her lap. Looking at the pile of chicken salad that had oozed out onto her paper wrapper, she grinned. How Margaret Culpepper's nostrils would flare if Jane displayed messy eating habits!

As she chewed, Jane began composing the description that she planned to jot on her class roster under the name Margaret Culpepper: "Slim, stiff, snobby, salt-and-pepper hair. Lives in St. Simons, formerly Gilbertville. Granddaughter - Maggie." Jane liked the alliteration of s words in the description of Margaret. The mnemonic would make it easier to remember. Although Jane doubted if she could ever forget who Margaret was - the woman had such an abrasive personality.

All around the patio, conversations dwindled as the painters unpacked their sandwich boxes and began eating. Jane noticed that their instructor, Alec, was seated at a table set for six, with Alicia and her husband Teddy, Sheryl the Golden Girl, and the only other male painter in their class. But the last seat at that table was empty. Jane looked around. Where was Catherine, the other Golden Girl? Perhaps her light-headedness had been the start of an illness? And Saundra Staunton had not come to lunch, either. Jane wondered if she was going to skip the rest of the workshop.

At their table, the quiet was interrupted by Donna's phone, which burst into a tinny version of "Old MacDonald Had a Farm."

"My grandkids," Donna said, by way of explanation. "They keep changing my ring tone, and I don't know how to change it back."

Margaret rolled her eyes as Donna fished her phone out of her large, floppy leather purse. Glancing at the screen, Donna said, "Oh, it's Bill. I need to take this," and she hurried off to the lobby where the reception was stronger.

The chicken salad was, of course, bountiful. Along with chunks of white meat, there were plump grapes, crunchy celery pieces, and sugared half-pecans mixed into creamy mayo. Somehow, the flaky croissant had retained its crisp consistency despite its overstuffed contents. Looking around the patio, Jane noticed that everybody seemed to be eating with relish - gathering up dropped dollops and licking their fingers. Everybody except Margaret Culpepper, who didn't approve of her meal any more than she approved of the company at her table. Frowning, Margaret had opened her sandwich box, unwrapped her sandwich, and emptied the chicken salad onto the waxy paper wrapper. Then she deposited the croissant in the box and ate the salad with her fork.

"Would you like my brownie, Maggie?" Grace asked. "This croissant is delicious, but it's as many carbs as I'd better consume at lunch. I'm trying not to bring home any unwanted souvenirs." Grace patted her tummy. "I find it so difficult to limit calories when I'm eating out three meals a day."

Hesitating, Maggie looked at her grandmother.

Margaret promptly answered for the teen. "I think one brownie will be enough for Maggie." Margaret looked at Grace and Jane. "Maggie is my namesake, the only child of my only child. As you can imagine, I'm very proud of her. She's a fine rider and a talented young painter. But I'm afraid she has inherited some of her father's undesirable qualities. Such as an unfortunate enthusiasm for dessert."

In the distance, a slim man was walking on one of the garden paths leading to the patio. Jane noticed that he was wearing the uniform of the garden's employees - an emerald green polo shirt with the logo Gardens and Horses on its breast pocket. He wore shiny rubber, knee-length boots, the boots of a man who tends a garden or livestock. A border collie frolicked along beside him.

As he neared the patio, the man called, "Maggie - there you are!" He waved, and a grin spread across his lean, clean-shaven face. "I hoped I'd catch you at lunch."

Jane guessed the man was in his thirties. He had dark, wavy hair and a contagious grin, made all the more endearing by a dimple in his right cheek. Judging by the dirt on his blue jeans, Jane guessed the man was a gardener. But as he approached their table, her nose led her to a different conclusion. He smelled of horse.

As soon as the man reached the patio, the border collie rushed to Maggie, its tail wagging gloriously.

The man nodded at Margaret before introducing himself to Grace and Jane. "I'm Dave," he said. "Head of the stables."

"Heard you were attending the art retreat with your grandmother," Dave said to Maggie. "You know, I've still got one of your helmets and a pair of your riding gloves. I keep meaning to send them to you. But since you're here, I thought you might want to stop by and pick them up."

Maggie smiled and started to answer, but Margaret inserted herself. "Maggie will be occupied during the day. I don't want her to miss any of the instruction. We should have a few minutes before dinner. Since you finish at five, Dave, why don't you leave those items on the bench in front of the stable after you lock up. We will come by and retrieve them at that time. Thank you for keeping Maggie's things safe."

Maggie's smile faded as soon as her grandmother took over the exchange. But Dave seemed determined to interact with the teen rather than the grandmother.

"That's okay," he said, his eyes locking on Maggie's. "I'll wait for you to come by. No hurry."

The dog perched its paws on the arm of Maggie's chair and licked her cheeks. Maggie giggled, then, glancing at Dave, she said, "Scott?" Her eyes darted sideways at Margaret before returning to Dave. "Does Scott still work here?"

"No," Dave said, his voice gentle. "I'm afraid not. You remember, his dad was military. They moved in January. A few months after you and Gwenny left. I guess he didn't have a chance to write and tell you."

Maggie looked crestfallen. "How about Izzy? Hannah?"

"I'm afraid we've got a whole new crew of interns at the stables since you and Gwenny were here. We have some new horses, too - you'll enjoy seeing them. Josie had a colt. He's a beauty. I think he's gonna be a real champ."

"As a matter of fact," he said, his eyes moving around the table to include Jane and Grace as well as Maggie and Margaret, "why don't all of you come? Who knows - maybe you'll be inspired to do some horse paintings."

Donna returned to the table as Dave was speaking. "Hello," she said, holding out her hand to shake his. "I'm Donna Norton."

Dave grinned. "Better not shake my hand before you eat lunch," he said. "I've been brushing horses. My hands smell."

"Oh," Donna said, "the stable man, are you? Well, I don't object to the smell of horses. I was raised on a farm."

"That clinches it," Dave said. "I've been trying to convince these ladies to come by the stables and take a tour. Maybe do some horse paintings. You'll come, won't you?"

"Sounds terrific," Donna said. "I love to paint horses. And so far, the only horses that I've seen here are what you might call 'still lifes' - if you know what I mean - not the living, breathing types."

Suddenly, all the faces at the table were staring open-mouthed at Donna. Margaret gasped. Maggie looked frightened. Jane winced and tried to catch Donna's eye - hoping to shush her before she said any more about the dead horse.

Grace, of course, galloped in for the rescue. "Yes, we so enjoyed seeing the magnificent bronze statues of champion thoroughbreds in the grounds around the museum. I'm sure the horses at your stable would be marvelous subjects for painting, Dave. And I'd just love to see that new colt."

"It's settled, then," Dave said.

"What time should we plan to come by?" Jane asked. "I'm not sure when our painting class will be finished."

"Whenever you get there is fine with me," Dave said. "I'm not going anywhere. Taking care of horses - it's not a job, it's a life. Isn't that right, Maggie? Gets under your skin." He grinned and held up his palms, which looked dusty, with brown etched in the creases. "Not complaining, mind you. Horses are my heart's blood."

Dave turned to leave. "See you later," he called over his shoulder. Tensing, the dog watched him. Then it whined as if reluctant to leave Maggie.

"It's okay, girl," Maggie said. She hugged the dog's neck and held out a bit of chicken salad. The dog gobbled up the treat, then pranced off to rejoin Dave.

"Well, he's a handsome fellow," Donna said. "Bet you enjoyed his company when your horse was here, Maggie."

Margaret fairly snarled as she lunged into the conversation. "Dave was very kind to Maggie. He has had some experience as a jockey. Not a pro, of course - he's much too tall for that. But he was helpful when Maggie was perfecting her posture for shows."

Jane picked up her bottle of water and took a sip to hide the smile dancing across her lips. Clearly, Margaret did not want anyone to think that Maggie had an inappropriate relationship with a stable man. Observing Dave as he threaded his way through the patio tables, Jane noticed that Alicia looked up with a bright smile. Jane couldn't see Dave's face, but she could see his fingers waggling a greeting. Dave's dog was not so subtle about its greeting. It pranced over to Alicia's table, tail wagging wildly. Alicia reached over and rubbed the dog's neck and back. Jane remembered Alicia saying that she was first attracted to her husband Teddy because of his horses. Clearly, Alicia loved dogs, too.

"Dave's a really sweet person," Maggie was saying. "At the stables here, they always have interns helping out. And Dave is like a big brother to all the kids. He knows everything about horses."

"Yes, he does seem like a kind person. And very enthusiastic about horses," Grace said. Turning to Donna, she asked, "Any news from home? How is Bill handling being an art widower?"

"Oh, he's doing fine," Donna said. "But he's awfully worried about me. That's why he called. I guess I shouldn't have told him that I nearly passed out yesterday." She turned to Maggie and Margaret to explain. "When we saw that dead horse in the pool, it was an awful shock. I've got high blood pressure."

"Yes," Margaret said, "I'm sure it must have been a shock. I suppose the topic can't be entirely avoided, but the mysterious death of a horse is not something that I want my granddaughter exposed to." She cast a pointed look at Donna. "I really would prefer to discuss something else at lunch."

"It's alright, Gram," Maggie said. "I'm fifteen, I'm not a child. You don't have to worry about me. I understand that accidents happen. Horses die."

"Anyway," Donna continued, "my husband is afraid this workshop is too much for me. He says he doesn't like me being here without my own car because I haven't got any way to get home if I need to leave early. You see," Donna explained to Margaret and Maggie, "Our son Max took the week off work. And Bill promised that he'd help rebuild Max's patio. Bill's the expert on all this - he used to be a contractor. And they've already delivered the wood and all the supplies. So Bill really can't get away, this week, and come get me. Oh, I suppose he could drop everything if there's an emergency. But there's no emergency. For me, anyway. The dead horse would probably see things differently."

At yet another mention of the dead horse, Margaret gritted her teeth, flared her nostrils, and glared at Donna. Again, Jane reached for her water bottle to conceal the smile that brushed across her lips.

Alec pushed his chair away from the table and stood up. Painters," he began. His napkin fell to the ground, and he bent to retrieve it. Then he waited for the talking to subside.

"Bill says he's going to talk to Pam," Donna whispered hurriedly to Jane and Grace. "To see if she could drive up. So there'd be another car here if I need to leave." Pam Gerald was another member of their Atkinsville painting group.

"Really?" Jane whispered back. "How can Pam join the class now? I thought it was full. And I thought Pam couldn't come because she didn't have anyone to take care of her dog."

Donna shrugged. "I don't know what she'll do with her dog. But I told Bill that Pam was welcome to share my room. I don't like sleeping up there alone. After finding that horse in the reflecting pool, the dead quiet of the place gives me the creeps."

Alec cleared his throat. "I think everyone's finished eating," he said. "And it looks like we've got a beautiful afternoon for our first plein air outing. Let's take a fifteen minute break, then meet in the rose garden. When you get your paints and easels, be sure to bring some water and a cup for washing off your brushes."

"Not a cloud in the sky," he continued, "so don't forget to bring extra water for drinking. I wouldn't want any of my students dying of dehydration," he added, with a grin at his own humor. "Or of any other cause, for that matter."

CHAPTER FIVE

As Jane, Donna, and Grace walked along the path to the rose garden, a gray-haired man joined them. He was dressed in a crisp white polo shirt tucked into belted khaki trousers. Jane recognized him. Except for Teddy Pickridge and their instructor, he was the only other man in their retreat.

"Hello," he said. "I believe you're the famous ladies who discovered the dead horse in the reflecting pool. Quite an introduction - that - to Gardens and Horses."

"Sure was," Donna said. "I just about passed out. Of course, it wouldn't have been the first time."

"Oh. Have you discovered many dead horses?" the man asked.

Donna giggled. "No, I meant that it wouldn't have been the first time that I passed out. I've got high blood pressure."

The man flashed a smile. "Too bad about the high blood pressure. But I see it hasn't stopped you from doing what you want to do," he said. "I was sitting with Alec at lunch, and he mentioned that three of the painters in our retreat had driven up from Georgia. I'm assuming that's you three?"

Jane noticed that even as the man chatted with Donna, he managed to sidle in beside Grace. There wasn't room on the path for four walking abreast, so Jane and Donna took up a position next to each other and in front of Grace and the man.

"That's right," Grace said. "We live about four hours from here. In Atkinsville. What about you? Do you live nearby?"

"Not too far. Gilbertville," said the man. "Name's Arthur. Arthur King."

"Glad to meet you," Grace said. "Grace Tanner. And this is Jane Roland and Donna Norton. We paint together at our local art center. In Atkinsville, near the University of Georgia."

"I'm familiar with the area," Arthur said. "Been there for conferences. Were you associated with the university?"

"No, but my husband was a professor there before he started his business," Grace said. "I taught elementary school. Fourth grade. Before I retired."

"You said your husband had a business?" Arthur said. "Is he retired, too?"

"He passed away," Grace said. Her voice grew quieter. "It's been just over a year. I still can't believe he's gone."

"I'm sorry," Arthur said. "I know how you feel. Painting was my wife's hobby. I enrolled in my first art class to keep her company. Then I discovered that I enjoyed it, too. She died three years ago. Cancer."

"How nice that you both shared an interest in art," Grace said. "You said you'd been to the university for conferences. What is your field of work?"

"I'm an accountant. I'm easing out, now, but I still keep a few clients," Arthur said. "Most of them are old friends - I've managed their accounts for years and years. I like to keep my hands in the business, but I'm not tied to a desk as much as I used to be. These days, instead of meeting people to go over tax forms, I meet them for a trail ride."

"Oh, you have a horse?" Jane asked, glancing back at Arthur. A light began to flash in the dashboard inside her brain. "You wouldn't happen to keep your horse in the stable here, would you?"

"How'd you know?" Arthur asked. "As a matter of fact, I have two horses here. My wife and I used to enjoy riding these trails. She's the one who introduced me to horses, as well as painting. You see, she started riding when she was a little girl. Her parents were friendly with Teddy Pickridge's family. Teddy's the other gentleman at our retreat. Teddy's sister and my wife went to school together.

"After I married, I started managing Teddy's books - for a very good fee, I might add." Arthur smiled. "And Teddy began selling me horses - for a very good price. I guess you could say we were horse trading."

Jane's head was beginning to spin. Arthur was connected to the Pickridges. And he might be connected to the teen, Maggie, as well, because he lived in Gilbertville - the town where Maggie lived. Arthur kept his horses at the stable here, and Maggie used to keep her horse here. The name of the dead horse was Lancelot, and Maggie's horse was Guinevere - both characters in the King Arthur legends. And this man's name was Arthur King. Surely, this couldn't be coincidental.

"Well, we'll probably see your horses this evening," Grace said. "We met Dave - the head of the stables - at lunch. He offered to give us a tour of the stables."

Arthur frowned, and his voice hardened. "He's a bit lax with security, Dave is. I'm afraid I'm going to have to speak to him about it. I was astounded that a valuable horse like Lancelot was outside lock and key yesterday. Unless the Stauntons had arranged for the vet or a trainer to remove the horse from his stall, there's simply no excuse for it. Nobody else should have access to these stables."

"Dave seems like a nice enough guy to me," Donna said. "He invited us to come paint the horses sometime. I'm really looking forward to that. I'd rather paint from a live horse than a photo, but I haven't been around horses for years. Not since we moved to the South."

"Well, I guess there's no need to worry about you ladies visiting the stables," Arthur said, his face softening and his voice resuming a cheerful tone. "Can't imagine a lady hurting a horse. And a paintbrush is hardly a deadly weapon!"

"Which of the horses are yours?" Grace said. "We'll be sure to look out for them."

"Why don't I come along and show them to you?" Arthur suggested. "What time is your tour? I'll meet you at the stables. Or, better still, I'll walk you over. I'd enjoy pointing out some of my favorite spots here in the gardens. There are quite a few out-of-the-way places perfect for landscape painting. I bet you enjoy painting landscapes, don't you?"

"Your bet is certainly on the money," Grace said. "I do love painting landscapes. That's why I was so eager to come to this workshop. Plein air seems ideal for landscape work."

Jane stole a glance at Grace. Her eyes were sparkling with delight, and her voice was practically singing. Jane hadn't seen her friend so effervescent for years - not since Grace's husband had taken sick.

Realizing that Grace would be too polite to invite Arthur to join them without first consulting her companions, Jane jumped in. "Dinner is at seven," she said. "According to our schedule, we'll finish this painting session at five. Why don't we all meet in the lobby at quarter til six? That should leave us plenty of time to tour the stables."

"It's a date," Arthur said.

At this, Jane snuck another glance behind her. She suspected that Arthur meant what he said - for him, this really was a date. He and Grace certainly made a handsome couple, Jane mused. Arthur stood about a foot taller than Grace. With his deep-set brown eyes, chiseled facial features, and the hint of a cleft chin, Jane guessed that he'd been movie-star handsome in his younger days. As an older man, he was still plenty good-looking. His expression was lively, he had a hearty voice, and his gait was as vigorous as a thoroughbred's.

When they reached the rose garden, Arthur ushered them to a spot under the shade of a magnolia tree. There, they had an unobstructed view of a white wooden gazebo surrounded by rose bushes. Acting the part of the perfect gentleman, Arthur helped each of them set up their easels. Jane noticed that Arthur managed to position his easel in easy conversational distance from Grace.

Jane took out a pencil and then paused to study the scene. She decided she'd paint the entire view - the gazebo surrounded by rose bushes and trees in the distance. With the afternoon light hitting the gazebo, its roof gleamed. The contrast between the gazebo's straight lines and the bushy shapes of the plants was very appealing. Jane did a quick pencil sketch, then poured some water into a cup and took out her brushes.

As the painters worked, Alec circulated among the easels. When he got to Jane, he said, "Squint your eyes. So you're seeing the big blocks of light and dark - not the small details. There. Can you see how the shadow from the roof across the railing slants at the same angle as the shadow from the railing across the grass?"

Alec seemed to be in his element out here. No need to fumble with an overstuffed backpack or a binder bursting with papers. Instead, he moved effortlessly from painting to painting - a sea lion in water. Jane could overhear his interactions with each of the painters. With one quick glance,

Alec seemed to be able to spot problems. To each painter, he offered a suggestion tailored to the person's level of experience.

Donna was struggling to judge the distance between the gazebo's rails by holding her paintbrush sideways in her line of sight. "Lock your elbow," Alec told her. "Like this." He demonstrated. "That's the way you can be sure that your arm is at the same angle every time you measure."

"You know, that makes perfect sense," Donna exclaimed. "I always wondered how I could be sure I was measuring the same way each time."

At quarter to five, Alec announced. "Let's stop now. Line up your easels so we can have a look at your work. I know some of you aren't finished. That's okay. You're here to learn, not to produce a masterpiece."

With the easels lined up in front of the gazebo, Jane marveled at the differences in each painter's approach to the same scene. Some of the paintings merely suggested the gazebo's structural details, while others resembled architectural blueprints. The application of color was also very different, with some painters emphasizing the deep greens and heavy reds of the rose bushes and others working in light, pastel hues.

A few of the painters, like Maggie and her grandmother, had worked on capturing a single flower. Jane was impressed by the teen's talent. Her rose was so crisp and realistic - it made Jane want to reach out and smell it.

Arthur's painting stood out from the rest of the group. Instead of the expected landscape or floral, his painting told a story. He had painted a woman standing in front of an easel, paintbrush in hand. The woman - who was clearly Grace - was painting a gazebo surrounded by rose bushes. Jane could see that Arthur was a talented artist. He had selected just enough details to tell the story and identify Grace.

After a short critiquing session filled with Alec's encouraging comments, the painters collapsed their easels, poured out their painting water, and arranged their supplies in their bags. Alec reminded them that supper was at the hotel restaurant at seven.

"How are you feeling after all that standing?" Arthur asked Donna. "Would you like me to carry your easel? Can't have you passing out, you know."

"I'm fine," Donna said. "But aren't you nice to offer! You and Grace make a fine pair. You're the two most polite people I've ever met."

When Donna's phone rang, she stepped off the path to answer it. Jane waited for her, while Grace and Arthur joined the rest of the group to walk back to the hotel.

"Oh, hi, Bill. Everything going okay with Max's deck?" Donna paused. "Tonight? Really? What about her dog? No, I didn't know there was a kennel on the grounds. Well, that takes care of everything, doesn't it? Do you know what time Pam will get here? She's going to stay in my room, right?"

Donna hung up and told Jane that Bill had spoken with Pam Gerald, another of the painters from their Atkinsville group. "It's all arranged," Donna said. "Pam's coming. Tonight. Bill told her he'd pay for everything if she'd drive up here and watch over me. He'll even pay her class fee if Alec agrees to let her join the class. Pam's already on the road. And she's bringing her dog. Bill says there's a kennel that boards dogs right here. Dogs aren't allowed to stay in the hotel rooms."

"My, that was quick. Sounds like he thought of everything. I guess Bill is really worried about you," Jane said.

As they walked toward the hotel, the tail end of the group was visible up ahead. But Arthur and Grace were already out of sight.

"I'm pretty sure our class is full. But maybe Alec will agree to take one extra student. I wonder if Saundra Staunton is dropping out, and Pam could take her place?"

"There's certainly enough space out here for one more painter," Donna said. "These gardens go on and on. But from now on, we'll have to be sure that we get to meals early so we can grab a table for five."

Jane looked puzzled. "What do you mean? When Pam gets here, there'll be four of us."

"Well, Pam makes four," Donna said. "But it looks like Arthur and Grace will be sitting together from now on. So that's five. It's a good thing Arthur's the only single man in our retreat."

"Huh. What do you mean?" Jane said.

"I didn't realize that we were going to have a romance at this retreat. Most of the patio tables only seat five, so we've got as much dating as we can handle."

As they reached the lobby, they spotted Maggie on the patio. She was sitting at a table and sipping from a glass of lemonade. Smiling a greeting, they joined her.

"Where's your grandma?" Donna asked.

"She went to get her sweater - she left it in the rose garden. She told me to bring our easels up to the room and wait for her down here. It's still warm out, so I don't know why she insisted on getting her sweater now. I told her we could pick up her sweater on our way to the stables."

"So you are still planning to walk over to the stables tonight?" Jane asked. "That's what I wanted to ask you about."

Maggie nodded.

"If you'd like, we can all go together," Jane said. "We're going to meet in the lobby at quarter til six. That should give us enough time for a quick tour of the stables before dinner."

"Okay," Maggie said. "I'll tell Gram when she gets back." Maggie took a sip of her drink. "Would you like me to get you some lemonade?"

"No, thanks, dearie. That's very sweet of you, but I have some things to do in my room," Donna said. Jane smiled at the teen as she headed upstairs with Donna.

At twenty to six, Donna knocked on Jane's door. "I've got all my stuff pushed over to my half of the room," Donna said. "And I left Pam a note, in case she arrives while we're out. Are you ready?"

They knocked on Grace's door on the way to the elevator, but nobody answered. In the lobby, they spotted Grace and Arthur sitting on one of the big leather couches. There were two stemmed glasses full of red wine on the coffee table in front of them.

"Arthur just called up to my room and suggested a glass of wine before the tour." Grace blushed. "I should have told you. I don't know where my head was."

Before Jane or Donna could reply, Margaret and Maggie stepped out of the elevator.

"Good," Jane said. "We're all here. Let's get started so we'll have plenty of time to see the horses."

Arthur gulped down his wine, but Grace left most of hers behind. As they walked, Donna announced that another painter - Pam Gerald from their painting group - was driving over and would be joining the group. "Only thing is, I don't know if there's going to be room in our class for her."

"Money is a strong driving force," Arthur remarked. "If Alec accepts another student, he collects another workshop fee."

Margaret told them that Catherine Manfred was still in the hospital. "I don't know when they'll release her. Pneumonia. She's prone to it. That's why she had to quit working at the Staunton's. A stable is pretty hard on allergies."

"I didn't know that Catherine worked for the Staunton's," Jane said. "She worked in the stable?"

"For years," Margaret said. "She was in charge of the whole staff - house, grounds, barns, and stable. But her office was in the entrance of the stable so she couldn't escape the hay and dust."

Yet another connection between the painters in the retreat! Jane made a mental note to add this detail to her class roster.

The Gardens and Horses stable was a short walk on a dirt road from the hotel. The group walked past the back entrance to the thoroughbred museum and some private residences before the road ended at a circular driveway and wooden fence surrounding a large pasture, a two-story barn, and the stable.

As soon as they came within easy sight of the stable, Maggie began to scream. The teen charged toward the fence, yelling, "Dave! Dave! Dave, are you okay?"

At first, Jane didn't understand why Maggie was screaming. Everything seemed peaceful enough. A large brown horse stood in the open doorway of the stable, its bit tethered with a rope to a hook on the wall. A brush lay on the ground beside the animal. Except for the brush, everything seemed neat and orderly.

But Maggie wasn't running toward the stable. She was heading for the barn. A large water trough stood beside it. A rubber boot jutted over the rim of the trough, its sole sticking up. The boot was standing erect, cocked like a flag on a pole. One ray of sun glinted on the boot s shiny surface.

Suddenly, Jane gasped. A boot could not stand in that position unless something was holding it up. Was the boot attached to a man's leg?

Afterward, Jane would remember that glint of sunlight on the boot. It would fuse in her mind with that other horrifying moment - when she'd seen the highlight in the eye of the dead horse in the reflecting pool.

CHAPTER SIX

Grasping the top rail of the fence, Arthur leaped over. He rushed to Maggie's side before the rest of them had managed to fumble open the metal latch on the gate.

"Does somebody have a cell phone?" he shouted. "Call 911." He helped Maggie tug Dave's head and shoulders out of the water.

Pulling her cell phone out of her pocket, Jane said. I don t have any reception."

Jane noticed a smear of blood on the rim of the trough. A shovel was lying on the ground a few feet from the trough. The handle of the shovel was coated with mud. Except for the blood and the shovel, the rest of the barn area was as neat as a hospital waiting room. Jane's intestines gave a twinge. Did somebody hit Dave with the shovel and try to drown him? Who would do such a thing?

"No reception on my phone," Donna said.

"I forgot to grab my phone when I left the room," Grace said.

Margaret felt for a pulse on Dave's neck. "Is he breathing?"

"I don't know. Help me get him out of the water," Arthur said.

Pushing and tugging, they all managed to get enough of Dave's body out of the water so Arthur could get his arms under Dave's armpits and around his chest. Together, they rolled him up and over the lip of the trough and onto the ground.

"Anybody know CPR?" Grace looked around.

"I do. But I can't," Donna said, her voice sputtering. "Oh, my."

"Donna! You look like you're going to pass out," Grace said.

"Oh, my. Gonna. Gonna pass out," Donna said, her words slurring.

Jane grabbed a large bucket, upended it, and she and Grace guided Donna to sit on it. Feeling for Donna's pulse, Jane gasped. It was racing. Beads of sweat were forming on Donna's forehead and neck.

"Maggie, you're our fastest runner," Jane said. "Run to the lobby. Tell them we need an ambulance. Quick. For two people." Turning to Grace, she said, "I'm not sure - Donna could be having a heart attack. Can you support her by yourself while I help with Dave?"

Grace nodded and positioned herself so Donna was leaning against her.

Jane hurried to Dave's limp body. "I had a CPR course," she announced, "but I'm pretty rusty." She kneeled down. "We have to tilt his head back and make sure there's nothing blocking his airway. I'll start the chest compressions. Arthur, watch me so you can take over. Put one palm over the other in the middle of his chest. Compress two inches. Go fast. Like this. At least one hundred compressions per minute. It helps to push to the tune of 'Stayin' Alive.'"

After several minutes, Jane told Arthur to take over. "I don't know how long he's gone without breathing," she said, "so I'm going to blow some air into his lungs." Jane pinched Dave's nostrils shut and blew into his mouth. As she leaned over, Jane caught a movement in the shadow between the stables and the barn. Was someone back there?

Just then, Dave groaned, and Jane turned all her attention to him. He spit up water.

"Help me roll him onto his side," Jane commanded. Arthur and Margaret did as she said, and Jane steadied his head as he spit up more water. Dave coughed then began to vomit.

When Jane looked up again, she couldn't see anybody in the shadows behind the buildings. Had somebody been back there or was it a trick of the light? She was about to ask if anyone else had seen a person back there, but Grace began shouting.

"She's fainted!" Grace cried. "Oh, gosh." Donna's body was slumped against Grace. "I need help. I can't hold her up, she's deadweight."

Arthur rushed over and grabbed Donna's shoulders. Kicking the bucket out from under her, he and Grace lowered Donna to the ground.

Grace loosened Donna's clothing, and spoke in a loud voice, "Donna! Donna, can you hear me?"

With enormous relief, Jane spotted Maggie running along the road toward them. The teen was followed by Mr. Horne, two women dressed in the uniforms of waitresses, and Dave's dog. Jane heard a distant siren followed by another. As the sirens grew louder, two ambulances approached from the service entrance.

The next few minutes were a blur - like the rapid beating of a hummingbird's wings. Stepping out of two ambulances, two pairs of medics sprang into action. One pair kneeled beside Donna, the other rushed to Dave.

As the medics worked on Donna, she roused and began babbling. The medics listened to her heart, took her pulse, strapped her onto a stretcher, and slid her into the back of one of the ambulances.

"Is she having a heart attack?" Jane asked.

"Don't think so," one of the medics answered. "But we need to get her to the hospital. Let 'em run some tests."

The other pair of medics was wrapping blankets around Dave, who was unconscious but seemed to be breathing. The dog whined and licked Dave's forehead.

As they worked on Dave, the medics questioned Arthur about what had happened. Arthur explained that they'd found Dave in the trough. "I don't know how long he'd been in there," he said. "He wasn't breathing when we found him."

Lifting Dave onto a stretcher, the medics transferred him into the back of the other ambulance. Maggie kneeled by the open end of the vehicle, crying softly, with her arms around Dave's dog. Margaret stood beside Maggie, stroking the teen's hair.

"He was in the trough when you found him?" Mr. Horne asked.

Arthur nodded.

Mr. Horne turned to the medics, "If you don't need me right now, I've got to go call the police." He hurried toward the hotel.

Jane watched one of the medics start an IV on Donna in the back of the ambulance. The medic was a poem in motion. With quick, efficient, strokes, he hung a plastic bag of liquid on a pole, slipped a blood pressure cuff around Donna's arm, clipped a small plastic device onto her finger, and hooked her up to a monitor in the vehicle. While the man worked, Donna mumbled about rolling veins and high blood pressure.

Jane approached the second medic, who was jotting something down on a metal clipboard. Which hospital?" she asked him.

"Mercy. About ten minutes from here." He opened the driver's door.

"We're her friends," Grace called. "Would it be alright for us to ride with her?"

"Sure," the driver said. "Both of you can sit up front with me."

"You go," Jane said to Grace. To the ambulance driver, she said, "My car's in the parking lot by the lobby, but I don't know the area. Can I follow you to the hospital?"

As Jane hurried toward the parking lot to get her car, she remembered to glance behind the barn. Although she had a wider view as she trotted along the road, she couldn't make out anybody back there. But there'd been plenty of time for a person to slip inside a building or to vanish into the copse of trees that edged the far side of the barn. If there was a person back there, why didn't he or she come out to help with Dave and Donna?

While she drove to the hospital, Jane used her bluetooth to call Bill's cell phone number. No answer. Then she called Pam's cell phone. Again, no answer. The ambulance pulled into Everlasting Mercy Hospital, and the driver motioned Jane toward a parking lot near the emergency room entrance. Jane parked and went inside. In a few minutes, Grace joined her in the seating area.

"They're moving Donna now," Grace said. "The medics told me to wait out here. Did you call Bill?"

"No answer," Jane said. "I couldn't reach Pam either. I just sent both of them a text."

"You think Donna had a heart attack?"

Jane shrugged. "Her heart was beating faster than a racehorse. And she was sweating like crazy. Do you know how Dave is doing?"

"No." Grace shook her head. "What a mess! If we hadn't gotten there when we did, I believe Dave would've drowned. It's a good thing that all of us walked to the stables together. With both of them passed out, we surely needed all the hands we could get."

Jane was just about to ask Grace whether she'd noticed any movement in the shadows behind the barn, but a nurse called to them. As the nurse led them through the locked double doors, the smell of disinfectant filled Jane's nose.

Donna, wearing a flowered hospital gown, was sitting up on a narrow bed in one of the rooms. The color was back in her face, and she greeted them with a bright smile. "Well, I guess I passed out again," she said.

"Yes, you sure did," Grace said. "Scared me to death."

Donna laughed. "Don't say that. We don't need another dead body. We've had enough of those already."

Grace shuddered. "Oh, gosh. Did you hear something about Dave? Is he ...?"

"Oh no, nothing like that. I haven't heard anything about him."

Donna's phone began ringing. Her belongings were in a plastic bag on the rolling cart beside the hospital bed. Jane fished out the phone and handed it to her.

"Bill," Donna said as she slid her finger across the screen to answer.

While Donna told Bill what had happened, Jane slipped out of the room. She approached the nurse's station.

"I'm Jane Roland," she said. "I'm here with my friend, Donna Norton." She gestured to Donna's room. "She just arrived in an ambulance from Gardens and Horses. There was a second ambulance coming from the gardens - carrying a man named Dave. We found him in a water trough. He wasn't breathing, and I'm the one who gave him CPR. Did he make it? Can you tell me how he's doing?"

Frowning, the nurse touched the keypad on the computer on her counter. "He's stable." She looked at Jane. "That's all I can tell you. I'm sorry. I can't give you any more information unless you're a family member."

"I understand. I'm just glad to know he's alive."

The nurse nodded, her face a grim portrait. "He's alive - right now, anyway."

A young male nurse was in the room with Donna when Jane got back. He was asking about her medical history and recording the information on a computer.

"Do you think they're going to admit her?" Grace asked him. "She's passed out before."

The nurse said he didn't know. "They'll run some tests tonight to rule out heart attack or stroke. But even if everything checks out, they usually keep patients overnight to observe them."

Jane glanced at her phone and saw a text message from Pam:

In hotel parking lot. Just saw your text. Donna passed out? again????? What's going on? Should I come?

Jane texted back:

Donna much better. They will run tests. Grace and I here. No need for you to come. I called front desk to let you in Donna's room.

Jane announced that Dave was alive. "But the nurse wouldn't tell me anything else. She said she can't give out information unless I'm a relative."

The male nurse looked up from his computer monitor. "You talking about the drowning victim? That guy's your friend? Well, I'm not allowed to give out any official information, but I don't like to keep people in the dark. So I'll tell you this: In the case of a serious head wound like his, there's usually lots of swelling. Maybe a brain bleed. So they get the patient onto the operating table as soon as he arrives."

"A brain bleed? I don't know what that is, but it sounds terrible," Donna said. "Will he have brain damage?"

"If someone has a brain bleed, they usually put them into a coma until they can bring down the swelling," the nurse said. "The big thing is they don't want the swelling to press against the brain. At this point, it's probably too early to tell how severe the brain damage is."

"You said he has a serious head wound? You think that could have happened when he fell in the horse trough?" Donna asked. "You know, I wonder how he ended up in a horse trough. I certainly can't imagine that he climbed in there on his own."

Eager to divert the conversation from the sensational, Jane returned to medical information. "How long do they usually keep patients in a coma?"

"Depends." The nurse shrugged. "Could be a couple of days. Could be longer. Just depends on the amount of swelling."

After the nurse left the room, Donna said what they were all thinking: "So they won't be able to ask Dave questions," Donna said.

"Gosh, he sure seemed like a nice young man. Not at all like the kind of person with deadly enemies," Grace said.

"Well, Maggie's grandma didn't like him much," Donna said. "She acted like there was some hanky-panky going on. I'm not saying she's the one who tried to kill him. But she certainly got huffy about Dave's relationship with Maggie."

"Oh, surely she didn't think that Maggie had a romantic relationship with Dave," Grace said. "Dave must be in his late thirties or even in his forties. He's too old for Maggie, and she seems like such a sensible kid. I don't think she'd get involved with an older man."

"But he sure was handsome," Donna said. "Oops, I should have said 'is.' He's not dead yet. At least I hope he's not."

CHAPTER SEVEN

When a loud and terrifying noise erupted, Jane's eyes flipped open.

Groan - her alarm. Every bone in Jane's body cried for more sleep. She hadn't had a full night's rest since she'd arrived at Gardens and Horses. Maybe she should shut the alarm and go back to sleep? What would it matter if she missed the morning session and caught up with the class after lunch?

But if she did that, she'd have to let Grace know. That meant getting up to figure out where she'd left her phone. And, by then, she was sure she'd be wide awake.

Besides, she'd paid so much money for this retreat. It was a shame to miss any of the instruction. As a compromise, Jane decided to hit the alarm's "snooze" button and give herself a few glorious minutes of extra sleep.

Turning over, she pulled the thick coverlet up to her nose. Mmm, this bed really is heavenly, she thought - soft and warm and luxurious. But in spite of the delightful bed and her determined attempts to enjoy it, Jane's brain would not go back to sleep. Groan. Maybe she should get up? That would give her time to call Donna at the hospital and see if the doctor had already been in for morning rounds. Jane fully expected that Donna was fine and this was just another of her fainting spells. But still, she was eager to hear the doctor's opinion.

Jane plumped the pillow around her cheeks. What a night that was! By the time she and Grace had finally left the hospital, it was after ten. They hadn't had any supper, and the hotel restaurant was closed. So they'd gotten a glass of wine at the bar and nibbled on a few pretzels. They were both yawning more than chewing and it was getting close to eleven, so they finished off their wine and got into the elevator. But as soon as they stepped onto their floor, Pam - who had left her door open so she could hear them - had charged out of her room to greet them in the hall.

Of course, Pam was bursting to hear the whole story. So they'd closed themselves in Grace's room and talked about their discovery of the dead horse in the pool and the unconscious man in the trough. Pam buzzed with questions. They'd devoted at least an hour to speculations about who had killed the horse and nearly killed the man. Was it the same person? Surely two such unusual events in the same place on two consecutive days had to be related? But who would have done these things? And why?

When Jane finally got into her own bed, it was long past midnight and her brain was whirling like a pottery wheel. Since writing always calmed her nerves, she'd piled the pillows behind her back and turned on the bedside lamp. Then she'd taken notes about what had happened at the stable. Jotting down the events in as much detail as she could, she found there were three important unsolved questions:

The first was the matter of someone lurking in the shadows when she'd been giving CPR to Dave. She made a note in the margin to ask around about whether anybody else had noticed movement back there. Then she crossed through the note. Perhaps it wasn't wise to mention this to anybody? Except for Grace and Donna, she didn't know who to trust. While the attack on Dave could have been done by someone from outside the gardens - there was a back entrance by the stable so somebody could have slipped onto the grounds unobserved - it might have been done by somebody at the gardens, too. Even someone at their art retreat.

Two other questions gnawed at her: Dave had said that he was going to return Maggie's riding helmet and gloves. That was the original inspiration for their outing. But Jane hadn't seen these things on the bench outside the stable. Dave knew they were coming for their tour before dinner. Had Dave kept Maggie's things in his office? Or perhaps Margaret had stopped by to pick them up when she went to retrieve her sweater from the rose garden? That would put Margaret at the stable at the likely time of the attack. Jane figured the attack on Dave must have happened just prior to their arrival because his face was underwater when they found him. A person can only survive without breathing for what? Four minutes?

Margaret didn't like Dave - she'd made that abundantly clear at lunch. Then again, Margaret didn't seem to like anybody except possibly her granddaughter. But surely Margaret didn't have the motive or, for that matter, the strength to knock a man into a trough? Did she?

Jane made a note in the margin to ask Maggie if she had her helmet and gloves. Jane would have to find a moment to speak to Maggie alone and ask the question inconspicuously. If Maggie had her things, then Margaret was a prime suspect.

The third question was Dave's dog. When they'd arrived at the stable, the dog had been nowhere in sight. That seemed odd. If the dog had been with Dave when he was attacked, why didn't it defend him? The dog had come running to the stable with Maggie, Mr. Horne, and the two waitresses. Where had the dog been before that? Did the dog go wandering off on its own? The dog had seemed so obedient when Jane had first seen it on the patio at lunch. Had somebody purposefully lured it away from the stables so it couldn't bark a warning or defend Dave?

After writing her log, Jane had glanced at the bedside clock. It was 2:30 AM! She turned off the lamp to claim what little sleep she could get. But she couldn't stop her brain from tossing around questions. Echoing her brain, her body tossed and turned for the better part of an hour.

When she'd finally dozed off, Jane had a terrifying dream. A flashlight was penetrating into her eyes like a demonic laser. It was made of soft, shiny rubber - like a flashlight designed to float in water. With horror, Jane recognized the same rubber material as Dave s boot. Despite all her futile attempts to turn the thing off or knock it aside, the light was searing Jane's face. Piercing her eyeballs. She twisted and leaped to grab it, but the flashlight, like a living creature, was determined to elude her grasp. Unable to reach the thing, Jane finally turned and fled from it, dodging its painful ray as she ran down the road from the stable. She turned to see if she'd managed to outdistance the thing, but it was no longer a flashlight. Now the reflective, liquid eye of a stallion confronted her. A menacing stallion whose front legs were raised high to stomp her into the dirt.

Jane awoke, hot and shaky. A pinpoint of light was peeking through her curtains, evidently from the lamppost on the lawn outside. She checked the clock - 4 AM - then she got up and tried to overlap the curtains so they would block out the intruding light. But she couldn't close the gap. Frustrated, she crawled back into bed and rolled onto her other side to face the wall. She must have fallen asleep after that, because the next thing she remembered was the shriek of her alarm.

All through Jane's shower, shreds from her nightmare and questions about the attack kept intruding into her thoughts. It was a relief to leave her room and go down to breakfast.

Entering the breakfast area, she spotted Pam and waved.

"G'mornin'! Did you sleep okay?" Pam asked. She looked as perky as a squirrel, her wavy black-and-silver hair sticking up in every direction.

"Not nearly long enough," Jane answered. "You?"

"Oh my god, yes," Pam said. "That bed is so wonderful, I could write a sonnet about it. Who knew that a mattress could be as deep as the ocean, topped with mountains of snow-capped linens?"

Jane giggled. Pam was the poet of their watercolor group. She loved verse, loved the sound, the texture of words. But dark and depressing was not Pam's muse. Instead, Pam greeted life with the zest of a toddler in a field full of jumpy grasshoppers.

"Did you speak with Donna this morning?" Pam asked

"I did," Jane said. "She said she feels great, and the doctor said she could leave as soon as they got the paperwork in order. Can you pick her up?"

"Sure," Pam said. "Tillie will love it. There's nothing my dog likes better than going for a ride. By the time I got in last night, the kennel was closed. So I left the windows cracked and let her sleep in the car. I knew she'd get fur everywhere, but what else is new?" Pam gave a goofy grin - her typical reaction to the misbehaviors of her naughty fur baby. "That's why I got up so early today. I've already taken Tillie for a long walk. If I left her by herself in the car too long, god knows she'd rip out every stitch in the upholstery."

"I guess she's still a puppy at heart." Jane remembered many a sunshiny afternoon painting in Pam's backyard. Tillie would scramble out of the pool and gleefully shake her thick black fur onto everybody and everything. Although the droplets of spray probably landed at random, it seemed to Jane that the dog purposefully aimed for anybody not wearing a bathing suit. With a few energetic shakes, Tillie would add a Jackson Pollack spritz to the watercolor paintings on their easels. As the painters scurried to cover their paintings, the dog would prop her big clumsy paws on the picnic table and snatch any tidbits that her tongue could reach. If Pam didn't manage to grab Tillie quick enough, the dog had been known to wolf down every morsel on the table and wash down the treats with whatever was left in the wine glasses.

Pam began to compose an extemporaneous ode to the splendid gardens that she'd seen on her morning walk. "Oh, and did I tell you?" Pam said. "Two of the painters were out walking. Lovely young women. Have you met them? Both of them are art teachers in the Charlotte school district. One teaches in elementary school, the other in either middle or high school. Amanda Golden is one of their names. The other is Rachel something. Or maybe it was Rachel Golden and Amanda something. I forget which one said she teaches which grades."

Jane giggled at Pam's scrambled description. "No, those are the only two painters in the retreat that I haven't met. Except Saundra - the one who owned the dead horse - she left at lunch on the first day, and I haven't seen her since. We got a class roster, though, so we can figure out which person belongs to which name. I've been making notes on my roster so I can remember who's who."

"That's a great idea," Pam said. "Tell me about the other painters."

Jane glanced at her phone. "Oops, it's almost time for class. I better go get some breakfast before we talk any more.."

Grace came downstairs while Jane was at the buffet. "Good morning. Pam says you've already spoken to Donna?" Grace said to Jane. "And the doctor said they'll release her today?"

"Yeah, she seems chipper," Jane said. "I guess it was just another of her fainting spells."

"Well, that's a relief," Grace said. She got up to load her plate.

When Grace returned to the table, they made a plan for the day: Pam would pick up Donna and bring her back to the hotel. If Donna felt well enough, the two of them would catch up with the painters at the museum. According to the class schedule, the painters were supposed to start the day at the thoroughbred museum. After painting, they'd be given a tour of the museum before lunch. Lunch was at one on the patio.

Jane suggested that Pam could talk to Alec about joining the class when she got back from retrieving Donna. If he said yes, then she could begin the class after lunch.

Just as they were finishing breakfast, Arthur strode into the breakfast area.

Grace smiled a greeting. "Oh, we were just finishing." She invited him to bring over an extra chair and introduced him to Pam.

"I hope your drive was pleasant," he said to Pam.

"As pleasant as it could be with a big lummox of a dog prancing all over the car and slobbering on my shoulder every five minutes," Pam said. She gave her goofy dog-mom grin. "See, I had to bring Tillie - my black lab - with me. All the kennels in Atkinsville were full."

Jane glanced at the time on her phone and held it up to show the others.

"I hope you've had a chance to eat breakfast?" Grace asked Arthur. "I think we've only got ten minutes before class."

"I ate at home before I left," Arthur said. "Did I tell you that I'm not staying here at the hotel? I live so close by. I'm sure these rooms are comfortable, but there's no place like home." Looking at Pam, he added, "And I've got my own big slobbering dog to look after."

"I didn't know you were a dog person," Grace said. "Do you have a fenced-in yard so you can leave your dog outdoors? I think it's a long day for a dog to be stuck inside."

"No worries. My housekeeper's main occupation seems to be letting Malory in and out. He's the real king of the King domain. Patrols the garden in search of wayward moles, chipmunks, acorns, whatever. Plenty to occupy him. Mind you, my gardens are nowhere as extensive as these." Arthur gestured toward the nearest window overlooking the gardens. "But they are really something, and, believe me, I'm not boasting. It's a tribute to my gardener, who has an amazing green thumb. And Malory, I suppose, who makes sure we never have a problem with moles or chipmunks."

Jane excused herself to run up to the room for her easel and supplies. As she left, she heard Arthur telling them that they should plan to come over and tour his garden some evening. "I'm sure Malory would be delighted to meet your lab," he said to Pam. "He'll introduce her to any hapless chipmunks that have hitherto escaped his surveillance."

Malory. Something flashed in Jane's memory. She was sure she'd heard that name somewhere.

The answer popped into her head as she was brushing her teeth: Malory - Sir Thomas Malory - the author of the King Arthur tales.

CHAPTER EIGHT

The other painters were already assembled in the courtyard of the museum when Jane, Grace, and Arthur hurried to join them. Alec was addressing the group. He nodded at the new arrivals, then continued his directions:

"Plan to finish your painting by eleven. Then we'll break for a short critique session here in the courtyard of the museum. Afterwards, I've arranged for the curator to lead us on a brief tour of the museum before lunch."

Jane marveled again at how different Alec was in the field. Out here, he was a decisive leader, a fish knifing through familiar waters. Inside the classroom, he was just the opposite - bumbling and clumsy, like a walrus on land.

This observation reminded her that people weren't necessarily what they seemed at first glance. Looking at the group of friendly, apparently-innocent painters gathered on the courtyard, Jane reflected that any one of them might have been the culprit who attacked and nearly killed Dave last night. She made a mental note to discuss this privately with Grace, Donna, and Pam and urge them to be cautious about what they said when they interacted with the others.

Dee Dee, one of the sisters who'd gone to SCAD, raised her hand. "Two hours - that's not much time. Usually, I spend days on a painting. Alec, given we have so little time, should we take the time to sketch before we paint?"

"The goal of a plein air painter is to capture a unique moment in time," Alec said. "A moment that can never be repeated; when the light is hitting the scene in just that way and on just that day. It's different than painting in a studio. So, yes, you can sketch if you want, but make it quick. Try to get your painting started in five or ten minutes. Seize the moment."

As soon as Alec told them to spread out and find a spot to paint, Arthur led Grace and Jane to a shady nook on the southern side of the museum. There, they faced a patch of irises. Behind the bulb plants, a deep green bush hugged a sturdy red brick wall. The morning sun, slanting in from the east, drenched a section of the irises.

Since they had so little time to complete their paintings, Jane was tempted to choose a single iris, concentrate on it, and leave her backdrop the white of the paper. She was attracted in particular by a bicolor iris in royal purple and violet. Such lovely petals! The flower seemed like a living breeze, its action halted mid-flutter.

But then Jane reconsidered: If she included the brick wall as her backdrop, with the thick bush as her mid-ground and made her foreground the delicate irises, the composition would be ideal. In the end, she opted to paint the whole scene - wall, bush, and flowers. She pulled out a pencil. Remembering Alec's advice from the day before and squinting her eyes, she noted the slant of the light and the angle of the shadows. After a quick sketch, she began to mix an adobe color for the wall.

Alec came by and watched her work. "Nice composition," he said. "You plan to make the irises your focal point?"

"Yes." Jane was proud that her sketch had communicated her vision for the painting.

"Then use a bigger brush for the wall," he said. "With that small brush, you'll be tempted to put in too many details. The wall is going to be a backdrop for your main subject, so suggest it with a few strokes - don't try to paint every brick. Painters love to linger on details, but that's counter-productive. Too many details can be distracting. Decide on the focal point and make it the most detailed part of your painting. That's the way to lure the viewer's eyes to the spot where you want him - or her - to look."

Jane thanked Alec, and he moved to Grace's easel. As Jane suggested the bricks with a few strokes with a large brush, she reflected: A painting was the opposite of a book in the handling of details. She loved to read mysteries, and in every whodunnit, the plot is always cluttered with details, clues, red herrings - so the reader can't sort out what's essential. That's the way the author keeps the reader from arriving at the solution before Poirot figures it out. But a painting is intentionally transparent, Jane mused. The painter wants to grab the viewer and lead him directly to the most important element - nothing hidden, nothing obscured.

Hmm, Jane considered. Could she use this insight to figure out who had killed the horse and attacked Dave? The viewer of a painting is always standing outside the scene, with a broad view of every part of the composition, and can see the big picture. That's the opposite of a mystery, where the reader is in the page, so to speak, and unable to stand back and view the whole picture. How, Jane wondered, could she step away from the clutter of their surroundings and see the whole picture?

Absorbed in her thoughts, eyes focused on her painting, Jane was startled by a rustling noise. Before she could look up, something pushed her arm - hard - and jolted her easel. Her painting fluttered to the ground.

"Tillie - noooo!" Pam hollered as she grabbed her dog's collar. "When am I gonna learn that I can't trust you?" Pam retrieved Jane's painting from the grass. "Did my dumb dog mess up your painting?"

There was now a big pinkish smudge in the shape of a dog's pawprint across the sun-drenched patch of irises. Jane had intended to leave the area around the irises the bright white of the paper. Quickly, she grabbed a clean brush, dunked it in water, and tried to swab off the pawprint. But it wouldn't come off. Jane frowned.

"I m so sorry, Jane," Pam said. "Tillie was behaving so well that I thought I could trust her off the leash." As Pam clipped the leash on Tillie's collar, she ordered her to lie down and stay. "You bad girl!" she scolded.

The dog lowered her big head to her paws and looked up at Pam with a pitiful expression. Jane tried not to giggle. The dog made such a convincing portrait of sincere remorse. Except for her big feathery tail, which was thumping ever so slightly as she waited for Pam to forgive her latest transgression and cuddle her.

"You're back from getting Donna already?" Jane asked. "That was quick."

"Yes, I was surprised," Pam said. "The nurse had already issued Donna's walking papers. Donna was sitting in the hall waiting for me when

I got there. Another woman was sitting out there with her. Catherine, her name was. Said she's another painter in this class."

"Yes, she's one of the Golden Girls," Jane said.

"Huh?"

"That's my nickname for them," Jane explained. "Catherine and Sheryl. They came to the retreat together. Both of them were wearing capri pants, matching tops, and Keds yesterday. They reminded me of the Golden Girls on TV."

Pam giggled. "Catherine mentioned that she came with a friend. Which one is she?"

Jane looked around and spotted Sheryl, who had set up her easel near Margaret and Maggie. "She's over there," Jane said. "See the gray-haired woman in the capri pants set. Do you want me to introduce you to her?"

"No, that's okay, I don't want to pull you away from painting. I can talk with her at lunch. Catherine told me that she wants her suitcase. I told her I'd bring it over to the hospital if her friend couldn't do it."

"Oh, so Catherine's not coming home today?" Grace asked.

"No, she's got pneumonia," Pam said. "That's what made her light-headed, she said. Thinks the pollen set it off. It's too much for her, everything blooming here. She said she has terrible asthma. It's gone into pneumonia a bunch of times. Double pneumonia once. So she doesn't dare take chances. She said they're planning to keep her in the hospital for a few days. She's gonna ask Alec if he'll refund her workshop fee. "

"Maybe Alec will let you take her place?" Jane said.

"That's what I was thinking," Pam said.

"How's Donna doing?" Grace asked.

"She seems fine. I dropped her off at the hotel. She said she was tired and wanted to change clothes. She'll see us at lunch. But I thought I'd come down and say hello. I thought maybe I could catch up with Alec and ask him about joining the class."

"Good idea," said Jane. "I think he went over there." She pointed behind the museum. "I wasn't so happy about his teaching abilities at first. But I think he's really good at giving one-on-one critiques. Don't you think so, Grace?"

"I do," Grace said. "I've been very impressed. He looks at a painting and - just like that - he can spot the problem. He's very insightful."

"Wow! I definitely want to be part of this class," Pam said. "Let me see if Alec's got a minute now. If not, I'll speak to him after I put Tillie in the kennel."

The dog looked up at the sound of her name and whined.

"Yes," Pam said, "I'm talking about you, Miss Troublemaker." Tillie stood up, her tail waving like a flag in a storm, and began dancing around Pam's legs. Her tail knocked over Grace's easel.

"Oh, Tillie," Pam groaned, "you're just a big klutz." Turning to Grace and Jane, she said, "I better get this dog out of here before she does any more damage."

At eleven, Alec called everybody to the courtyard. The painters lined up their easels in a row. Again, Jane noted the wide range of responses to the assignment. A few people had chosen to paint closeups of flowers. The schoolteachers, Amanda and Rachel, had borrowed Arthur's idea from their session in the rose garden yesterday. Both of them had painted a scene of painters at work at their easels in a lush garden.

Once again, Jane thought Arthur's work stood out from the others. He had done a painting within a painting: A closeup of a floral painting stood on an easel, surrounded by greenery, against a backdrop of the museum's brick wall. Arthur really was talented, Jane thought. And his compositions were clever and unexpected.

"Why, look at your painting!" Grace told him. "What an interesting approach. How did you come up with that?"

Arthur gave her a rakish grin. "Oh, I don't know. I've got all kinds of tricks up my sleeve."

Alec stroked his chin as he stood in front of the first painting in the row. He hesitated. Then he complimented the painter on her choice of bright colors. "Did you decide to limit your palate to just a few colors?"

Dee Dee answered. She said she'd felt too rushed to mix colors so she'd just picked out three tubes to work with - a bright opera pink, an emerald green, and a turquoise. As Jane listened, her admiration for Alec grew. It couldn't have been easy to think of something positive to say about Dee Dee's painting. First of all, it was so crudely drawn that it reminded Jane of a child's work. Evidently, Dee Dee really did need to take time with her sketch, Jane thought.

Alec walked along the row of easels, commenting on each painting. As she waited for his evaluation, Jane compared her own work with the others. She was very pleased about how her painting had turned out. She had managed to scrub away enough of Tillie's paw print so the area looked as if she had intended it to be bathed in a hazy pinkish light. Not too shabby, she thought, and hoped that Alec would single out her work as an example of a successful composition.

A pair of police officers approached the group as Alec was critiquing the painting beside hers. Jane recognized one of them. He was the policeman who had interviewed her, Grace, and Donna in Mr. Horne's office on the night they had discovered the dead horse. He was a short man, shorter than his companion, but he had an energetic stride. Jane guessed he was Irish, with his gray-blonde hair, blue eyes, and turned-up nose.

The shorter police officer waved at Alec. "Sorry to interrupt," he said. Need to talk with a few of the painters. Is this a good time?"

"We're in the middle of critiquing of our morning's paintings," Alec said. "But I guess we can finish after lunch."

The policeman glanced at the row of easels and smiled. "Look good to me. Better than I could do. I promise this won't take too long. I understand that several of you went to the stable last evening. Please step over here if you were part of that group." He gestured toward a wooden bench between two large potted bushes that was tucked in a shady nook under the museum s roof.

Jane, Grace, Arthur, Margaret, and Maggie followed the two policemen to the bench.

"Is this all of you?" The shorter policeman took a notepad out of his breast pocket. "Mr. Horne said there were six painters at the stable."

"Donna isn't here," Jane said.

"She's not in this class?"

"Yes, she is," Jane said. "But she fainted. They took her to the hospital in an ambulance."

The policeman nodded. "She still in the hospital?"

"No, they released her this morning. She's at the hotel now."

"Alright, we'll check with her later. Meantime, we'll get a few statements from you," the police officer said. "I'm James Goode, and this here's my partner, Randall Kennedy." Goode looked at Jane and Grace. "You're the women who found the dead horse two nights ago, aren't you?"

Jane and Grace nodded.

"Some painting retreat, huh?" Goode said, shaking his head. "More like a mystery writers convention. How about if you two follow me. And Officer Kennedy, here, will interview the others."

Jane and Grace followed Officer Goode along the path leading to the stable. The wooden fence enclosing the stable and barn was wrapped in yellow police tape.

"We'll have to stay outside the fence," Goode said. "Don't want to add our footprints to the mix. You two don't mind standing? It won't take long."

Jane and Grace described what had happened while Goode took notes. He questioned them closely about what time they'd left the hotel to tour the stables. "You're sure you started out from the lobby at quarter to six? All of you together?"

Jane and Grace both nodded. "That's when we agreed to meet. I checked my phone before I left the lobby," Jane said. "I actually wrote all this down, if that would help you."

Goode raised his eyebrows and looked at her. "You wrote it down?"

"Writing calms me," she explained. "Last night, when I got back to the room, I wrote down all the details I could remember while they were fresh on my mind." She hesitated. "I'll be glad to show them to you, if you think it would help. But I haven't edited them. There might be some, um, too-straightforward descriptions of some people in the retreat."

Goode grinned. "Don't worry. I won't share them with anybody else."

"Do you want me to go get my notepad now?"

"It's in your room?"

Jane nodded.

"If you wouldn't mind. I'll walk with you to the hotel," Goode said. "I want to time how long it takes to walk from the stable to the lobby, anyway. Why don't you both come along? Walk at about the speed you went yesterday."

At the hotel, Jane and Grace went upstairs while Goode headed for the patio to wait for them.

Upstairs, when they got off the elevator, Grace knocked on Donna's door. "Donna, it's me. Are you alright?"

"Wait a minute," Donna yelled. When she opened the door, her hair was tousled. "I didn't get much sleep last night. I was taking a nap. Is it lunchtime already?"

"Sorry to wake you," Grace said. "We came back early. There's a policeman downstairs."

"Oh my. Did somebody else get drowned?" Donna asked.

"No, nothing like that," Grace said. "He just wants to interview everybody who was at the stable last night. Says he wants to speak with you."

Jane let herself into her room to retrieve her notepad. Should she tear out the pages she'd written last night or bring the whole pad, which included the notes that she'd taken about their discovery of the dead horse? What about the notes she'd written on her class roster? They showed the connections between the painters. She shrugged. Might as well show the policeman all of it, she thought. She had a suspicion that the dead horse and the drowned stable hand were related. And it was possible - maybe likely - that someone at the retreat was involved. She was sure these suspicions had also crossed James Goode's mind.

The patio had already been set for lunch with the same emerald green tablecloths as yesterday. Goode was sitting at one of tables when the three women joined him. Jane handed him her notepad.

"I'll make a copy and get the pad back to you. I'll leave it at the front desk," he said. He turned to Donna. "You're Donna Norton? I understand you were hospitalized after the incident at the stable?"

"Yes, I fainted. High blood pressure. Happens to me a lot."

Donna told Goode everything she remembered from their visit to the stables. "I'm kinda foggy about what happened after we saw the fellow in the water. You know, Dave, the stable man. He is still alive, isn't he?"

"Far as I know," Goode said.

"That's a relief," Donna said. "I'm kinda afraid to take a bath here."

Goode raised his eyebrows. "Huh?"

"Seems like every time we get near some water, there's a body in it."

CHAPTER NINE

"I think I'll skip the museum tour," Grace said. She leaned her head back and shut her eyes. "I'd like to sit here and relax for a few minutes before lunch. I can look at the museum another time - I don't care about the tour."

"Sounds good to me," Jane said. "The tour is probably over by now, anyway."

"Oh, that's what our class did this morning? Toured the museum?" Donna asked. "Did I miss anything else? Did Alec manage to get to class on time?"

"Actually, he arrived before we did," Jane said. "He's really a different person when he's outdoors. That's his milieu."

"Yes, he is such a different teacher when we're painting outdoors, isn't he?" Grace said. She opened her eyes and looked at Donna. "We painted on the grounds outside the museum this morning, Donna. Then we lined up our easels, and Alec critiqued. I think his suggestions are just so helpful."

"He's very tactful," Jane added. "I couldn't imagine what he was going to say about that first painting. The one that Dee Dee did. But he managed to find something to compliment her about."

"Which one is Dee Dee?" Donna asked.

"She went to SCAD," Jane said. "She's got short hair. Came with her sister, the redhead with freckles."

"Oh, yes," Donna said, "I remember them. Her sister has a funny name. Hairy or something. I guess they call her that because she has that big, bouncy red hair."

Jane laughed. "Actually, I think it's Harry. H-A-R-R-Y. Short for Harriet."

"Oh. That makes sense. She probably got the nickname when she was a little kid. And how could they have known, back then, that she was gonna wear her hair all puffed up like that?" Donna said. "So Dee Dee's a lousy painter? But she went to SCAD. I thought that was supposed to be a ritzy art school. Those two sisters sure seem snooty to me. I wonder if they have rich parents, and that's how they got into such a fancy art school."

"The problem was Dee Dee's drawing," Grace explained. "Everything was out of proportion. But, of course, we were on a strict deadline. Alec said we had to finish our paintings in two hours. Maybe Dee Dee is very talented but she's the kind of artist who needs more time to develop a sketch."

As they talked, the kitchen staff began carrying out warming trays, containers of food, and pitchers. Jane glanced along the path that led to the museum. The other painters were beginning to walk in small clusters toward the patio.

Arthur, with two easels folded under one arm and two bags of supplies looped over his shoulder, emerged from the trees. He called out, "There you are!"

As soon as he reached the patio, Arthur placed the two collapsed easels on the brick half-wall. "I grabbed your easel and supplies, Grace. But I couldn't carry everybody's. I'll help y'all carry the rest after lunch. I didn't want to leave anybody's paintings out there, though. Never can tell if a wind or a sudden shower will come up." He put a sheaf of paintings on the table.

"I forgot all about our paintings and supplies back there," Jane said. "Guess my brain is kinda foggy. I didn't get much sleep last night."

Donna picked up the paintings and began leafing through them. "These are really beauti.... Oh, there's Sheryl," Donna said. She waved at the Golden Girl and motioned for her to come over.

As she approached the table, Sheryl smiled at the women. But when she greeted Arthur, she frowned and gave him a curt nod.

Have you spoken to Catherine today?" Donna asked her.

"No, I was going to call her after lunch," Sheryl said. She glanced at her watch. It was a thin, silver circlet, an old-fashioned watch with a glass dome covering a round dial. The kind of watch that women used to wear before cell phones. More like a piece of jewelry than a utilitarian object.

"I talked with her this morning," Donna said.

Sheryl looked puzzled.

"You know I was in the hospital last night? Same floor as Catherine."

"Rupert did tell me that two ambulances came to the stable last night. He said they took two people to the ER - Dave and a woman who fainted."

"That was me," Donna said. "When I saw Dave in the trough, I passed out."

"Oh dear. But you're feeling better now?"

"Yes, I pass out a lot. High blood pressure."

"Well, I'm glad you're better today," Sheryl said. "I guess it was quite a shock seeing Dave like that. I can't get over what happened. I've been coming to these gardens since I was a little girl. Never heard of any violence here."

Sheryl turned toward Arthur. "Of course, I know that some people have been very vocal about objecting to the way Dave handles the thoroughbreds. But to attack him? Who would do such a thing?"

Jane noticed that Sheryl's face tightened into a school teacher's stern look of disapproval as she faced Arthur. Looking directly into his face, Sheryl pressed him to answer, "You've been coming to these gardens for years, Arthur. Could you have imagined such a thing?"

"No, of course not," Arthur said. He glanced off toward the stable. "I agree, it's unimaginable. Rupert must be at his wit's end."

"Who's Rupert?" Jane asked.

"Oh, that's my nephew," Sheryl explained. "Rupert Horne, the manager. He took this job about six years ago. Before working here, he managed the Sleep Inn in Gilbertville and that place ran him ragged. When he came to Gardens and Horses, he said it was so peaceful that he felt like he'd died and gone to heaven."

"Oh my. I hope he doesn't say that anymore," Donna said. "Dying seems to be an awfully common occurrence around here. 'Course I don't know about going to heaven. Do horses go to heaven, you think?"

Pam came bustling out the double door from the lobby and plopped onto the seat next to Donna. She greeted Sheryl. "You must be Sheryl," Pam said, reaching over Donna to offer Sheryl her hand to shake. "You're

Catherine's friend, aren't you? I'm Pam. I met Catherine at the hospital this morning, when I went to pick up Donna."

Sheryl gave Pam a pleasant smile. "Nice to meet you, Pam."

"Did you speak to her today?" Pam asked Sheryl. "Catherine told me they re going to keep her for a few days so she needs her suitcase. I told her I'd be glad to bring it over to the hospital if you can't do it. I guess Catherine is dropping out of the retreat. As soon as I get a chance to talk to Alec, I'm going to ask if he'll let me take her place."

Hearing his name, Alec turned toward their table. He stormed over and confronted Sheryl.

"So Catherine is dropping the workshop? You realize this is the third time she s dropped out of one of my retreats?" As he spoke, Alec's nostrils flared like a high-strung horse.

Yet another side of Alec Treville! When they'd first met him, Jane reflected, Alec had seemed the stereotypical teacher with his well-worn introduction and recycled jokes. Then, during his initial demo in the conference room, he'd revealed a second side to his personality - the burned-out prof; bored and disorganized. Outdoors, when they worked en plein air, Alec blossomed into the consummate teacher - clear, encouraging, insightful. Now, he was revealing an explosive temper. Jane wondered if there was another side to this complex man. Perhaps a darker side?

"I'm thoroughly fed up with it," Alec continued. "Inconsiderate! Irresponsible. Disrespectful. You name it! I suppose she's going to expect me to refund her workshop fee. AGAIN. I told her last spring that she couldn't keep doing this. If you're prone to asthma and you know that being outdoors sets it off, then don't enroll in a plein air painting workshop. When her application arrived, I told Rupert that I didn't want to accept it. But he insisted I'd give the gardens a bad name if I started refusing students."

Sheryl looked as if she'd been scolded. "I do understand how you feel, Alec," she said in a stiff voice. "But if they're keeping Catherine in the hospital, she really doesn't have any choice about whether to drop the workshop, does she? She needs her suitcase, so I'm going over there this evening before dinner. I'll talk with her then about the class fee."

As soon as Alec marched away, Pam raised her eyebrows. "Whoa, he's got a hot temper, doesn't he! This is the instructor who's so helpful and encouraging?"

"He seems to have a multifaceted personality," Jane said.

"I guess so. I was going to ask him about joining the class," Pam said. "But I think I'd better wait until he gets a little food in his belly."

Donna giggled. "If it's hunger that's making him so grouchy, he must be starving! It sounded like he was going to bite your head off, Sheryl."

"I guess everybody's tense," Sheryl said, frowning. "I know Rupert is at his wit's end. This is certainly not the relaxing retreat that I was expecting." She looked around. "Do you know where those policemen went?"

"I think they left. After they interviewed us. I saw them walking out the front door of the lobby," Jane said.

"Oh," Sheryl said, biting her lip. "I wanted to have a word with them. I wonder how late they stay at the police station? Well, it looks like lunch is ready." She waved goodby and found a chair at the table where Margaret and Maggie and the two schoolteachers were sitting.

As Jane waited in line to collect her lunch, she noticed that Alicia and Teddy Pickridge were sitting at separate tables. Teddy was beside Alec at a table for three. Saundra Staunton, who was apparently rejoining their retreat, was sitting with the two men. At the other table set for three, the two SCAD sisters, Dee Dee and Harry, were sitting with Alicia.

Lunch was an Asian salad bar. In addition to a heaping platter of spring mix lettuces, there were bowls of slender carrot sticks, honeyed almonds, and pineapple chunks. A warming tray held grilled teriyaki chicken, shrimp, and tofu pieces. Crispy spring rolls and crab Rangoon were in another warming tray. A large cooler held pistachio and coconut ice cream bars. Jane helped herself to a heaping salad bowl, a spring roll, two crab Rangoons, and a glass of iced tea. She decided she'd return later for an ice cream bar. After skipping supper last night, she felt like she could afford to indulge in an ample lunch. The food smelled delicious!

As they ate, Arthur regaled them with tales about the early days at the gardens, when wealthy New Yorkers vacationed in the vicinity during the winter. These East Coast barons inhabited palatial estates up North during the spring and summer. In fall, they moved here to their winter vacation homes. They brought their thoroughbred horses, their house servants, and their gardeners with them. Three of these "snow birds" lived on adjacent properties and they donated a portion of their estates to establish Gardens and Horses. The Gardens' current schedule - of horse events and flower shows - was originally developed by these wealthy patrons.

Arthur was a great storyteller, with an eye for intriguing details. But Jane found her attention drifting. All around the patio, conversation stilled as the painters leaned back in their chairs to savor the ice cream bars. As Jane licked her ice cream bar, she wondered if there was time for a short nap after lunch? She'd left her class schedule in her painting bag - which was in the museum courtyard - so she couldn't check to see when their next session would begin.

As if he'd read her mind, Alec stood up to announce the afternoon's schedule. "We'll take a break after lunch, then meet at the reflecting pool," he said.

Jane perked up as soon as Alec announced the location of their next session. Her eyes met Donna's and Grace's. "The reflecting pool?" she mouthed. That's where they'd found the dead horse. Jane didn't know if she was ready to face that scene again.

"You'll need your easel and painting supplies," Alec continued. "I want to start with a short talk. Afterward, we'll fan out and choose a spot for painting. I think you'll find that the play of shadows from afternoon lighting is very different. Water accentuates these effects. Let's plan to get started at three."

After Alec sat down, Jane announced her intention to go up to her room and nap before their next session.

"I'm gonna go speak to Alec about joining the class," Pam said as she stood up.

"Wait a minute, both of you, if you wouldn't mind," Arthur said. "I was hoping I might convince all of you to skip dinner tonight."

Jane was about to object. They'd missed dinner with the group last night as well as the night before. She was about to point this out when Arthur said, "I want to invite you to join me for dinner at my home tonight. My housekeeper is a consummate folk artist. Her paintbrushes are the spoon, the whisk, and the spatula; her canvas the heirloom china." He smiled, obviously pleased with his clever metaphor. "How about it? After everything that's happened, I think you're all ready for a change of scenery."

Grace answered first. "I think that sounds delightful," she said, "especially if we're going to have to spend the afternoon staring at the pool where we found that drowned horse." Then she hesitated as she looked at the others. "I didn't mean to speak for all of us. Would you rather stay here?"

"I'd kinda like to see how the natives live," Donna said. "Count me in."

Pam shrugged. "Suits me. I'm always up for an adventure."

"Okay by me," Jane said. "I can drive, if you like."

"You don't think this will be too much of an imposition for your housekeeper?" Grace asked.

"Not at all," Arthur said. "I'll call her right now. She'll be relieved to show off her culinary talents for somebody besides me. Think of this as a one-woman gallery show." He stood up.

"One thing," Grace began, "I hope you'll be willing to give us a brief tour of your garden? You've told us so much about it."

"I thought you'd never ask!" he said with a grin. "The irises are spectacular this year."

"Should we meet in the lobby after class and follow you to your house?" Jane asked.

"No need," Arthur said. "I live on the same road as the hospital. It's not hard to find. I can give you directions. Or if you prefer to use GPS, it'll bring you right to my door."

"I just thought it might be easier...." Jane began.

Grace broke in. "I'm sure we can find it." She looked at Jane. "I'm guessing that Arthur will want to take care of some things before we all descend on him."

"Exactly," Arthur said, smiling. "Shall we say between six-thirty and seven?"

Arthur left to make his phone call, and Pam went to speak to Alec. Donna and Grace decided they'd enjoy a stroll after lunch.

But Jane felt like she was dragging. "I really think I'd feel better after a nap," Jane said. "Especially if we're going to Arthur's tonight. It might be another late night."

Maggie was getting off the elevator as Jane walked through the lobby. The teen was carrying a riding helmet and lavender gloves, and she was practically bouncing as she headed toward the door.

"Going for a ride?" Jane said.

Maggie grinned. "Such a beautiful day! Mr. King said his horses need some exercise. He hasn't ridden them for a few weeks. And now, with Dave ...." She trailed off.

Jane gestured at the helmet and gloves. "Looks like you packed riding gear along with your art supplies? I guess that's the true sign of a horse lover - always prepared for a ride."

Maggie blushed. "No, Ma'am. Actually, I left my helmet and gloves here from when Gwenny was at the stable. Dave held onto them for me."

"So these are the riding things that Dave mentioned at lunch yesterday?"

"Yes, Ma'am. Mrs. Calhoun brought them to me."

"Mrs. Calhoun?" Jane asked. "You mean, Sheryl?"

Maggie nodded. "She and Gram are friends."

Jane tried to keep the tone of her voice and her facial expression from displaying her eagerness to probe this revelation. "I thought you were planning to pick up your things when we went to the stable last night - that was the reason Dave invited us for a tour. How'd Sheryl get them?"

Maggie shrugged. "I don't know. She brought them to me this morning at breakfast. She and Gram started talking. I never got a chance to ask her."

Jane's head was buzzing like a hive about to swarm, but she tried to sound nonchalant as she waved goodbye. "Be safe out there."

Maggie froze. The color drained from her face.

"Oh. Did I say something wrong?" Jane said.

Stammering, Maggie said, "No, no, of course you didn't. It's just that Dave always said those exact same words whenever any of us went out to ride. Thoroughbreds - they're high strung, you know. Difficult to handle. So are their owners. With those horses, there's a lot of money at stake. All the interns were terrified that a horse would break a leg or something."

"I guess that would be a lot of responsibility - riding somebody's expensive racehorse. Have there been, um, other problems with the horses at this stable? You know, before Lancelot drowned?"

"Not that I know about." Maggie lowered her voice to a whisper. "But there were always rumors. You know. About drugs."

Jane looked at Maggie, puzzled.

The teen shrugged. "You know how race horses are given stuff so they'll run faster? And pain killers so they can run even if they've gotten injured."

"I had no idea," Jane said. "Is that why your dad didn't want Gwenny stabled here?"

"No, I don't think so," Maggie said. "Gwenny was already retired from racing before we got her. But some of the horses, like Lance, they're still in competition."

"I see," Jane said.

Maggie looked around the lobby. She seemed nervous. "Gram doesn't like for me to talk about horses being drugged. It's probably just rumors, anyway. You know how people are when a horse is winning. They get jealous."

Jane raised her eyebrows. "Was Lancelot winning?"

"Oh, yes," Maggie said. "He was a champion. Well, I gotta go. "

Jane smiled. "Have a good ride."

As she pushed the elevator button, Jane realized that she was not the least bit sleepy anymore. As soon as she got upstairs, she decided to get online and read everything she could about drugs and horse racing.

CHAPTER TEN

Jane opened her laptop and typed in "racehorses and drugs." Nineteen screens full of articles popped up.

She learned that racehorses can reach speeds of 30-40 miles per hour, but speed comes at a mighty cost. Track injuries are unavoidable. A horse achieves maximum speed on a track with a firm, hard surface, but hard tracks cause percussive injuries to a horse's leg bones. Softer tracks produce other problems - they're like running through mud, which fatigues a horse's muscles and overloads its soft tissues. Running on a track with a loose surface is like running on slippery silt, and a horse can easily pull a tendon.

Jane assumed that an injured horse would be given time to heal before it raced again. But racehorses began their careers as two-year-olds, and their careers are finished by the time they're six. So owners resort to a variety of painkilling drugs - patches, shots, IV's - to keep an injured horse on the track. Jane had heard of some of the painkillers, like fentanyl and pentobarbital, because they're also used to block pain in people. All these drugs have various side effects. Dosing is critical. Jane read that even the most carefully-handled champion horses had sometimes died of overdoses.

During their brief conversation in the lobby, Maggie had said there was lots of money at stake. But Jane was astounded to discover how much. Buying a champion racehorse involved an investment of millions of dollars. Just the stud fee for a proven stallion might run as high as $100,000. Add that to the billions spent in gambling each year, and Jane's head started spinning like a moon in orbit. A combo of drugs and money - that's a perfect recipe for crime, Jane thought.

Caught up in her research, Jane completely lost track of the time. A knock on her door roused her. "Jane, are you awake?" Pam's voice called through the door. "It's almost time for class."

Opening her door, Jane found Pam in the hall, with an easel over her shoulder and a painting bag in hand. Donna was standing behind her, her purple floppy hat on her head.

"Were you asleep?" Donna asked. "You look like you've just gotten back from the Twilight Zone."

"Actually, I've been reading about racehorses," Jane said. "And it was sort of like being in the Twilight Zone." She glanced up and down the corridor. Nobody else was in sight, but still.... Reluctant to talk about what she'd just learned in a public hallway, Jane ushered Pam and Donna into her room and closed the door.

"The amount of money involved in horse racing is mind boggling," Jane said. She pointed at her laptop on the desk. "Champion racehorses have sold for as much as seventy million dollars. At U.S. tracks, legal betting brings in over eight billion dollars a year. That's billions - not millions! Under-the-table betting brings in lots more - something like a hundred billion. Just maintaining a racehorse can cost an owner about $55,000 every year."

"I'm not surprised," Donna said. She sat on the edge of Jane's bed. "There's no such thing as a cheap horse. It used to cost my dad plenty just to keep a little pony for me to ride. Then you add the rest - fancy stables and trainers and jockeys. Horse racing isn't a sport for the average Joe."

"I never thought about it," Pam said, "but it makes sense. Everybody's heard of the big races, like the Kentucky Derby and the Preakness. Any sport that makes front-page headlines has to rake in big bucks."

"With so much money riding on these four-legged athletes, there are all kinds of scandals," Jane said. "Drugs are a big issue. Owners give the horses steroids to boost performance, and since that's perfectly legal in many states, a horse doesn't really stand much chance of winning unless its owner resorts to drugs."

"I've heard of that," Pam said. "I think horses are given painkillers if they get injured, too. So they won't miss a big race."

Jane nodded. "And they get injured all the time. One writer said racehorses were basically 'thousand-pound athletes on toothpick legs.'"

Pam giggled. "That's a great description. They do have awfully skinny legs."

"You can say that again," Jane said. "I read that a racehorse's ankles are no wider than a person's. You wouldn't believe some of the stories I read. Let me show you what I ...." Jane started to pull up an article on her laptop, but stopped when she noticed the time. "Hmm, our class starts in ten minutes. I guess we'll have to talk about this later. We've still gotta go by the museum and pick up our stuff."

Donna and Pam stood up, but before they opened the door, Jane said, "Wait a minute. There's something I've been meaning to talk to you about. This is important, even if it makes us late for class. And I don't dare mention it where anybody else can hear."

Donna raised her eyebrows. "Don't tell me you found another dead body?"

Jane laughed. "No, nothing that dramatic. But I was thinking about everything that's happened since we got to the gardens. Somebody killed a champion horse. Somebody attacked Dave."

"Maybe the same person," Pam suggested.

"Maybe," Jane said. "But the point is we don't know who. Could be one of the people in our retreat. Could be somebody on the hotel staff."

"Now there's a cheerful thought," Donna said

"If I realized things would turn out this way, I never would've signed up for this retreat," Jane said.

"Now she tells me!" Pam exclaimed. "Here I thought I was getting such a great deal when Bill called and offered to pay for everything if I'd drive up here."

Jane shrugged. "Well, we're here, so I guess we may as well make the best of it. But we need to be careful. We know that whoever did those things to Lancelot and Dave is violent - capable of murder. So we better watch what we say when we're in earshot of anybody. Say we happen to notice something suspicious, and we don't even realize it. We don't want to announce what we saw and give the attacker a reason to get rid of us."

"Jeesh," said Pam, "you're making it seem like we're right smack in the middle of an Agatha Christie movie."

"And from now on," Jane continued, "I think we better operate on the buddy system. None of us ought to go anywhere alone."

"Okay with me," Donna agreed. "Mum's the word. And two by two, like Noah's ark." She moved toward the door. "I guess we won't have to worry about telling Grace about that."

"What do you mean," Pam asked. "You don't want Grace to stay safe?"

"Well, she's never alone, anymore," Donna said. "Every time she turns around, that Arthur fellow is with her. He's like her shadow. That's where she is right now. Arthur called and invited her for a little stroll before class."

Jane grabbed a straw sunhat and ushered them out the door. One of the two young schoolteachers in their class was in the elevator when they got on. She was a petite woman with curly brunette hair bouncing merrily against her shoulders.

Pam introduced them. "Hello, Amanda," Pam said. "These are my painter friends from Atkinsville that I told you about: Jane Roland and Donna Norton."

Amanda smiled, revealing a pair of adorable dimples. "Glad to meet you."

As soon as she smiled, Amanda reminded Jane of a dark-haired Shirley Temple. "Pam told us about meeting you," Jane said. "You were out walking this morning when Pam was walking her dog. I think Pam said you're a teacher? From Charlotte."

"Good memory," Amanda said. "I teach middle school art. I drove up here with Rachel Sanchez. She teaches elementary school in my district. I recall Pam telling me that some of her friends were teachers, too?"

"That would be me," Donna said. "I taught fourth grade. In a teeny little rural school - probably nothing like the schools in Charlotte."

"But I thought you told me that there were four of you from the same art center?" Amanda said to Pam. "And you got here late because one of your friends had fainted and her husband was worried about her health."

As they exited the elevator, Pam said, "Now look who's got the good memory! There are four painters from our painting group. The fourth, Grace Tanner, is out walking with a fellow that she met here. She's the other former teacher. And it's Donna, here," Pam said, nodding at Donna, "who fainted."

"I guess you're feeling better?" Amanda said.

Donna nodded. "High blood pressure. I faint all the time."

Jane said to Amanda, "I'll bet you really need a good memory to keep track of all your students. How many kids do you teach every day?"

"Lots," said Amanda. "We have a huge school - almost 3,000 kids - grades six, seven and eight. Every sixth grader has to take one semester of art. So I get to know one group of kids and then the schedule changes. Poof, they're gone, and another crew comes in. For the seventh and eighth graders, art is an elective, but a very popular elective."

"Sounds exhausting," Jane said. "I don't know how you do it."

"I love it," Amanda said. "But there are some days when I'm so tired, I wonder why in the world I ever decided to teach."

As they exited the patio door, Jane reminded Donna, "Speaking of memory, let's not forget. We need to go by the museum so we can pick up our easels and supplies."

"You left your stuff out there?" Amanda asked. She raised her eyebrows. "I guess nobody would steal anything. I mean an art retreat seems like it would be safe enough. But there have been some crazy things going on. That man from the stable who was attacked. And weren't you the ones who found a dead horse in the reflecting pool?"

Donna nodded. "Yeah, that's why I keep fainting. You know, I've heard a lot of people talk about a gorgeous painting and say it's 'to die for.' But until we got to this retreat, I never thought they meant that literally."

Donna laughed at her own joke. And Amanda laughed, too. Donna's laugh was a gruff "heh, heh, heh," but Amanda had a melodious laugh that sounded like a bell ringing in a Christmas concert. The contrast between the sounds of their laughter made Jane burst out laughing, too. Jane decided that the popularity of art class in Amanda's school probably had more to do with this art teacher's personality - plus her dimples and tinkling laughter - than with the subject matter.

After Jane and Donna collected their art gear in the museum courtyard, the four joined the class. Jane was afraid that the reflecting pool area would be cordoned off with yellow crime tape, like the stable was. But - much to her relief - there was no such reminder of their shocking discovery of the dead horse.

Far from a crime scene, the reflecting pool and surrounding plantings looked idyllic, like a glossy photo from an art school catalogue. Alec was pointing out the shadows in the pool; how a subtle dance of light and color was created by overhanging leaves from the trees reflected in the water. The students, themselves a dance of summer colors, arrayed themselves among the foliage. Some approached the pool as Alec gestured, others receded, weaving in and out, like an elaborate minuet.

Jane stood back and watched the scene, reluctant to approach the pool. When she finally did force herself to step forward and look into the depths of the water, she saw only a lovely pattern of shapes and shadows. Gone was the horse's eye, pierced by the last rays of sunlight, that had populated her nightmare. As she stepped back, she sighed audibly.

Behind her shoulder, Donna said, "I know what you mean."

Jane startled and whirled around.

"Doesn't make any sense, does it?" Donna said. "I was afraid to look into the water, too. I mean, I knew that poor horse wasn't going to be in the water, anymore. But I can't get that image out of my mind, so I kinda expected I'd see it when I looked into the pool."

Pam had begun to set up her easel at one end of the reflecting pool. Jane and Donna joined her. They had a lovely view of the pool framed by arcing trees. A pathway led from the far end of the pool into a forest of greenery. The pathway seemed to beckon the viewer to walk along dappled shadows to some splendid but unknown future.

As they began to paint, Jane smiled across the pool at Grace, who had set up her easel next to Arthur's. Grace beamed back - obviously enjoying herself - and waved her index finger in greeting. Looking at Grace and Arthur painting beside each other, Jane was torn about the subject of her afternoon painting. She could capture the perfect landscape or she could create a Renoir-like scene of a perfectly matched couple happily engaged in their outdoor environment. In the end, Jane opted for the landscape - people were a lot of trouble. They always complicate a scene.

The afternoon session seemed to fly by. Jane noticed that conversation grew sporadic and finally muted entirely as the painters became entranced by their work. Movement stilled, until the dip of paintbrush in color and water became a sort of rhythm. The gentle rustling of leaves and the aroma of greenery and soil animated the scene. It was as if the painters were gradually transformed into the words of a poem. They created an ever-so-subtle alliteration, an echoing rhyme-scheme, a metaphor that hung like perfume in the air. When Alec called for the group to finish their paintings and line up the easels along the path for critiquing, Jane was reluctant to relinquish the harmony and return to the ordinary chaos of human interaction.

As she looked at her own work in the context of the others, a sense of satisfaction washed over Jane. Maybe when she was tired, she became more absorbed in her work and therefore she painted better? She had allowed her mind to quiet and become immersed in the task and scene. It was a good feeling and it produced good work.

Alec was very complimentary when he paused along the line of easels and discussed her landscape. His words gave Jane a heady feeling of a job well done and justly acknowledged.

The painters gathered their supplies. Jane, Donna, and Pam met Grace and Arthur for the short walk to the hotel. Still absorbed in the vibes from the successful painting session, Jane was jarred back to the moment by Grace's voice. "Jane?" Grace said. "Did you hear me? We're still planning to be at Arthur's around seven?"

Jane glanced at her phone. They had two hours before they'd need to leave. Maybe she'd better take a short nap - her mind seemed as cloudy as pond water.

"Yes," Jane responded. "Let's meet down here in the lobby at, say, ten past six? That'll give us plenty of time to get my car and drive to Arthur's. Okay?"

"Sounds great," Arthur said. "I'm going to pick up a few things on my way home. I've invited the Stauntons to join us, by the way. They're fine people. I think you'll enjoy getting to know each other." He waved goodbye as he headed out the hotel's front doors toward the parking lot.

As they rode up the elevator, Jane listened to the conversation between Grace, Donna, and Pam. But none of the words penetrated into her mind. Instead, a golden feeling pervaded her, as if she'd gotten drunk on painting.

I must be really overtired was Jane's thought as she flipped the lock and dropped her painting gear into a corner of her room. The bed seemed to wait with soft and loving arms. She was dreaming as soon as her head sunk into the pillow. As consciousness vanished, the expression, "dead tired," washed into her mind. For some reason, the truth of it filled her brain and soothed her muscles.

It was the last time during the retreat that Jane would think of death and find any comfort in it.

CHAPTER ELEVEN

Jane woke up to the buzzing of her phone. A text message was coming through. She wiped sticky drool off her cheek with the edge of her pillowcase. I must have been sound asleep, she thought.

She glanced out the window at the fading light. What time is it? she wondered. Then she remembered that they were going to Arthur's house for dinner, and she sat up. Hopefully, she'd have a few minutes to freshen up before they needed to leave.

The text was from Pam, who had sent it to Grace as well as Jane:

Let's glam it up. I'm wearing a dress. Donna is too.

Jane glanced at the time. If she hurried, she'd have time for a quick shower before she put on her favorite evening outfit: the hand-painted blouse that she'd bought on her last trip to Hawaii and the matching silky pants.

She was just running a comb through her hair when she heard the knock on her door.

"Ready!" Jane called out. "Just gotta find my car keys."

She opened her door. "Wow!" she exclaimed at the sight of her three friends in the hallway. "Don't we look fabulous!" In her most exaggerated fake French accent, she said, "Les mademoiselles attending une Parisienne art exhibit, n'est-ce pas? Love your mauve turban, Donna - with rhinestones, yet! And look at you, Grace Tanner, I've never seen you in that dress."

"I got it before the retreat," Grace said. "Do you like it?" She twirled, lifting her arms so the flounce above the bodice would float.

"Ooh, I love it," Jane said. "That shade of pink was invented for you."

"If that doesn't make Arthur drool, nothing will," Donna said.

"Why would she want Arthur to drool?" Pam said. "Tillie drools all the time, and I'm here to tell you there's nothing desirable about drool." Looking at Grace, she said, "But that dress is gorgeous, Grace, and it looks terrific on you." Then, turning to Jane, she said: "Love that blouse, Jane. Was it painted by that artist in Hawaii that you like so much?"

Jane nodded. "And it looks like your scarf would match this blouse perfectly."

Pam gave her scarf a protective pat. "Can't have it. Sorry," she said. "It was a gift from my sister. She knows I love this color."

The elevator door opened. Amanda and Rachel, the two schoolteachers from Charlotte, were inside.

"Room for us?" Pam asked.

"Sure," Amanda said, skooching back to make room. As the doors closed, she introduced Rachel to Pam, Donna, and Jane. "And you must be Grace," Amanda said, "the fourth member of the Atkinsville group and the other former schoolteacher."

"Seems my reputation precedes me," Grace said.

Rachel was a head shorter than Amanda but both young women had dark eyes and dark curly hair. Jane thought they could have easily passed for sisters.

"Y'all look stupendous," Rachel said. Were we supposed to dress for dinner? I'm still wearing my sweaty painting clothes."

"If we looked as good in sweaty painting clothes as you do, we'd be wearing them, too. But, actually, we've got a dinner date," Pam explained. "Arthur King has invited us to his house for dinner."

Amanda raised her eyebrows. "Oh, I see. A royal dinner! I understand he's quite the high-roller."

It was Pam's turn to raise her eyebrows. "Really. Why do you say that? Do you know him?"

The elevator came to a stop, and the women spilled out.

"No, not really," Amanda said. "Just rumors. He's quite the talk of the Charlotte artsy gallery set. Rich. Eligible. Known as the out-of-towner who lives on a storied estate near THE gardens of South Carolina." She looked at Pam. "Are you planning to take your dog for a walk in the morning? I'll fill you in on the gossip then. If you promise you'll fill me in on your royal dinner."

"Deal. I need to walk Tillie in the morning." Pam nodded. "She gets pouty if I don't check on her at least once a day."

"We'll be down around seven for our walk," Amanda said.

Jane raised her eyebrows. "I guess you girls aren't planning to stay up late partying."

"Schoolteacher's hours," Rachel explained. When she shrugged, her slender shoulders brushed against two-inch-long beaded earrings. "That's what we're used to."

Jane smiled. Rachel's eyes were as shiny as anthracite coal and her eyelashes seemed nearly as long as her sparkly earrings. If all the schoolteachers in Charlotte were as adorable as these two, Jane thought, the school district must be recruiting faculty at beauty pageants.

Amanda winked at them as she and Rachel headed toward the hotel restaurant. "Have fun at the palace tonight, ladies!"

As the Atkinsville painters waved goodbye to the schoolteachers, Jane sidled close to Pam and whispered, "If you come down to walk Tillie in the morning, but you don't catch up with them in the lobby, please call me. I'll walk with you. Remember, we're not going off anywhere alone."

"Are you saying that Tillie wouldn't protect me?" Pam said, a smile twinkling across her lips.

"What are you talking about?" Grace asked. "Pam can't go off alone?"

"Shh," Donna said and slid her arm through Grace's as they walked out the hotel doors toward Jane's car. "You weren't in the room when we were talking about this. We'll tell you in the car."

Jane turned on the ignition and brought up Maps on the dashboard screen. She fiddled around until she located what looked like an upscale wine and cheese shop on the route to Arthur's house. "I don't think we should show up empty-handed to Arthur's. Especially if it's such a palace," she explained to Pam, who had taken the front passenger seat.

While they buckled their seatbelts, Donna told Grace about their conversation in Jane's room and their resolution: "We're going to be on the buddy system from now on," she said. "Jane thinks we shouldn't trust anyone, not even the other painters. Not with all the drugs and scandal involved in racehorses."

"That's probably a wise precaution," Grace said. "But I'm going to have a hard time believing those two schoolteachers are capable of anything sinister. Aren't they just adorable?"

"Yes!" Pam said, and she chuckled. "Can you imagine how much those middle school boys look forward to art class?"

As Jane pulled her car out of the hotel parking lot, they agreed to split the price of a fancy bottle of wine. Pam and Grace volunteered to run into the shop to pick it out.

Jane pulled to a stop in front of The Cheese Board, a cute little shop in an upscale strip of boutiques and eateries. As Pam reached for the door handle, Jane said, "Get something sophisticated, okay? Maybe aged. At least with cursive lettering on the label."

"Yes," Donna added. "Get something suitable for royalty."

"And you better hurry," Jane added, pointing to the chalkboard in front of the shop. On Tuesdays, the shop closed at six-thirty.

"Oh, gosh," said Grace. She scrunched up her mouth. "This is a lot of pressure. How are we supposed to know which wines are sophisticated?"

Pam slid her hand through Grace's arm. "Come on, I'll teach you," she said. "No problem. You just look for the bottles with corks and then you choose by price tag."

After getting back on the road, they passed a red brick hospital, a neat little city park that circled a manicured lake, a red brick city hall, a red brick courthouse, and a red brick police station. They were definitely going to be fashionably late, Jane realized. The GPS listed their estimated time of arrival as 7:15.

Following Maps directions, Jane turned onto a private road. Matching pairs of tall trees bordered the roadway, standing like sentries to witness their arrival.

Donna's phone started playing "Old MacDonald." She answered, "Hello, Bill. Everything alright? Oh, good. Yes, Pam got here, and Alec let her join the class. Let me call you back in the morning, okay? We've been invited to dinner at Arthur King's place, and we're pulling up to his house now. He's that fellow at the retreat that I told you about. Yes, the man who keeps sniffing around Grace." Donna hung up.

Grace scowled at Donna's description of Arthur. "He is NOT sniffing around me!" she said. "I think he's been very courteous. And considerate. To all of us."

At the top of the lane, there were a series of buildings. Guessing by degrees of elegance, Jane assumed the first was a large barn, the second a larger horse stable, and the third what Amanda had dubbed the palace. But that descriptor was not really apropos, Jane thought. This house didn't look at all like a palace. Instead, it was a dead-ringer for a manor house plucked off a postcard from the English lake district. She pulled to a stop beside three vehicles - one a sporty coupe with buttery leather seats open to the sky, the other a late-model hybrid sedan, and the third a large truck.

"I'm guessing the king owns the coupe and the big truck," Pam said.

"So you think the Stauntons drive the eco-conscious sedan?" Jane said. "That wouldn't be my impression of them - not after seeing the business suit he wears, anyway."

Further speculation over car ownership was halted by the sound of another vehicle coming down the road; a large, black Lexus SUV. The Lexus careened to a stop, and Arthur popped out.

"Forgive me," he said. "I promised Nan that I'd pick up the cheeses. The salesgirl kept offering me various possibilities to sample, each more delicious than the last. I probably bought enough cheeses to feed our entire retreat and then some."

"Did you stop at The Cheese Board?" Jane asked.

"Yes, I love their selection," he said.

"We just came from there. I didn't see your car."

He nodded. "I always park around back," he said. "You take your life in your hands backing up onto that road."

Pam handed him the bottle of pricey wine.

"Thank you," Arthur said as he led them along a path paved with gray stones. It passed under a covered entranceway. In front of massive, mahogany front doors, the paving stones formed a pattern that looked like a family crest. The architecture of the entranceway looked Tudor to Jane, but together with the gray stones, the ancient Nordic poem, *Beowulf*, sprang into her mind.

"Welcome to my modest abode," Arthur said with a gallant flourish as he ushered them into a front hall with a floor made of big, irregular-shaped field stones.

"What's that old saying?" Donna said. "Be it ever so humble, there's no place like home."

"Exactly," Arthur said. "Do you ladies have any coats that you'd like me to hang up?" He flipped on the light switch, then touched a second button and doors slid open to reveal a spacious hall closet the size of a child's nursery. The overhead lamp was made of heavy, black iron forged into the shape of a horse's head.

Jane mused: It's late spring in the South - who brings coats on a night like this? She decided that Arthur was showing off. But who could blame him? The entranceway really was spectacular.

"How unusual," Jane said, pointing at the iron horse lamp. "Was that designed for this house?"

"Indeed it was," Arthur said.

"It's magnificent," Grace said.

He shrugged. "Client of mine. Talented guy. I'm fortunate to be an accountant. The most creative people have shared their skills - as well as their business secrets - with me."

"That's called tax fraud, isn't it?" Donna said. "When you have business secrets and you're creative about them?"

"Perhaps so," Arthur replied. He flashed an impish grin, then led the group down a hall overhung with massive beams. They entered an enormous dining room. To their left was a stone fireplace worthy of the abode of the gods on Mt. Olympus. On its carved mantle was an Asian-style pot holding a bonsai tree in full bloom. The little tree was no taller than five inches, with a gnarled trunk that looked ancient. On the other three walls hung life-sized portraits of men who looked like the barons of industry. At each corner of the room stood a brass planter containing a four-foot-tall topiary trimmed into the shape of a rearing horse. In the center of the room, a titanic banquet table of polished wood gleamed under three iron chandeliers. On the table were two large urns holding generous displays of cut flowers.

"I thought we'd dine outside on the patio," Arthur explained as he led them through open double doors onto a patio bordered with tall brick walls. "The dining room has such a formal feeling. I wanted you to relax and feel comfy, after your long day's toil with paintbrush and palette."

The Stauntons were on the patio, drinks in hand. Walter stood at their arrival. Although he wasn't wearing a custom-made business suit, he'd paid serious attention to his appearance. His casual attire had never been sullied by an event, casual or otherwise. He wore a crisp Henley shirt in royal blue, khakis that looked like he'd unpacked them an hour earlier from a Land's End shipment, and boating shoes that had likely arrived in the same box. With his chiseled facial features, trim mustache, chin dimple, and salt-and-pepper hair, he reminded Jane of David Niven.

Saundra's version of casual, on the other hand, looked more genuinely casual but every bit as pricey. She wore a flowing royal blue caftan that was clearly made of silk, not polyester. Her raven black hair flowed down her back but was pulled up over one ear and fastened with a deep red cattleya orchid. She didn't spoil the dramatic effect with fussy jewelry. Except for the ocean-blue sapphire studs in her ears, all she wore was a filigreed wedding band and a sapphire ring the size of a small goldfish bowl.

"Walter and Saundra, I have the pleasure of introducing you to the watercolorists of Atkinsville," Arthur said as he brushed his arm through the air in a grand gesture that reminded Jane of a ballet movement. "This is Grace Tanner, Donna Norton, Pam Gerald, and Jane Roland."

"My, my," Donna said to Arthur, "you're quite the politician."

Walter gave an elegant continental bow as he stepped forward and took each woman's hand by way of greeting. After Donna received her bow, Arthur gave her a quizzical look and asked, "A politician?"

"You've only known us for two days and you've already memorized each of our names. First and last," Donna said. "The only other person I've ever met who did that was running for mayor."

"Well, I've never thought of running for mayor," Arthur said. "But I'll take it under consideration."

"There's no way Arthur would ever run for office," Walter said, smirking. "Not the way the press scrutinizes a candidate's background, these days. Arthur's otherwise brilliant reputation would be totally destroyed."

"Now, now, Walter, whatever are you implying?" Arthur said with his own smirk. Striding to the outdoor bar, he uncorked the bottle of wine from The Cheese Board. "Who'd like a glass of wine? Or, if you prefer, there's beer or cocktails. What can I get you?"

A small, wiry man with a bushy mustache peeked out the double doors from the dining room. "Ah, there you are, Mr. Arthur."

"Henry," said Arthur. "I almost forgot. Here are the cheeses." He handed a black plastic bag to the man. "Tell Nan we're ready for the hors d'oevres. Then we'll take a little stroll around the gardens before dinner. I hoped you wouldn't mind joining us, Henry? To show off your handiwork?"

"Of course, Mr. Arthur. Just let me run the cheeses back to Nan." Henry took the bag and vanished into the house.

"Henry is my gardener," Arthur explained. "And he's every bit as talented as his wife, Nan. They're master craftsmen, both of them, and I'm lucky to have them."

"Do they live on the grounds?" Jane asked. She took a stemmed glass of wine from Arthur.

"Yes, there's a cottage on the western edge of the garden," Arthur said. "It's small but sufficient for two adults."

Jane thanked Arthur for the wine. Judging from what she'd already seen, Jane guessed that 'small but sufficient' would not be her choice of adjectives to describe any structure on this property.

Arthur freshened up the Stauntons' glasses. Then, drinks in hand, the guests meandered along gray stone pathways as Arthur narrated a tour of the king's gardens. Henry walked along with the group, and he seemed as proud of his botanical triumphs as any parent would be of their child prodigies.

At an extensive patch of irises, Grace stopped. "Oh, how lovely! I didn't know irises came in that color."

"It was a first for me, too, Ma'am," Henry said. "Mr. Arthur, he found them in a specialty catalogue. I was afraid they'd be finicky. Require special handling and all. But Mr. Arthur insisted. And he was right, as usual - they're hardy bulbs. Not a bit of a problem. Perfectly content with the very same soil preparation and location as a standard iris."

"Well, they're spectacular," Grace said. "And I suspect you're much too modest about the skill required to produce those blooms."

In addition to its rich assortment of flowers, the King garden was remarkable for its topiaries. Henry explained that Mr. Arthur had sent him all the way to Washington State to attend a workshop so he could learn how to shape these unusual plant statues.

"You created these topiaries? Yourself?" Pam exclaimed. "I've always wondered how people do that. Do you begin training the bushes when they're small - like doing bonsai? You know, so they'll form certain branches to support the future figures?"

Saundra smiled and slipped her hand through Pam's arm. "I can tell you're a passionate gardener. But if you get Henry started on topiary, we're never going to have dinner. And bonsai - that's a whole other story! Did you know that Arthur has an entire greenhouse of bonsai trees? Henry tends them. Some of them are over one hundred years old. Most of them are imports from Japan."

Arthur led them to the center of his rose garden, where a painted gazebo with gingerbread cutouts stood. "This gazebo is nearly as old as the house," he said. "People made things to last back in those days, and last it has."

"So you're not the person who built the house?" Jane asked.

"Oh, no," Arthur said. "The house was originally built by the Parkhursts. Perhaps you've heard of them? Famous horticulturist, he was. Taught at Harvard. My wife was a descendant."

"Are the Parkhusts one of the wealthy families that lived in New England and summered in this area?" Jane asked. "The ones you were talking about at lunch?"

"Exactly," Arthur said.

Suddenly, a dog rushed along the path toward them. It was a great gray, shaggy animal, as leggy as a pony and nearly as tall. The dog threaded through the group until it reached Arthur's right thigh. At the snap of its owner's fingers, the dog sat obediently. It looked up at Arthur's face as if waiting for a command.

"Malory, who let you out?" Arthur said. He fondled the dog's ears. To the group, he said, "This is probably a message from Nan that dinner is ready." He slipped his left hand through Grace's arm as they headed back toward the patio. As Arthur walked, the dog kept a matching pace beside his owner's right leg. "There's lots more garden to see, but we don't want to spoil Nan's masterpiece by being late to dinner. It's just as well, I suppose. It'll be dark soon. And I don't want to bore you to death on your first visit."

"I don't think we're the least bit bored," Grace said.

At the intersection of two garden paths, Henry stopped and said, "If you wouldn't mind, Mr. Arthur, I'll hurry back and see if Nan needs my help in the kitchen."

Arthur nodded, and Henry darted off.

"I'm guessing Malory is an Irish wolfhound?" Pam said. "Did you train him yourself? He's got the best manners of any dog I've ever seen."

"Yes. A sturdy, old-fashioned breed," Arthur said, turning to face Pam. "Seems to suit the house, don't you think?"

"I'll say," said Donna. "He's the same color as the paving stones."

When they returned to the patio, the table was already set with a white linen tablecloth, black iron candelabra, china embossed with the family crest, and silver goblets. Individual bowls of spring greens were laid at each setting. Nan was placing a basket of warm biscuits on the table. The yeasty aroma was irresistible.

"Mmm, these are terrific," Pam said after sampling a biscuit. "They're lighter than feathers. You make them yourself?"

Nan nodded, a smile on her small, round face. "My mother's recipe. She called them angel biscuits. Mr. Arthur, he requested something grilled. You know, for outdoor dining. But I always like to add a touch of local color. Nothing says the South like a biscuit."

"Well, these angel biscuits certainly paint a heavenly picture of the South. Even the smell is celestial," Pam said. "Promise me you'll share the recipe with us."

While the basket of biscuits made a second circuit around the table, Nan began serving the main course - skewers of shrimp and marinated steak, with red peppers, mushrooms, zucchini, and onions. The sweet and smoky aroma of the marinade tickled Jane's nose. Henry poured glasses of red wine, then served buttered corn on the cob from a silver platter.

"Yes, please," Grace said to Nan, who was offering a skewer of steak. "You know, when Arthur invited us, he compared your culinary skills to an artist," Grace said. "I can see why."

Beaming, Nan thanked her and then aimed an elfin grin at Arthur.

"So tell me about yourselves, ladies," Walter said. "I understand that you're part of a group of painters who work together at an art center in Atkinsville. You were the ones who discovered poor Lancelot in the reflecting pool on Sunday evening." He looked at Donna. "I hear you almost fainted."

"Yes, I almost fainted that night. And I did faint the next night when we found that poor stable man in the trough," Donna said. She turned to Arthur. "You don't have any bodies of water here, I hope?"

Arthur chuckled. "No need to worry. There used to be a goldfish pond near the gazebo, but the raccoons kept raiding it, so I had it bricked in. Henry planted rhododendrons around it."

"Well, that's a relief!" Donna said. She gave her hearty heh-heh-heh laugh that Jane always found so comical. Saundra began to laugh, too, and her laugh burst forth like a cackle from a full-breasted hen. Was it a reflection of the red cattleya in Saundra's hair, or were the woman's cheeks flushed with drink? In the candlelight, it was hard for Jane to tell.

"And how about you, Walter?" Grace asked. "You and Saundra live nearby? Are you long-time residents, like Arthur?"

Walter told them that he was born in the area. "Except for college and a few trips abroad, I've always lived here. As a matter of fact, I was actually born - as well as conceived - in the master bedroom of our house."

Saundra tittered as she finished off her wine. "I did NOT follow that Staunton family tradition when our son Wally was born. I went to the local hospital." She reached for the red wine and poured herself another glass.

Were Saundra's words beginning to slur? Jane recalled that the Stauntons had arrived - and begun drinking - before them.

"Is yours also one of the original estates of the New Englanders who summered in this area?" Jane asked Saundra and Walter.

"Exactly," Arthur answered for them, "the Stauntons of New England." Arthur said to Jane, "I'll bet you were an A-student. You not only listened to that history lesson, but you remembered it."

It was Jane's turn to flash an impish grin. "I like to think I'm an attentive listener."

"And how about you?" Grace asked Saundra. "Are you also from this area, Saundra?

"No, I'm one of those New Englanders who did not come South for the summer." She cackled at her own joke. "I'm from Connecticut. I met Walter when he was at Yale."

"You didn't find it difficult to adjust to life in the South?" Donna said. "I've been here for four years, and I'm still getting used to the place."

Arthur smiled at Saundra. "Saundra? Not at all. From the start, she fit in like a hand slides into a glove. As soon as she married Walter, Saundra became my wife's best friend. Everything about them - horses, gardening, art - was a perfect match."

"And you two have been friends for a long time?" Jane said as she looked back and forth from Arthur to Walter. Jane didn't want to make it obvious that she was probing. But she had a hunch that the background and relationships between all the people attending the retreat might be important in understanding the disturbing incidents that had darkened their visit to Gardens and Horses.

"Walter and Arthur were best of friends when they were schoolboys at Lawton Academy," Saundra said. "Actually, there were three of them: Walter, Arthur, and Teddy Pickridge. Two heirs to their family's fortunes, the Stauntons and the Pickridges. And one clever little scholarship boy." Saundra winked at Arthur. "The three became inseparable. The Three Mischief-eers. Their reputation trailed behind them like tin cans behind a just-married limo. Clang clang. The first time I came here for a visit, I heard tales about their escapades. Naughty, naughty boys." She raised her glass to Walter and then to Arthur and took a swig worthy of a drunken sailor.

Grace looked at Arthur. "I'd love to hear some of those tales. If you think they're fit for mixed company."

Walter jumped in. "I'm afraid they're best told in the wee hours." He gave a naughty grin, "After several rounds of beer."

"Okay, I'm game," Pam said. "I'm usually more of a wine drinker, but If the tales are spicy enough...."

"Now, now," Walter said. "Remember: You ladies have to wake up early for class tomorrow."

"That's right, I forgot." Pam snapped her fingers. "And I've got to get up even earlier. I've got to take Tillie on an early morning walk; she pouts whenever she's away from me. I'm walking with the two schoolteachers, and they want to get started at seven." She looked at Arthur. "They told me you're quite the high-roller, by the way. They're planning to fill me in on all the gossip from the artsy set of Charlotte."

Jane wasn't sure, but she thought a shadow of irritation pass over Arthur's face. In a second, it was gone, replaced by his charming smile.

"I hope you won't believe a word those schoolmarms tell you," Arthur said. "If you want to hear the true tales of the Mischief-eers, you'll simply have to return for another of Nan's exquisite dinners. Next time, without any curfew." Arthur turned to Grace and stroked her neck.

Jane noticed that Grace's shoulders seemed to tense when Arthur touched her. The man certainly was a charmer, Jane thought, but perhaps he was coming on too strong. They'd only met him yesterday.

Saundra began to giggle, and they all looked at her. Jane thought the giggle was a little too vivid for the degree of humor in their conversation. Was the woman completely soused?

"If you really like spicy tales, you'll definitely have to come back," Saundra said, leaning in as if to spread juicy gossip. She giggled again. "I've heard those tales more than once. Let me tell you, they get spicier every time they're told."

Henry began to clear the dinner plates as Nan brought out a tray with individual servings of peach cobbler. "More local color," she said. She handed around a large bowl of whipped cream to top off the cobbler.

"Mmm, if only all local color smelled like this cobbler," Pam said.

"Then we'd need to go on a cooking retreat," Donna said.

Sensing that the evening was coming to a close, Jane decided to probe into the relationship between the Pickridges and Arthur and the Stauntons.

"So Teddy Pickridge was the third mischief-maker in your merry band?" Jane said. "But I thought Alicia said he was living in Savannah when they met. She seems quite a bit younger than he is, by the way."

There was an awkward silence. Jane wondered if she'd pushed past the bounds of etiquette.

"Teddy's first wife was from this area," Saundra said, leaning in toward Jane and Donna. She pursed her lips. "They grew up together, and everybody expected he'd marry Bunny. Isn't that right, Walter?" She looked at Walter for confirmation. He nodded, but Jane thought he looked uncomfortable.

"Well, he married Bunny. But, unfortunately, alcoholism runs in her family." Saundra licked her lips, then arched her eyebrows and tilted her head forward. "Always has, that's what I've heard. When the marriage fell apart, Teddy moved to Savannah. He was a train wreck. All he wanted was to get away from here. That's when he met Alicia. She's the exact opposite of everything he grew up with. Full of youthful passion, righteous indignation. Women's rights. Animal rights. Pockets full of granola bars - Little Miss Wholesome. You know the type. From a completely different culture. Oh, her family has money all right. Jews. But not what Teddy grew up with. I mean, plenty of people have affairs, but to marry..."

Stunned, Jane stared at Saundra. Had the woman just intimated that Jewish people were not Teddy's - and, by extension, Walter's and Arthur's - kind of people? Oh, my! Realizing that she would cut off any further intimacies from the Stauntons if she objected to this blatant prejudice, Jane forced herself to ignore the remark.

Walter shrugged. "Alicia was a pretty girl when she was a college student. Teddy's life was in tatters. He blamed himself for the mess with his marriage. He got swept away, that s all."

Another silence.

"Well," Arthur exclaimed. "We seem to have wandered into a dark alley." He stood and glanced at the Rolex on his wrist. "Oh dear, it's close to midnight. I promised myself that I'd get you home before your carriage turned into a pumpkin."

They all stood and said their goodbyes and thank-you's and compliments on the food.

"Are you staying at the hotel or at your home?" Grace asked Saundra as they walked through the doors into the dining room.

"I got myself a room at the hotel for the retreat," Saundra said. "It's more convenient. But Walter has an early work meeting tomorrow, so he's going to drop me off tonight and then drive himself home."

Jane was relieved that Saundra was not going to be driving drunk. "My car only seats four," Jane said, "or I'd offer to take you and save Walter the trip."

"Doesn't matter," Saundra said. "You know, it's already so late, I might as well go home instead." She looked at her husband. "I think I'll do that. I'll leave my car here. One of us can get it tomorrow."

As they went out the front door, Arthur switched on the flood lights. "You'll be alright driving home?" he asked Jane as he opened her car door.

"I feel fine. Thanks again for the wonderful evening," Jane said.

Arthur opened the car door for Grace and took her hand to help her get inside. "I hope I haven't kept you up too late."

"Not at all. It was a delightful evening," Grace said.

"See you in the morning." Arthur waved as they drove off.

"Well, wow! That's quite the country cottage!" gushed Pam as they drove down Arthur's private lane.

"And Arthur is quite the host," Jane said.

"Isn't he!" said Grace. "I think his manners are impeccable. Just a charming man."

"Yes! The way he took our hands and bowed when we met him," Donna said. "I never met anybody who did that. And all those topiaries. It was like being in a movie set. Downton Abbey. Complete with the drunk aristocrat's wife."

As they pulled into the hotel parking lot, Jane wondered why the lobby was so brightly lit. "I wonder if they had an event here tonight? Maybe a wedding reception? Or a graduation party?"

They walked into the lobby, where painters from their retreat were milling around. Alec, their instructor, was there, his elbows on the countertop at the front desk and his forehead in his hand as if he was exhausted. Jane wondered if he'd had too much to drink. If Alec had gotten tipsy and all the artists were up late, perhaps they had an impromptu party.

Then Jane noticed the two policemen who had interviewed them after lunch. They were seated on armless chairs across the cocktail table from Alicia, who sat on the couch, her shoulders sagging. Was it the lighting, or were Alicia's eyes red from crying? The police had notepads and pens in their hands. Police at a party? Either this party had gotten seriously out of hand or something terrible had happened. Looking around the room, Jane spotted young Maggie, who was leaning against her grandmother, her face in a crumple and tears running down her cheeks.

The elevator doors opened and Mr. Horne stepped out. He caught the eye of the policemen and shook his head. Perhaps the manager had brought a cold draft from the air conditioning on the upper floors. Because suddenly Jane shivered as if ice water had splashed down her back.

CHAPTER TWELVE

Pam made a beeline toward the two schoolteachers standing near the open patio door. Jane, Grace, and Donna followed like a hive on the swarm.

"Hey, girls! What's going on here?" Pam said.

Amanda and Rachel looked at each other, then at Pam and her friends. "I guess y'all haven't heard," Amanda said. "A woman was found dead in that little lake in the downtown park."

"Oh, my. Another dead body in water? Maybe I better sit down," Donna said. "I really don't want to faint again." She staggered over to the settee by the window and plopped down. Grace went with her and sat down with her arm encircling Donna's back.

Jane and Pam watched to see if Donna would remain upright. When she did, Pam turned to the schoolteachers and said, "A woman drowned?"

Rachel shrugged. "That'd be my guess. The police aren't giving out any information."

"But why are the police here?" Pam asked. "Was it somebody staying at this hotel? Not somebody in our retreat?"

"They're not revealing the dead woman's identity," Rachel said. "I don't know if the police have identified her yet."

"Maybe they need to notify next of kin before they can release her name," Amanda said.

Jane's mind began to race. If the police were here in the hotel lobby and had rounded up the people at their art retreat, they must have a pretty good hunch that the dead woman was a member of their retreat group. Jane began looking around the room, trying to account for all the women in their class. They had just left Saundra Staunton, so it couldn't be her. Both of the schoolteachers were here. Alicia Pickridge was sitting on the couch, and Jane had already noticed Maggie sobbing beside her grandmother. Together with the four Atkinsville painters, that made ten of the thirteen women enrolled in the retreat. Who was missing? The two sisters who had attended SCAD, Dee Dee and Harry - where were they? Jane scanned the lobby, but there was no sign of them. Taking a step outside, she noticed some movement at the far end of the dimly-lit patio. As her eyes adjusted to the dark, Jane could make out the two sisters sitting at a table. They were both wearing bathrobes and slippers. Harry's hair was in rollers.

So who hadn't been accounted for? The Golden Girls! Assuming that Catherine was safe in her hospital bed, the only woman left was Sheryl Calhoun. Jane glanced around the patio and went back into the brightly-lit lobby, but there was no sign of Sheryl. Since Mr. Horne had just stepped off the elevator and then shaken his head at the policemen, Jane guessed the manager had unlocked Sheryl's door with his master key but hadn't found her in her room. Thinking back to the conversation with Sheryl at lunch, Jane remembered her saying that she was going to take Catherine's suitcase to the hospital this evening. Jane had driven past the hospital on the way to Arthur's house, so she knew it was across the street from the complex of red brick buildings that bordered the city park. That would have put Sheryl in the vicinity of the lake.

Did the police officers know that Sheryl was planning to go to the hospital tonight? Had they spoken to Catherine to find out whether Sheryl had arrived? This information might be critical. It could help them determine the time of death. Jane looked at James Goode, the policeman who had interviewed her this morning. She raised her hand and waved her fingertips, hoping the movement caught his eye. Nodding at her, he tipped his head toward the patio. Then he stood and joined her outside.

"Hello, Officer Goode," Jane said. "I'm Jane Roland. Do you remember me? We spoke this morning. I'm one of the Atkinsville women - we were the ones who found the stable hand last evening and the horse in the reflecting pond on Sunday. My friends and I just got back from a dinner party at Arthur King's house. I understand that a woman was found dead tonight in the lake by the city park," Jane said.

Goode waited without speaking or gesturing. So Jane swallowed a gulp of air and plunged in. "I think it might be Sheryl Calhoun. She's the only woman from our retreat that I don't see down here. Except for Saundra Staunton, but Saundra was at the dinner party with us. She left at the same time as we did - about midnight - and was on her way home with her husband."

Goode didn't confirm or deny Jane's suspicion that the dead woman was Sheryl.

His facial expression seemed chiseled in stone.

"If it is Sheryl, I have some information that may be helpful," Jane said. "Today, at lunch, Sheryl told us that she was planning to take Catherine's suitcase to her this evening. Sheryl and Catherine came to the retreat together. They were roommates. Catherine had to drop out of the retreat - she has asthma, and they're keeping her in the hospital. So she wanted her suitcase, and Sheryl said she'd take it to her. After class this afternoon."

"When did the class end?" Goode said.

"About five," Jane said. "We were painting by the reflecting pool."

Goode nodded. "Did you happen to notice whether Sheryl returned to the hotel after class?"

"No, but she probably did," Jane said. "She would've had her easel and painting supplies with her. She'd probably drop off that stuff in her room before going to the hospital."

"Unless she was in a hurry to get going," Goode said.

"But why would she be in a hurry?" Jane said. "Unless hospital visiting hours are over early? Anyway, if she stopped here, her painting supplies should be in her room."

"I'll check," Goode said.

Jane hesitated.

"Something else?" Goode asked.

"Well, it may not be relevant," Jane said. "But at lunch, Sheryl asked us whether you and your partner were still at the hotel. She said she wanted to have a word with you. We told her that you'd already left. Sheryl wondered how late you'd be at the station this evening."

Jane thought that Goode's eyebrows rose ever so slightly. "Who else heard her say that?"

"All the people at our table. The four of us from Atkinsville. And Arthur King. But everybody was out on the patio, so I suppose anybody could have heard. I forget if Alec was standing by our table when Sheryl said that. But he did come over after he heard Sheryl say that Catherine was dropping out of our retreat. He was pretty angry."

"Angry?"

"Seems that Catherine has dropped out of his retreats before," Jane said. "Because of her asthma. He seemed irritated about having to return her fee."

Goode nodded. "And The wait staff? Did they hear what Sheryl said?"

Jane shrugged. "They were in and out. You know, setting up. Bringing out food. So I suppose, yes, they might have heard her talking."

"And did Sheryl sit at your table during lunch?"

"No, there were only five chairs at our table," Jane said. "Sheryl went to sit with Maggie - the teenager - and her grandmother. Maggie told me that Sheryl is good friends with her grandmother. And the two young schoolteachers," Jane pointed at Amanda and Rachel, "were sitting at their table, too."

"When did Maggie tell you that her grandmother and Sheryl are good friends? At lunch?"

"No," Jane said. "In another conversation." Jane debated whether to continue and tell the policeman about Maggie's riding gloves and helmet. Was it important that they were planning to pick up the girl's things last night, when Dave was accosted? Later, Sheryl had brought them back to Maggie. Jane frowned. Maybe the policeman would find something useful in this seemingly-trivial information, but Jane wasn't sure. With a woman dead in the pond, he probably wouldn't want to be burdened by such picky details now.

Just then, Goode's partner signaled to him.

"Thanks," Goode said. "That's good information - excuse the pun on my name." He flashed a reassuring smile. "If you think of anything else, don't hesitate to call me." Reaching into the pocket of his pants, he brought out Jane's notepad and handed it to her. "Or write it down in your notepad. Your notes were very helpful." Then he turned and walked over to the coffee table, where the other policeman was standing.

Jane tucked her notepad under her arm. She found herself glowing at James Goode's compliment - like she did when Alec had complimented the composition of her painting. Goode hadn't been effusive in his compliment, but he had smiled. Jane was sure that Goode was more of a listener by nature, rather than a talker, and that his few words were meaningful. If he was encouraging her to take notes and share them with him, he must believe that she was a good judge of people, that she had an eye for critical information. Jane had always thought of herself this way - as a sort of natural Miss Marple. It was good - excusing another pun on his name - to have an expert agree with her.

Before rejoining her friends, Jane paused to look around the lobby. As she did, a terrifying thought sizzled through her: Had Sheryl been killed? What other reason would there be for her to be in the lake? Following this line of reasoning, another sizzle: If the police suspect foul play, the people in this retreat are probably their main suspects. After all, the stable hand had been attacked and a champion racehorse had been killed - all in the short span since this retreat began.

Instead of rejoining her friends, Jane sank into a wingback chair to process these disturbing thoughts. Who in this room would want to kill a kindly older woman like Sheryl? A friendly stable hand like Dave? A champion racehorse? Who had the motive? Or, for that matter, the strength? None of the people in the lobby seemed likely to be such a villain.

The hard edges of her notepad were cutting into Jane's arm, so she tucked it into her pocketbook. She decided that from now on, she'd take notes at every class break, when details were fresh in her mind. After all, she could analyze the people in the retreat from a viewpoint the police didn't have. She was inside the group; part of the painting. From her vantage point, she might be able to offer critical insights. She vowed to pay close attention to everything she was seeing and hearing. A casual remark, a just noticeable change in the placement of an everyday object might make the difference between a murderer brought to justice and an unsolved crime.

Teddy Pickridge, with a drink in his hand, joined Alec at the front desk. That's odd, Jane thought. Teddy's wife is sitting alone on the couch, and it certainly looks like the woman is upset. In addition to Alicia's red-rimmed eyes, her cheeks are blotchy. Why doesn't Teddy go and comfort his wife? And why is Alicia so upset? At dinner, Saundra had said that Alicia was full of youthful passion and righteous indignation when she was a college student at SCAD. Maybe Alicia's a very sensitive person? Suddenly, it occurred to Jane that she and Alicia could be useful to each other: The woman looked like she was in need of comfort, and Jane was in need of information. Jane got up and walked to the couch.

"Mind if I sit here?" Jane said.

Alicia shook her head and slid to the end cushion so Jane had plenty of space.

"Pretty horrible, isn't it?" Jane began. "Who would've thought we'd be up to our ears in bodies at a painting retreat? First, the horse, then Dave, and now a woman. I'm wondering if it's...."

"Dave is dead?" Alicia's face drained of color. "When did you hear that...?"

"Oh no, I didn't mean that," Jane said. "I don't know how Dave's doing. When I asked at the nursing station last night, they wouldn't tell me anything. Said I had to be next of kin. But the nurse told me they'd probably induced a coma. After a traumatic head wound, that's what they usually do to control swelling around the brain. I haven't heard anything about how he's doing today."

Alicia let out a ragged sigh and wiped her eyes with a crumpled tissue. "I'm sorry. I thought maybe you'd heard something. I called his mom this afternoon. She said they're keeping him in a coma until tomorrow, at least. Maybe for several days."

"I guess you and Dave are close friends?" Jane said.

Unsmiling, Alicia stared at Jane.

"I mean, because you know Dave's mother," Jane said. "You must be very close friends."

Alicia frowned. "You could say that."

Was there a note of irony in Alicia's voice? Jane couldn't tell but judged it best to shift to a different subject. "We were at Arthur King's for dinner tonight," Jane said in a chatty tone. "The Stauntons were there, too. Saundra said Teddy grew up with Walter and Arthur. I guess all of you enjoy horses."

Alicia rolled her eyes. "Hmm, let me guess. I suppose Saundra also told you about the Mischief-eers and their merry exploits."

Jane smiled. "Yes, as a matter of fact, she did."

"And about how I swept poor distraught Teddy off his saddle after his disastrous marriage ended."

Jane giggled. "Well, she didn't put it that way, of course, but that was the implication. I gather this is a tale told often, then? And it gains spice with each retelling?"

"Loves her gossip, does salty Saundra," Alicia said. The sarcasm fairly dripped from Alicia's voice as she continued. "Almost as much as she loves her drink. By the way, that she had in common with Teddy's first wife. In addition to both of them being the 'right kind of people.' I assume she mentioned that, too? That I'm Jewish. Perfectly alright for Teddy to have an affair with a Jew. But to marry one? Well, that's not the sort of thing that WE do, is it?"

Jane nodded. "Saundra did allude to that. I found it a bit shocking, actually. I thought antisemitism had gone out with the wind, and good riddance to it. For Saundra to talk openly like that - especially around people she hardly knows." Jane shook her head. "Well, I was speechless."

"Yeah, Saundra is a trip. Like time travel, isn't it?" Alicia said. "This whole antiquated scene: the inherited family estates. The servants. The bored, alcoholic women. The weird notions of privilege, lack of morality." Alicia stuck her pinky in the air and feigned a snobbish British accent. "I mean, really, dahling. It's simply not 'done' to marry an outsider. Particularly not one of 'them.' Of course, it's perfectly fine to have a dalliance with them."

"I guess you've always felt like an outsider when you're around them?" Jane said. "Saundra told us that Teddy fell in love with your passion, your youthful indignation, when he met you at SCAD. Sounds like you grew up with a completely different idea of what's acceptable, and you've held fast to your ideals."

Alicia shrugged. "I admit that over the years, I've dismounted from my high horse."

Jane looked at her, puzzled.

Alicia looked down at the tissue that she was twisting in her hands. "Let's just say that, since moving to the Pickridge estate, I've come to appreciate the benefits of a dalliance."

Jane blinked. Did Alicia just confess she was having an affair? Surely she hadn't gotten involved with one of Teddy's friends? Suddenly, like the flash of a firefly in the dark, Jane realized who Alicia had been dallying with. Alicia's red-rimmed eyes, her white-faced reaction to the suggestion that Dave had died. Dave! Alicia and Dave were lovers. It all made sense. Dave was closer to Alicia's age than Teddy was. She and the handsome stable hand shared a passion for horses. With Dave, Alicia would not have been ostracized as the outsider, the 'wrong sort' of person.

Before Jane could think of a way to confirm her suspicion, the silver bell on the front desk dinged. Everybody looked up.

Officer Goode stood by the counter. "Thanks for your patience, folks," Goode said. "I think we've learned all we can tonight. I know you have lots of questions. Hopefully, we'll have some answers for you soon. Meantime, go on up to your rooms. Lock your doors. Get some sleep."

Everybody stood, but before Jane could rejoin her friends, the manager stepped forward and cleared his throat. "Regrettably, some of you may not be feeling totally safe in the hotel at this juncture," Mr. Horne said. "To reassure you, Officer Kennedy, here, has generously offered to remain in the lobby during the night. If you should have any concerns, don't hesitate to call the front desk.

"It's very late, and I know you're exhausted," he continued. "Please forgive tonight's inconvenience. Of course, you understand that these are extenuating circumstances. In consideration of the late hour, I've decided to extend breakfast for a half-hour, until 10:30. Alec has agreed to adjust your morning class schedule.

"I suggest we plan to meet in the breakfast area at ten. Alec and I will have an important announcement for you at that time."

CHAPTER THIRTEEN

As they waited for an elevator to go up to their rooms, Jane glanced at her phone. It was 1:45 AM - much later than she usually got to bed. And this was the third late night in a row. Just anticipating how she was going to feel when her alarm went off in the morning, she groaned inwardly.

One of the elevator doors opened, and Alicia and Teddy stepped inside. Alicia pressed the hold button and beckoned to Jane, so the four Atkinsville painters had no choice but to crowd in with them. Nobody spoke until the elevator discharged the Pickridges on the second floor. Then Jane turned to Pam. "Are you still planning to meet the schoolteachers in the morning for a walk?"

"Yup. If I don't go check on Tillie, no telling what my crazy dog will do. But it's so late that we decided we'd sleep in and meet at 9."

"Remember," Jane said, "we're on the buddy system. Please don't go walking by yourself. If you don't connect with the schoolteachers, call me from the lobby, and I'll walk with you and Tillie."

"I hope my alarm isn't going to wake you in the morning, Roommate," Pam said to Donna as the elevator discharged them.

"I won't even hear it," Donna said. "I don't know about you but I'm so tired that I could fall asleep like a tree trunk right here in the hallway."

"Tree trunks sleep?" Pam asked.

Donna shrugged. "I guess so. Isn't that where they get the expression: sleeping like a log?"

"Well, I never thought of it like that. But maybe," Pam said. "Anyway, this was quite the night."

"It really was," Grace said. "That lovely supper. Then the shock of discovering that a woman had been found in the lake."

Pam looked at Jane. "Did you figure out who the dead woman is? I saw you sitting with Alicia after she'd been talking with the police. Did Alicia know who it was?"

"Alicia and I didn't talk about that," Jane said as they paused in the hall in front of their rooms. "I'm not certain, but I'm guessing the dead woman is Sheryl. Sheryl Calhoun. She's the only person from our retreat who wasn't in the lobby or accounted for."

"That's what I was suspecting, too," Grace said. "How awful. She seemed like such a nice person. Was she swimming, do you think? Do you know if there's a swimming beach at that lake?"

"I doubt it," Jane said. "I couldn't see the whole shoreline when we drove by, but I think it was too small to have a swimming beach. It looked like one of those shallow man-made lakes. You know, the ones they build to make a pretty setting for a downtown park. With a walking path around it."

Jane said goodnight to the others and let herself into her room, took one glance at her bed, and gave up her determination to take notes before she went to sleep. She was so worn out that she could barely force herself to brush her teeth.

She was sound asleep when her alarm went off the next morning. Before jumping into the shower, she checked for a text from Pam. No message, no call. Hopefully, Pam had joined up with the schoolteachers before she went to get Tillie for their morning walk.

Jane showered and dressed quickly, then sat down to scribble a few notes before heading down to breakfast. There wasn't enough time to describe everything that she'd seen and heard at Arthur's house. But maybe that setting wasn't so important? After all, there were just a few people from their retreat involved, and none of the suspicious incidents had taken place at the King estate.

At 9:50 AM, Jane texted Grace, Donna and Pam:
Going to breakfast now. Meet u in hall?

Pam texted back:

Returning Tillie 2 Dog Prison. See u at breakfast.

Grace texted Jane:

We r in hall.

As Jane opened her door, she saw Grace and Donna in the hall. "How'd you sleep?" Grace asked.

"Like a tree trunk in a hallway!" Jane laughed.

Donna grinned. "Me, too," she said.

While they waited for the elevator, Jane saw Officer Goode coming out of what had been Sheryl's and Catherine's room. He checked to be sure the door was locked, then adjusted the yellow crime tape stretched across the jamb casing. Jane nodded at him, and he tipped his head toward her.

Pam was sitting in the lobby waiting for them. They went into the breakfast area together, filled their plates at the breakfast buffet, and found a booth to sit in. A waiter came to pour coffee and offer juice.

"Learn anything interesting on your walk?" Jane asked Pam.

"Only that Arthur King is considered THE most eligible man in the Southeast," Pam said.

"I figured." Jane smiled. "I wouldn't be surprised if every widow in the Charlotte area has tried to throw her reins around his neck."

"He enters paintings in all the juried shows in Charlotte," Pam said, "and Amanda says his work ALWAYS gets chosen." She smirked. "Mind you, it doesn't hurt his chances that ALL the gallery owners want him to attend their meet-the-artist galas."

Grace frowned. "I don't think that's fair. It seems to me that he's a very talented artist, and his work would get chosen on its own merits. I've been very impressed by the paintings he's done on this retreat."

"That's true," Jane said. "But it never hurts to know people - or for them to know you. Even if you are talented. Did Amanda happen to say whether he's dating anybody in Charlotte?"

"No, but she did mention that Arthur's late wife wasn't nearly as talented as he is," Pam said. "She had her degree in art. But as soon as Arthur got into painting, his talent outshined her. Apparently, everything about him outshined her. Amanda says he was the peacock in the family, but his wife supplied the funds for all the fancy feathers.

"But listen," Pam leaned in and lowered her voice, "never mind about Arthur. Wait until you hear what they said about the Stauntons: Saundra used to enter all the Charlotte shows, too. And won gobs of ribbons - she's a master painter. Has all those initials - South Carolina Watercolor Society, Southeast Watercolor Society, National Watercolor Society - you name it - on the corners of her paintings. She's taught workshops all over everywhere. At the art receptions, Saundra basked in the admiration of the artistic set, while her husband did his own basking - if you get my drift."

Smirking again, Pam raised her eyebrows to emphasize her point. "Apparently, while the artists admired Saundra's work, the women admired Walter. And their admiration had nothing to do with talent - at least not his painting talent!"

"Maybe that's why Saundra took up drinking," Grace said.

"How do Rachel and Amanda know all this gossip?" Jane said. "I think they're too young to be hanging around with Walter and Arthur, aren't they? And they're schoolteachers. I can't believe they have enough money to collect art. "

"I asked the very same question," Pam said. "Amanda said that since they're both art teachers, they get asked to volunteer at the receptions. They like staying active in the city's art world - keeps them up to date with trends in painting. But there's more to it than that." She leaned forward again. "Rachel's dad made a fortune in real estate, but gambled away every penny. Rachel says the family lost everything."

"Let me guess," Jane said. "He gambled on horses."

"You got it," Pam said.

"Oh my," Donna said, "the plot thickens. Hey, look over there," she said, and pointed in the direction of the door to the breakfast area. The two sisters, Dee Dee and Harry were just coming in. Each of them was rolling a suitcase and carrying a large leather purse. It looked like they were packed to check out of the hotel.

Donna said. "They're packed up? Does that mean the rest of the retreat is called off?"

"Evidently, it is for them," Jane said. "I wonder if that's what the announcement is going to be."

"Well, Bill will be relieved to hear that we're coming home," Donna said. "He's been really worried about me. Fainting and all. I haven't even told him about the lady in the lake yet."

"I bet that's what the meeting is about," Grace said. "I guess it would make sense for them to abort the retreat, given everything that's happened. But I kinda hate to leave. I've enjoyed Alec's instruction. And the setting is lovely."

"And some of the painters are nice to look at, too," Pam said. This time she aimed her biggest smirk at Grace, who stuck out her tongue in response.

"Well, you can certainly say this setting is to die for," Donna said. "That is a proven fact."

Standing by the buffet, Mr. Horne cleared this throat. "If you're part of the art retreat, please gather at the far end of the room for a brief meeting." He pointed to the tables at one end of the room. "You're welcome to bring your plates and your coffee if you haven't finished breakfast."

Jane got up and dropped off her plate on the cart for dirty dishes. When she walked to the far end of the room, most of the chairs were filled. She found an empty seat beside Harry and Dee Dee. "Looks like you two are heading home today?" Jane said.

Harry nodded. "Things have gotten a little too crazy around here for my taste," she said, her nostrils flaring. "I told Dee Dee that painting is fun. But not fun enough to risk my life."

Dee Dee shrugged. "My sister's a true redhead."

Jane looked puzzled.

"You know," Dee Dee explained, "high strung. Hot headed. Once Harry gets a notion in her head, that's the end of the discussion."

Harry pursed her lips. "Well, do you feel safe here?" she asked her sister. "First, it was Walter's horse. Then the stable man. Now some dead woman in a lake. Tell me these are coincidences. It's only Wednesday morning; this retreat isn't even halfway over. What's going to happen between now and Friday? Is the instructor going to drop dead in the middle of a demo? Are we gonna find poison in our paints? Serrated edges on our palette knives?"

"See what I mean?" Dee Dee said to Jane. She rolled her eyes. "My sister, The Drama Queen."

Jane smiled, but before she could come up with a clever rejoinder, Mr. Horne cleared his throat again. Everyone quieted.

"I asked you to meet this morning so Alec and I could make an announcement," he said. "We realize this retreat has been, well, let's say ... somewhat problematic. Not what any of us would have hoped - or anticipated - from an event at Gardens and Horses.

"If any of you feel uncomfortable about remaining with us for the duration of this event," Mr. Horne paused and looked directly at Dee Dee and Harry, "we will - under the circumstances - accommodate you. While it is the hotel's policy to refund room fees only when a request for cancellation is made at least two weeks prior to the date of stay, we have decided to make an exception. We will issue a full refund for any remaining nights at the hotel. And your instructor, Alec, has generously agreed to offer a refund for the remainder of the class." Mr. Horne tipped his head in the direction of Alec.

Jane glanced at Alec. She thought he looked none-too-pleased about what had been described as his generous agreement. Surveying the faces of the other painters, she wondered: Would most of them decide to go home? If there was a murderer among them, would that person decide to stay or go?

"That said," Mr. Horne continued, "we would prefer for you to remain. To assure your safety, the police will supply a uniformed officer to accompany the group during all instructional activities. As well as during meals. And for those of you who are staying here at the hotel, we will have a police officer in the lobby at night." Mr. Horne tipped his head toward Officer Goode, who gave a firm nod.

"Indeed, Officer Goode has joined us this morning to tell us what he can about the disturbing incidents that have occurred. But one more thing before I turn the meeting over to him," Mr. Horne said. "By staying, I want you to realize that you will be assisting the police in their investigation. Officer Goode has told me that the sooner evidence can be gathered, the better the chances that a perpetrator will be caught. The police need to interview each of you, and it will greatly aid their investigation if you remain here. Therefore, to encourage you to stay, and to assist the police in their efforts, Gardens and Horses is making what I hope is an irresistible offer: We will issue a voucher for a complimentary stay of two nights at the hotel, to be redeemed anytime during the next year. And Alec, you have something to add to this?"

Alec stood up. "As Mr. Horne explained, I'm willing to refund half your workshop fee if you decide to leave. But I want to encourage you to remain. I've enjoyed working with each of you, and I look forward to a few more days of painting together. In spite of what I can only describe as bizarre circumstances, painting at these gardens really is a privilege. This is an ideal setting for watercolor, for plein air painting.

"And, like you, I want the police to be successful at finding and punishing whoever is responsible for the terrible things that have happened in the last few days. Their job will be much easier if we remain here. So, to entice you, I'm going to offer a voucher: If you stay, you can sign up for any of my workshops for half price. Any workshop that I offer, either here or anywhere else. I'll make the offer good for the next five years."

Officer Goode stood up. "Thanks, both of you for doing what you can to encourage people to stay." He looked directly at Dee Dee and Harry. "I realize that some of you are frightened, and that's understandable. But I wouldn't be encouraging you to stay if I felt that you were being placed in a risky situation. You will have a police officer with your group for the rest of your time here. Of course," he continued, looking at Arthur and Saundra, "we cannot offer the same degree of safety off the premises."

Goode paused, and various people began to whisper. Jane looked at Harry. "With a policeman in residence, would you feel any better about staying?"

Harry bit her lip. "Not sure. The whole vibe has changed, you know? I came here for a vacation - a carefree retreat at a garden. Now it's like we're the key witnesses in a mob investigation. Or Agatha Christie characters on the Orient Express."

Dee Dee mouthed: "Drama Queen, Drama Queen."

Harry gave her sister a dirty look. "Would you quit it? This is not a game. A woman has been found dead and ...."

Officer Goode began speaking again. "While you're making up your minds, I promised you some information. The woman found in the downtown lake was, as some of you have surmised," he took a breath and looked at Jane, "a member of your painting class. Sheryl Calhoun."

Several people gasped. Amanda raised her hand and spoke up. "Officer Goode, I assume that Sheryl drowned?"

"I'm not at liberty to reveal the cause of death," Officer Goode said. "But in my business, I've learned it's best to assume nothing."

"Can you tell us if you are investigating Sheryl's death as a murder?" Amanda asked.

"Yes, we are," Goode said.

"Are you investigating the three incidents - the dead horse, the assault on the stable hand, and Sheryl's death - as related events?" Margaret asked.

"For now, we are considering all possibilities," he answered. "I can tell you that the results of the necropsy are back. The horse found in the reflecting pool on Sunday night did not have water in its lungs."

"That means the horse did not drown?" Margaret asked.

"That's right," Goode said. "The horse died of an overdose. Painkillers."

Jane looked at Margaret. She was sitting beside Maggie, whose cheeks had turned tomato red. The teen covered her mouth with her hands, and tears trickled down her face. Beside them sat Alicia. Tears streamed down Alicia's face, as well. But the face of Saundra, who was sitting with Arthur at the corner of that table, was as dry as the Sahara. That's odd, Jane thought. Saundra seems to have no emotional reaction to the news about her own horse's demise.

"Sheryl's car was found in the hospital parking lot," Goode announced. "We are going over its contents, now. As for the attack on the head of the stables, we will have more information soon. My partner, Officer Kennedy is at the hospital now. The doctors have decided it's safe to bring Dave out of his coma."

Jane looked at Alicia. Her mouth was open like a guppy gasping for oxygen. Beside her, Teddy listened with steely eyes, a rigid jaw, and what seemed like an irate expression.

"So Dave is gonna be alright?" Maggie blurted out.

"I didn't say that. It's too early to tell," Goode said. "But the doctors are hopeful that he will not sustain permanent brain damage."

"And his memory?" Margaret said. "Will he be able to identify his assailant?"

"Not sure," Goode said. "I'll know more when I hear from my partner."

All over the room, people were murmuring. Jane couldn't help hearing the conversation between Dee Dee and Harry.

"Why not stay one more night?" Dee Dee was saying. "If you don't feel safe, we can drive home tomorrow. You heard what the cop said. If we don't leave the gardens, we'll have police protection day and night."

Harry harrumphed. "I'll think about it. I'm not making any promises."

"Do you live far away?" Jane asked them.

Dee Dee shook her head. "No. In Columbia. Just an hour from here."

Pam and Donna came over to Jane. "What do you want to do?" Pam asked.

"I'm enjoying the instruction, and I think the gardens are spectacular. I think it's safe to stay. We just need to be careful," Jane said. "How about you?"

"I feel safe. In addition to the police, I've got Tillie to protect me," Pam said with a grin. "But I'm here on Bill's dime, so I'll do whatever you want, Donna."

Donna scrunched up her lower lip. "Well, Bill doesn't know about the lady in the lake." She shrugged. "And I guess there's no need to tell him until I get back home. I'm kinda curious about how everything will turn out. When you think about, it's pretty interesting - like taking a vacation inside a true-crime novel."

Jane grinned. "Then it's up to Grace. I don't want to force her to stay if she's uncomfortable." They turned to look at Grace, who was standing with Arthur and Saundra. She was smiling at something Arthur had said.

"Don't worry, she'll stay," Donna said. "For her, it's like taking a vacation inside a romance novel."

"I wonder who else will decide to stay," Pam said.

Mr. Horne cleared his throat again. "Anybody who needs to talk to me, please follow me to my office. Alec will remain in the lobby for several minutes, in case you wish to explore your options with him."

"I suggest you take your time deciding what you want to do," Alec said. "For those of you who are going to stay, let's set up our easels out on the patio this morning. We'll paint until lunch, then critique after we eat. The afternoon will begin with a tour of the greenhouse at two-thirty. Afterward, we'll stay there to paint. With the afternoon sun slanting through the glass-topped roof, we'll have an opportunity to capture a spectacular phenomenon. There's a technique to painting light through glass, and I want to give you some pointers during a brief demo after our tour."

Jane saw Margaret and Maggie heading toward the elevator. If she hurried, she might be able to get on the elevator with them. She wanted to ask them about Sheryl. "I need to run up to the room for a few minutes," Jane said to Pam and Donna. "I'm gonna jot down a few things in my notepad. Then I'll see you on the patio in, say, thirty minutes?"

CHAPTER FOURTEEN

The elevator doors were starting to close, so Jane thrust her arm in front of the sensor. As the motion of the doors clanged to a stop, then reversed and reopened, Margaret scowled at Jane. Maggie gave a tiny nod of greeting.

The elevator doors closed with all three of them inside, and Jane looked at the teen. "I'm so relieved to hear the doctors are bringing Dave out of his coma. I assume that means the swelling is down and he's going to be okay."

Maggie managed a weak smile.

"He'll recover quickly, you'll see," Jane said. She tried to make her voice as reassuring as possible. "He seemed to be in great shape before the assault. That's got to be in his favor."

Turning to Margaret, Jane asked, "Have you decided to stay for the rest of the retreat?"

"Yes, we intend to stay," Margaret said, her voice as icy as her face. "I've never been one to shirk my civic duty. With a police escort, we will certainly be safe." Her nostrils flared. "Whoever is responsible for these crimes must be brought to justice."

When the elevator stopped at the third floor, Jane did not get out. Instead, she leaned against the door to hold it open and faced Margaret. "Maggie told me that you and Sheryl were friends. I'm very sorry for your loss."

"Sheryl was a good and loyal friend," Margaret said. "And a dear, dear person." Her voice cracked, but she swallowed and continued. "I've known her for over forty years. When I taught second grade at the Gilbertville

Elementary School, she was my teaching assistant. When I became principal, she became my secretary."

"I didn't know you were an educator," Jane said. "Sheryl seemed like a very nice person. I'm sure she was wonderful to work with." She paused. "It's hard to imagine how this could have happened. Did Sheryl know how to swim?"

"Oh, yes, she certainly knew how to swim," Margaret said. "In fact, she swam laps at the local swim club. For years. If you're asking whether she drowned while swimming in that lake, there's no way. It's a manmade lake, just for decoration - not even three feet at its deepest. There are signs all around telling people to keep out. Ducks get in there; it's not clean enough for swimmers. Sheryl knew that."

Jane nodded. "One quick question: I remember that Dave had some of Maggie's things - her riding gloves and helmet. We were going to pick them up when we toured the stable. In all the confusion, that errand was forgotten. But Maggie said Sheryl brought the things to you. When?"

"She handed them to me at breakfast the next morning," Margaret said. "Come to think of it, I never asked how she got them. All we could talk about was Dave. He was one of our students, you know." She shook her head. "Not a standout, got into some mischief; but overall a good boy. What could you expect with a sorry family like his?"

Jane said goodbye. As the elevator doors closed behind her, she sighed. Every time, I try to tie up one loose end, she thought, it seems like I find another; and it's even more frayed than the first. Frowning, she decided it was a lot more fun to solve a mystery in a novel than in real life. Then again, she mused, I never can guess the culprit when I'm reading a whodunnit. There's always one missing piece or I end up chasing suspects down dead ends.

She let herself into her room, brushed her teeth, and sat down to work on her notes. On a clean sheet of paper, Jane wrote the heading, "Maggie's Riding Helmet and Gloves." Then she listed what she knew and what she wished she knew;

- *How* did Sheryl get Maggie's things? Maybe Sheryl was walking by the stable and stopped to chat *with Dave? Why did he give them to her if Maggie was coming for a tour at 7 pm?*

Dave was a student at Gilbertville Elementary. Sheryl worked there. Margaret - teacher & principal - said he came from a "sorry" family. Meaning? Did Sheryl take a special interest in him because of his "sorry" family?

- When did Sheryl pick up Maggie's things?

Items weren't on bench when we arrived. If Maggie's things were in Dave's office, Sheryl couldn't collect them after police arrived - police blocked off area as a crime scene. So Sheryl was there before he was attacked. Or earlier in afternoon?

- Could Sheryl be Dave's attacker?

Jane frowned as she wrote this section. Sheryl seemed like a nice person. Friendly. Reasonable. Easy to talk to. It was hard to imagine a woman like her attacking Dave. Sheryl was slender, average height. She looked like she was at least in her sixties, maybe seventies. Wasn't she too old to assault a man like Dave, a strong fellow in his prime of life? Then again, Margaret said Sheryl swam laps for exercise so maybe she was stronger than she appeared.

But what would have been her motive?

Jane drew a line under her page of notes. She felt frustrated. There was certainly a lot she didn't know about Sheryl. Maybe the woman did have a reason to want Dave dead. But if Sheryl had assaulted Dave, then there was a second murderer out there. Who would have wanted Sheryl dead? And then there was the matter of the dead horse.

Turning to a fresh page, Jane wrote, "Person Lurking Behind Barn?" She was about to jot down everything she remembered about the movement that she thought she'd seen in the shadows while they were administering CPR to Dave. Was there a person back there, or was it an illusion? Perhaps it was Sheryl?

Jane glanced at her phone and realized it was time for their painting session. So she closed her notepad and gathered up her sunhat, easel, and bag of painting supplies. Before she let herself out of her room, she checked to be sure she had a clean sheet of watercolor paper in her bag.

Donna, Pam, and Grace were already set up when she joined them on the patio.

"How would y'all feel about taking a drive this afternoon? After lunch?" Donna said. "I want to go visit Catherine at the hospital. I chatted with her when I was there overnight, and I was thinking it must be rough for her, all alone. She told me she hasn't got any family living near here. And now her friend is dead."

"That's very sweet of you," Grace said. "But I can't go after lunch. I promised Arthur I'd pose for him. He's been working on a series of watercolor portraits. Women in Sunhats."

"Figures," Donna said. "Everybody says he's a lady's man."

"Where - exactly - are you going to do this posing?" Pam raised her eyebrows and scrunched up her mouth into a naughty grin. "Not in your hotel room, I hope!"

It was Grace's turn to scrunch up her mouth, but hers was a frown. "No nothing like that! For one thing, he's doing all the portraits outdoors."

"Then I guess you'll be wearing something besides a sunhat," Donna said.

Grace exhaled and heaved her shoulders down with dramatic flair. "Stop that, you two. You're too much!"

Returning the conversation to the hospital visit, Jane said, "It would be a nice gesture to visit Catherine."

She didn't say the rest of what she was thinking out loud, but she hoped that a visit might yield some useful information. Not just about Sheryl. Jane remembered that Catherine had worked for the Stauntons but had quit because of her asthma. So there might be something to be learned about the other mystery - the horse they'd found in the reflecting pool. "I'll be glad to drive you."

"If you don't need me to drive, then I'd rather stay here," Pam said. "I was looking forward to a nap after lunch. We were up so late last night." She looked at Grace. "That's if you think you'll be safe alone with the portraitist."

"Oh, come on," Grace said, her eyes rolling. "You don't think he's going to lure me into the bushes and have his way with me. We're a bit old for that sort of thing."

"Well, I didn't think about that, but now that you mention it ... hmm." Pam giggled. "Actually, what I was thinking about was our buddy system. We agreed to go everywhere with a buddy. Does Arthur count as a buddy?" She looked at Jane.

Jane nodded. "I suppose he does."

"What's this about me being a buddy?" Arthur said as he joined them.

Grace blushed. "Just ignore them," she said. "I think they've all gone slap happy. What with the terrible news about Sheryl. And staying up so late last night."

"I understand the police gathered you together last night in the lobby?" Arthur said.

"Yes. When we drove up, the lobby was all lit up," Grace said. "It looked like the painters were having a party. Then we came inside and heard the news."

"I'm sorry. That must have been a shock," Arthur said. "I hope it didn't cast a shadow on our evening together."

"You don't need to worry about that," Donna said.

"Good," Arthur said. "I'd hate to think that every time you thought about my house, you thought about Sheryl's death."

"Well, as a matter of fact, that probably **is** how we'll remember the evening," Donna said.

They all looked at Donna.

"I thought you just said it would **not** cast a shadow over the evening?" Jane said.

"Well, it won't," Donna said, in a matter-of-fact voice. "It was too dark for shadows when we got back here. You need sunlight to cast shadows."

That exchange left everybody speechless, so they pulled out their pencils and began to sketch.

Jane decided she'd rather paint the patio than the green lawn surrounding the wood and brick structure. The tables and chairs cast angular shadows on the wooden floor, creating interesting criss-cross patterns over the wood grain and bricks. Maybe Donna's peculiar remark about shadows has inspired me, Jane thought. She'd seen watercolor paintings of cafes in exhibits, and she'd admired the patterns cast by the shadows of the furniture, but she'd never tried to paint this type of composition.

Jane sketched quickly, then stood back to check her drawing. She frowned. Something was wrong. Either the tables and chairs or their shadows looked odd. She erased some of the legs and tried again. Were the shadows too long? She held up her pencil and squinted, trying to compare the lengths of the legs to their shadows. Then she erased and drew again. Frustrated, she was just about to turn the paper over and start again when Alec came by.

"Pay close attention to the colors," he said to her. "A lot of painters automatically decide that every shadow is a cool color. But one of the advantages of painting from life is you can see complexities. Shadows are often warm tones, especially in the earlier part of the day."

"I'm thinking of starting over," Jane said. "I just can't get these lines right. See how close together those shadows of the chairs are? Mine aren't like that. But I keep squinting and measuring. I know I'm doing something wrong, but I can't figure out what it is."

Alec studied her drawing. "It's the angle of that table," he said, his finger running along the length of the table. "But actually, I wouldn't worry about accuracy in the placement of the furniture," he said. "That doesn't matter so much; it's not necessary to depict the scene with photographic accuracy. I'd concentrate on the angles of the shadows. Are all the shadows falling in same direction? Are they all representing the sun's height at the same time of day? May I?"

He held out his hand, and Jane handed him her pencil and a gum eraser.

Alec made three adjustments in the placement of chair legs. He enlarged the table in the foreground and lengthened the shadow under it.

"There," he said. "Does that read better?"

Jane said, "Yes. Thank you." She marveled at how a few small adjustments had rescued her drawing.

Alec smiled. "Remember about warm versus cool tones." He handed her the pencil and eraser and moved on.

Jane checked her phone. Barely an hour left to complete the painting before lunch. She decided to use a number ten brush and lay down paint quickly. But she soon discovered that was a mistake. The lines of the furniture should have been straight and angular, but hers were wobbly and the legs were not of uniform thickness. Well, it's a workshop, she reminded herself. I'm not here to produce a masterpiece; I'm here to learn. Maybe this painting will have a spontaneous, "painterly" look. Some people call that charming, she mused, even if I call it amateurish.

Her painting wasn't anywhere near finished when the servers began setting up lunch. The other painters began lining up their easels in a row along the far end of the patio for the after-lunch critique. Jane was tempted to collapse her easel and hide her painting under her bag so Alec wouldn't evaluate it. But she decided that wasn't fair. They were all here to learn, and they probably learned more from each other's mistakes than from their successes. So she carried her easel over to the others and set her painting on it. Then she went and got herself a glass of lemonade while she waited for the servers to finish laying out the trays of roast beef and veggie sliders, platters of paprika-sprinkled curly fries, and bowls of mixed spring greens.

After lunch, the painters walked over to the easels for the critique session. In addition to Jane, three other painters had chosen to concentrate on the patio and its furniture: Dee Dee, her sister Harry, and Amanda, the middle school teacher. In Jane's opinion, Harry's painting was the most successful of the four. She had used a ruler to draw in the furniture then painted with a small brush. In the resulting painting, all the lines looked precise, almost like an architectural rendering. Amanda's handling was the most unusual. She had zoomed in close to a single table and chair, casting gigantic shadows across the paper.

Alec critiqued the four patio paintings together. He paid the most attention to Amanda's unusual composition. To Jane's relief, he didn't have much to say - good or bad - about her painting. Then he moved on to Grace's painting of distant bushes and trees at the far end of the lawn. Jane had already admired Grace's landscape. She thought it was the most painterly of the lot. Grace had started with a quick wash of pastels to create sky and lawn, then while the paper was still wet, she'd dabbed in bushes and trees at the horizon with a large soft brush full of green pigment. This "wet on wet" technique yielded blurry edges. Alec praised Grace's work as "spontaneous-looking" and said she'd controlled the pigments perfectly so they'd retained their freshness. Grace beamed at his praise.

After the critique, the painters collapsed their easels. Jane deposited her painting supplies in her room and grabbed her purse and car keys. In the hall, she peeked into the open door to Donna's and Pam's room. "You sure you don't want to come with us?" she asked Pam.

"No, thanks," Pam said. "I've already taken off my bra, and that bed is calling my name."

Donna came out of the bathroom, an orange beret plopped on her head. (Jane thought it looked like a mandarin orange on an upside-down white bowl, but she decided against saying that.)

"Ready," Donna announced.

In the lobby, Jane stopped to tell the police officer where they were going. "We'll be back in time for the afternoon painting class," she said.

"If we're not back by three, you can check the lake," Donna said.

The police officer blinked and stared at Donna.

Jane whirled toward her friend. "Huh?"

Donna smirked as she laced her hand through Jane's arm and began walking toward the parking lot.

"Why'd you say that?" Jane said. "Are you nervous about us getting attacked at the hospital? You really rattled the policeman."

"I wouldn't go if I was nervous," Donna said. But I wanted to be sure the policeman was paying attention. Just in case anything does go wrong, he'll be sure to remember where we're going."

"Let's go by that little store," Donna said while they fastened their seat belts. "The Cheese Board, where we got the wine for Arthur last night. We ought to get Catherine some flowers. Or chocolates, whatever. To cheer her up."

Jane pulled up in front of the shop, but there were no lights on inside. A chalked sign on a little blackboard hanging on the door read "Closed" and listed the hours: Monday, Tuesday, Thursday - 11 to 6:30. Friday, Saturday, Sunday - 10 to 8. The shop was closed on Wednesdays.

"Maybe they have a gift shop in the hospital," Jane suggested.

Although several people were entering and leaving the hospital when they pulled into the parking lot, Jane decided to park as near to the front entrance as possible - just as a precaution. After all, Sheryl had been on her way to visit Catherine yesterday when she was killed.

Turning off the ignition, Jane said, "I wonder where Sheryl parked her car yesterday?" The hospital was in the same complex as the city hall, police station, courthouse, and city park. All the buildings looked like they'd been constructed at the same time. They were connected by a series of sidewalks and staircases bordered by green lawns and shrubbery. Jane eyeballed the distance from the hospital parking lot down three sets of stairs to the lake. It was an easy stroll, not much more than the length of a city block.

As they entered the hospital, they spotted a small gift shop tucked in the corner of the lobby.

"Not much of a selection," Donna remarked. "Maybe a small bouquet and something to read? What kind of magazine do you think she'd like?"

Jane looked over the wooden rack of magazines. There were two or three magazines with glossy covers full of gardens and some standard women's magazines promising interviews with doctors, trainers, and chefs. Scattered among the magazines were books of crosswords and sudokus. Jane spotted one magazine with a cover featuring a woman in jodhpurs jumping a horse over a brick hedge. Donna nodded when Jane slid that one out of the rack.

In a narrow refrigerator with a glass front, they found a selection of bouquets in small colored-glass vases. Donna picked out a green vase containing a mix of cut flowers and greenery.

After paying for the gifts, they headed for the elevators in the lobby. A woman was stationed at an information table near the elevators. Jane told her that they were visiting Catherine Manfred, and the woman checked a list. Yes, Catherine was still on the fifth floor. Room 521.

As they rode upstairs, Donna said, "I hope Catherine knows about Sheryl. I don't want to be the one to break the news to her."

"I'm sure the police have spoken to her by now," Jane said.

They found Catherine on a reclining chair in her room, her legs up, watching television. Donna handed her the flowers and magazine.

"Why, thank you," Catherine said. She turned off the TV and adjusted the chair to a sitting position. "This is an unexpected pleasure. Nice hat."

"Thanks," Donna said. She pulled the beret off her head. "I figure if I ever run out of things to paint, I can always use this. Reminds me of a navel orange."

Catherine squinted. "I would have said a mandarin."

Jane laughed. "Exactly what I was thinking: a mandarin orange on an upturned white bowl."

Donna introduced Jane. "Jane's the one who drove us up here from Atkinsville. Me and Grace. Then Bill got nervous about me fainting and arranged for Pam to join us, so we'd have a second car in case I needed to come home early. Alec is letting Pam take your place in the workshop, by the way." She looked at Catherine. "How long are the docs going to keep you?"

"They're releasing me tomorrow. My daughter is driving up from Atlanta to get me. Kitty will stay with me for a few days. Until we're sure my asthma is under control again."

"Oh, good," Donna said.

They chatted for a while about the workshop, about Catherine's family, about her sometimes-serious bouts with asthma. When they ran out of mundane topics, Donna said, "I assume you heard the news?"

"You mean Sheryl? Yeah," Catherine said. She bit her lip. "I still can't wrap my mind around it."

Donna shook her head. "It's terrible."

"I'm so sorry for your loss," Jane said. "Sheryl seemed like a such a nice person. I guess you were close friends."

"She was a close friend. And a nice person - at least to the people she cared about." Catherine smiled. "She could be - shall we say - salty when she didn't think much of somebody."

"Margaret told me that Sheryl worked with her. As her classroom aide then her secretary at Gilbertville Elementary," Jane said.

"I didn't know they both worked at a school," Donna said. "Well, if Sheryl had a salty personality, I guess the two of them made a bag of potato chips," Donna said. "With Margaret supplying the vinegar."

Catherine chuckled. "Yeah, Margaret is definitely not the soft, sugary type! But she'll do anything in the world for you if you're in trouble. No telling how many kids at Gilbertville Elementary had coats in the winter, sneakers when they grew out of their last pair, school supplies, food on their table - because of her. Whatever their families couldn't afford, Margaret would buy for those kids. Sheryl told me she made a trip to the Walmart every week or so to pick up something that Margaret knew those kids needed."

"I guess Dave, the stable hand, was one of the recipients of Margaret's generosity?" Jane said.

"Yeah, Sheryl said he used to come to school dirtier than a donkey," Catherine said. "Didn't have a pair of shoes to his name. The mother spent every penny on drugs." She shook her head. "At school, the teachers like to never taught little David to read. My guess is he was bright enough, but it's awfully hard for a kid with a home life like that to concentrate. I swear, some parents deserve to be shot."

"How did Dave's mother earn her pennies?" Jane asked.

"Hung around the stables all over town, doing odd jobs." Catherine raised her eyebrows and pursed her lips to communicate her meaning. "Not a bad-looking woman. I guess there'll always be men willing to pay for a woman like that."

Donna chuckled. "So you could say that Dave's mother earned her living through stud fees."

"Yeah, something like that. You know, Sheryl's the one who got him the job at Gardens and Horses," Catherine continued. "Mr. Edmonson, the owner of the place, is - well, was - a good friend of hers. Sheryl encouraged Dave to apply for work at the stable, and she vouched for him. By that time, Margaret had washed her hands of the boy. Can't blame her, really. He was a wild teenager. Nearly dropped out of high school, hanging out with the wrong sort, fooling around with drugs. What do you expect with a mother like his? But Sheryl never gave up on him. Said Dave was just acting out, like teenagers do. Once Sheryl got him that job, it turned his life around. He's terrific with horses."

"That's quite a story," Jane said. "Do you think Sheryl's death and Dave's attack had anything to do with each other?"

"I've been wracking my brain trying to figure that out," Catherine said. "But I can't think of anything. The police asked me if I thought Sheryl might have committed suicide. But that doesn't make any sense, either. She didn't seem the least bit depressed. She was enjoying the retreat. She was on her way over here with my suitcase in her car. Why would she go drown herself in a lake before she dropped it off?"

"So she never delivered the suitcase?" Jane said.

"Nope. She called me in the afternoon and said she was coming by after class. But she never showed up."

"I guess the police still have your suitcase?" Jane asked. "Do you need anything? We could run over to a store."

"I'll be fine," Catherine said. "Kitty will be here tomorrow. But thanks for the offer."

"You know that business about Dave fooling with drugs? Like his mother?" Donna said. "You think that could have anything to do with the horse we found in the reflecting pool? That policeman who came to talk to us at the hotel this morning said the horse didn't drown. It died from an overdose of painkillers."

"That's interesting," Catherine said. "Are you thinking Dave got sloppy and gave the horse too high a dose?"

"After what all you said, something like that might make sense," Donna said.

"I guess it's a possibility," Catherine said. She bit her lip again. "But Sheryl never said anything about Dave getting back on drugs. He was almost like a son to her, so she might not have wanted to mention it. But she was forthcoming about his other shenanigans. I know she didn't approve of his carrying on with that Pickridge woman."

"Sheryl knew about Dave's affair with Alicia?" Jane asked.

"Everybody knew," Catherine said. "Including Alicia's husband. It's a small town. And the horsey crowd is its own little world. With an emphasis on 'little.'"

"Well, I guess that's always true," Donna said. "Where I grew up, the horse people were the 'in' set. They looked down their noses at the farmers. I always thought it was ridiculous, myself. A horse has four legs - just like a cow, just like a pig."

"On that bit of wisdom, nobody could say 'neigh.' Get it? N-A-Y, N-E-I-G-H." Jane giggled at her own lame joke.

"Heh, heh." Donna chuckled. "I guess you were a member of the horsey crowd," she said to Catherine. "You used to work for the Stauntons, right? And they're the ones who owned the horse that got killed."

"I managed their estate, so I knew plenty about their horses," Catherine said. "But no, I don't have a personal interest. If you ask me, the only thing a horse is good for is eating up your income. You may as well fill their feed sacks with hundred-dollar bills, as much as it costs to own them. Especially race horses."

"I heard Lancelot was a champion," Jane said. "That's what Maggie said. So I guess the Stauntons were pretty skilled at breeding race horses."

Catherine wrinkled up her face. "The Stauntons? They never bred horses."

Jane looked at Catherine. "So how'd they get Lancelot?"

"Bought him," Catherine said, "as an investment. When Teddy Pickridge's attempt at a winery went belly up, he needed cash so he decided to sell Lancelot. Walter and Arthur King went in together to buy principal shares in the horse. It about broke Alicia's heart. That horse was like her baby. Personally, I think that was the reason she took up with Dave in the first place. He's tender-hearted, just like she is. To them, a horse is a living, breathing creature - not some asset on a balance sheet."

A nurse came in and took Catherine's temperature and blood pressure, then handed her a waxed-paper cup of pills.

Jane glanced at her phone. "It's about time for our afternoon painting class," she said. "And we better not be late." She looked at Donna. "Since you told that policeman that he should check the lake for us if we're not back on time."

Donna grinned as she stood up. "Well, it got his attention, didn't it?" She put her mandarin orange back on her white bowl of hair.

Jane rolled her eyes. "One more thing," she said to Catherine, "when Sheryl called you, did she say anything about stopping at the police station?"

"No, why?"

"She asked us at lunch if the police had already left the gardens - they came to interview us, you know, about Dave in the morning. Sheryl said she might stop by to talk with them when she went to see you."

"She never said anything about that to me," Catherine said. She peered at Jane. "You think that might have something to do with her death?"

"I wish I knew," Jane said.

As Jane and Donna said goodbye to Catherine, they exchanged phone numbers. "Maybe we'll see you at another painting retreat sometime," Donna said. "Preferably one without flowers. No bathtubs either."

Catherine smiled. "I guess you're referring to my asthma? But what's wrong with bathtubs?"

"No place to find dead bodies in," Donna explained. "You get asthma from the flowers; I faint every time somebody finds a body in the water."

Catherine laughed and waved goodbye. "Thanks again for coming by."

In the hall, Jane and Donna waited for the elevator. When it stopped, a uniformed policeman stepped out. They nodded at him.

"Well, I'm glad to see him. I was worried about Catherine being here by herself," Donna said, "after what happened to Sheryl."

Inside the elevator, Donna said, "I guess you pumped her for all the info you wanted?"

"Was it that obvious?" Jane asked. She grinned. "We do know a lot more than we did before."

"You know whodunnit?" Donna said.

Jane shook her head. "No idea. In mystery novels, the motive always seems to be money, love, or revenge. The more I learn about all the people at the retreat, the more people I'm finding with one or more of those motives. What about you? Any ideas?"

Donna adjusted her beret. "Whenever Bill and I watch a whodunnit on TV, the criminal is the character who seems the most innocent," Donna said.

"And that would be?" Jane asked.

"I don't know," Donna said. "The schoolteachers. Probably the one with the dimples."

CHAPTER FIFTEEN

By the time Jane and Donna returned from the hospital, the afternoon had turned uncomfortably warm. But the Gardens and Horses greenhouse - to Jane's relief - was air-conditioned.

As she entered the sunny glass-walled building, Jane inhaled the earthy aroma of moist, black soil. After the antiseptic smell of the hospital halls, the greenhouse smelled wholesome and fertile. She put down her painting supplies on the tiled floor inside the entrance door, then crowded around Alec to watch his demonstration. After he finished, the painters spread out to find spots for their easels along the long, narrow aisles that ran between raised shelves of plants.

Most of the painters headed for the middle of the greenhouse, with its shelves of colorful, blooming plants. To avoid the crush, Jane decided to set up at the far end of the building. She wanted to sketch a view of the long interior, showing the tiers of wooden shelves holding rows of black plastic plant trays. That would give her another chance to paint angular furniture legs and their shadows. While her earlier attempt on the patio was fresh on her mind, Jane wanted to see if she could master this type of composition.

Saundra began setting up her easel next to Jane's. "Dammit," Saundra said as she unpacked her bag. "I forgot to fill up my water bottle. I've got to go find a sink."

"Here," Jane said, "my bottle's full." She poured some water into Saundra's cup. Saundra thanked her with a smile.

As Dee Dee and Harry edged by them, Jane said hello. "Are you feeling more comfortable about staying?"

"Out here, we're painting in full sight of everybody," Dee Dee said. "I just don't see how anything could happen."

Jane nodded. "How about you, Harry?"

"Let's put it this way: I'm not unpacking my suitcase yet," Harry said.

Dee Dee rolled her eyes and mouthed, "Drama Queen."

Look, Dee, there s room for two easels over there." Harry grabbed her sister's wrist and pointed at the policeman, who was leaning against the wall near the bedding plants. "Not much in the way of interesting flowers, but I've always wanted to paint a policeman." Harry winked, flashed a Hollywood grin, and headed toward the man. As she pushed forward, her bag knocked against Saundra's easel.

"Watch where you're going, would you!" Saundra snapped.

"Yes, ma'am, excuuuse me!" Harry said in an exaggerated voice, pulling in her chin to make a mocking grimace and waggling her head like a bobble-head doll.

After the sisters were out of earshot, Jane glanced sideways at Saundra. "I guess there's no love lost between you and Harry."

"You can say that again," Saundra said. "Can't abide either of them. The SEXton sisters."

"Sexton?" Jane asked. "I thought their maiden name was Thaxton?"

Saundra snorted. "Yup, and maiden name is most definitely the only part of them that could be described as 'maidenly.' If you ever want to observe tigers on the prowl, you should attend an opening with those two. I mean, that cop had better keep a firm grip on his zipper because any male in the room is fair game for those man-eaters. The redhead with the big hair, she doesn't even bother to camouflage her intentions. Just pounce, prick, and purr."

Jane giggled. "I guess you've known them awhile? They're from Columbia, aren't they? Not around here."

"Oh, everybody in a five hundred mile radius knows the SEXton sisters." Saundra snorted again. "At least, every MAN, and that includes - I suspect - my darling Walter. It was Teddy who first introduced them. He's known them since he lived in Savannah. Might I add: When I say 'known,' yes, I am talking in the biblical sense."

Jane wanted to probe Saundra about the history of her relationship with the Thaxton sisters, but Walter had just entered the greenhouse. He waved at Saundra and began threading his way along the aisles toward them. As soon as he sidled up beside his wife, he leaned in and whispered in Saundra's ear. Jane could only make out part of what he was saying, but she distinctly heard the words, "Dave," "police," "coma," and "Lance." Jane kneeled down and began to fish through the tubes of pigments in her bag. Although she didn't want more paint, she did want more information, and she hoped she'd be able to hear better if she positioned herself a bit closer.

Jane's attempt at subtle spying became unnecessary when Saundra chimed in. With a whisper as loud as the color scarlet, Saundra said, "Didn't I tell you it was going to be something like that? An apple doesn't fall far from the tree. If you'd listened to me in the first place, that druggie never would have gotten anywhere near our Lance."

Again, Walter leaned in to whisper. This time, Jane caught enough of his words to piece together what he was saying: Walter's informant - who was someone on the local board of commissioners - had seen the transcript of the police interview with Dave at the hospital this morning. Dave admitted that he'd overdosed Lancelot! He swore it was an accident. He told the police that he'd forgotten to indicate the time on horse's medication chart and administered a second dose of painkillers too soon. This interview was on record, and Dave had been acting as the owner's proxy. So Walter said their insurance wouldn't pay for the loss of the horse.

"And it's no use in us trying to sue the little jerk for negligence," Walter continued. "Even if we won the case, Dave doesn't have a pot to piss in. He'd never be able to pay the lawyers' fees, let alone the value of the horse. We'd just be out god knows how much for court costs, on top of everything else. The only thing we can do is pressure Edmonson to fire him. And that I will most joyously do."

Saundra pursed her lips. "Does Arthur know about this yet? Teddy?"

Walter shook his head. Saundra snorted. "Well, I'm guessing it's not going to be pretty when they hear the news. And wait 'til Alicia gets wind of it!" She tilted her head at Arthur and Grace, who had set up their easels near a table full of potted orchids. "Maybe wait and talk to Arthur when he's not courting this summer's Guinevere."

"Alright," Walter said. "I'll go find Teddy. You know when this class is over?"

"Five-thirty? Six?" Saundra looked at Jane for confirmation. Evidently, Saundra was well aware that Jane had been eavesdropping on the whole conversation.

As soon as Walter left, Jane said, "I guess you're pretty upset about what happened to Lancelot?"

"Yes, I'm upset. I'd have to be a damned fool not to be. You can't imagine how much we shelled out for that horse. We were counting on him as an investment. Just a few more wins. Then Walter planned to retire him from racing and ride on his stud fees.

"To tell you the truth, I had my doubts about Walter's plan from the get-go," Saundra continued. "Lance's legs have been a problem since he started training. And then there's the fact that Alicia raised him. Little Miss Wholesome insists on doing everything the organic way. When Lance was at the Pickridge stable, Alicia refused to give him any meds. Didn't matter how much he was limping."

"You can treat an injured horse without meds?"

"Yup. Let 'em heal 'naturally,'" Saundra said.

"Oh? What does that entail?"

"Whenever they limp, you let 'em rest. Sit out the next race," Saundra said. "Trouble is, with a horse like Lance, that would've meant sitting out every race."

"So he would've become a pet," Jane said, "not a racehorse? I guess he would've been a pretty expensive pet."

"You can say that, again," Saundra said. "After you pour that kind of money into stud fees, then into training, you can't afford to keep a horse like Lance as a pet. But try telling that to Little Miss Wholesome."

Alec had started to circulate among the easels. He came and stood beside Saundra, who stepped back to share his view of her composition. Saundra had drawn a panoramic view of the ceiling of the greenhouse, with its glass panes around its domed top. She had applied a masking liquid to preserve the white of the paper where a shaft of light was slicing through the glass dome. After masking that area, she'd wet the rest of the paper and dropped in intense blues, greens, and yellows to create a dramatic interpretation of the sky.

"You realize you're going to have hard edges when you peel off that masking?" Alec said.

Saundra laughed. "That's the Staunton signature style. Hard edges, bold colors."

Alec chuckled. "Then I'll leave you to it," he said. "Most watercolor painters are aiming for soft and suggestive, but I know you've got your own style. I was actually a little surprised that you decided to sign up for this workshop."

"Never hurts to refresh the basics," Saundra said. "Dust off techniques that I haven't used in a while. Rub shoulders with a new group. " She rinsed off her brush, then tipped the bristles toward Jane and winked. "Get out of the house and listen to some new voices."

Alec moved to Jane's easel and began talking about her painting, but he was interrupted by an outburst coming from the knot of painters in the center of the greenhouse. A woman was shouting. Jane looked up and tried to pinpoint the source of the yelling.

"That's impossible!" the woman yelled. "The police must have pressured him. He couldn't possibly have overdosed Lance. It's a false confession!"

All the other painters stopped and stared in the direction of the shouting. Jane gasped when she realized the outburst was coming from Alicia!

Walter and Teddy were both trying to calm Alicia down. But there was no quieting her. "Don't you dare!" Alicia screamed at Walter. "I'm warning you! Don't you even think about it. You know how important this job is to him. It's his life."

"Alicia, please. Get control of yourself," Teddy said. His deep voice boomed across the large greenhouse. "Nobody is going to speak to Edmonson. Or to the police, for that matter." He reached out and put a hand on Alicia's shoulder.

Alicia shoved away Teddy's hand. "And what makes you think you'll have any choice? When the police come to arrest you for assault. Or better yet, attempted murder!" Alicia flung her paintbrush at her husband, pushed past the cluster of onlookers, and swept out the greenhouse door.

Glancing sideways at Jane, Saundra smirked. "I'd say that conversation didn't go too well. What would you say?"

Jane watched Walter help Teddy gather up both of the Pickridge's painting supplies. Both men left the building.

"I would have to say I'm speechless," Jane said. True to that sentiment, and with her mind in a torrent, Jane proceeded to paint in silence for the remaining hour of class.

At quarter to six, when the painters set up their easels for Alec's critique, it seemed to Jane that everyone was just going through the motions. The usual enthusiasm of artists for discussing art had been drowned by Alicia's outburst. Alec spent most of the time talking about Saundra's unusual painting - which stood out from the others as a flamingo stands out from songbirds - and about developing a personal style, a unique vision, as a painter.

Then they all gathered up their supplies and headed for the hotel. Jane caught up with Donna and Pam.

"Well, hello," Donna said to Jane. "I saw you were painting next to that Staunton woman. Learn anything about the big outburst in there? At the hospital, you said Alicia and Dave had an affair, right?"

Jane nodded. "When I was talking to Alicia last night, she admitted it."

"Oh," Pam interrupted. "First I've heard about that. So that's why Alicia lost it in the greenhouse?"

"Catherine said their affair was common knowledge in the horsey community," Donna explained. "Even Alicia's husband knew about it. That got Jane and me started on the ride home about what motivates the murderers in whodunnits," Donna explained.

"Love, money, or revenge. Right?" Pam said.

Jane grinned. "You've been reading the same novels as me."

"Well, seems to me that Alicia's husband has all three," Donna said.

As they neared the hotel, they saw Officers Goode and Kennedy sitting at a table on the patio with Teddy Pickridge. None of the three men had a drink in front of him. None of them were smiling. They certainly did not look like fellows enjoying a sociable chat.

"I guess I'm not the only one who's thinking about murderous motives," Donna said.

They entered the lobby, where Alicia was sitting on one of the couches. She sprang to her feet and said to Jane, "Do you have a minute?"

"Sure," Jane said.

"Not here. Can we go somewhere?"

"Um. Okay." Turning to Donna and Pam, Jane handed over her painting bag. "Will you take my things upstairs for me?"

As she reached for Jane's bag, Pam whispered, "Does she qualify as a buddy?"

Jane did a double-take, then realized what Pam was referring to - their agreement to take along a buddy, for safety sake. "I guess she'll have to," Jane said sotto-voice as she slid her easel off her shoulder and handed it to Donna. "This is probably not a good time to suggest bringing somebody else along. Alicia seems pretty distraught, doesn't she?"

Alicia was gazing at Teddy and the police through the open door to the patio when Jane joined her.

"Do you want to take a ride somewhere?" Jane asked. "I've got a car in front. Or we could walk around the gardens?"

"Let's sit in your car. That way nobody can listen."

In the parking lot, Jane slid into the driver's seat. Although it was in the shade of a tree, her car felt stifling inside. Alicia settled herself in the front passenger seat as Jane turned on the ignition to start the air conditioner. She turned the fan up to high and fiddled with the vents.

"I don't know who else to talk to," Alicia said. "I mean, I guess this is kind of weird - it's not like we're old friends or anything. But you seemed so understanding last night. Calm. Since you don't know all the gossip around here, maybe you can be, well, objective. But if I'm making you uncomfortable, I mean if you don t want to, then ....."

"I'm fine," Jane said. She tried to make her voice steady, soothing, reassuring. "You need a sounding board, and I'm glad to help. There's no way I can ignore what's been going on, anyway. Not after finding Lancelot dead in the reflecting pool and then finding Dave drowning in that water trough."

Alicia nodded, her eyes staring blindly out the windshield. "I'm pretty sure they're going to arrest Teddy. I can't tell the kids. I mean, I'll have to eventually, but...." Her voice broke. "I guess I should call my mom. But she's never liked Teddy, and when she hears about this.... Mom still blames him for me dropping out of college. Never understood what I wanted with him, in the first place. He's so much older than me. Mom thinks the whole

Pickridge family is a bunch of snobs." Alicia dabbed at her eyes. "She's probably right. I don't know, I just don't know."

Alicia covered her eyes with her hands and began to cry. At first, her crying was muted, but it intensified until she was weeping with the abandon of a small child. Her shoulders heaved. Tears streamed through her fingers and rolled off her chin.

Leaning across Alicia, Jane pressed the button and the glove compartment sprang open. "I have some kleenex. Here." After handing Alicia the box of tissues, Jane waited, wondering if she should rub Alicia's back or pat her shoulder - a physical gesture - the way she might comfort an upset child.

Finally, Alicia's sobbing began to subside. She drew a few ragged breaths of air, mopped her face with a soggy tissue, and closed her eyes.

"You think the police are going to arrest Teddy," Jane said. "For attacking Dave?"

Alicia nodded. "They were arguing at the stable Monday evening. I heard them. They were really going at it. I was in the barn. I guess I should have gone outside and tried to stop them. But I thought I'd just make things worse. Teddy's never hit Dave before."

"Arguing about you?" Jane asked. "About you and Dave?"

Alicia bit her lip. "That and other stuff. Pretty screwed up, huh? I offered Teddy a divorce when he found out about me and Dave. But Teddy doesn't want that. When he and Bunny split, it was really ugly. Totally messed up their kids. He says anything is better than divorce."

"Is murder better than a divorce?"

Alicia gave a tiny smile. "No, Teddy's not like that. He's not a monster. He wouldn't have gone to the stables in broad daylight to attack Dave. They were arguing and things got out of hand, that's what I think. I wish I hadn't left, but I just couldn't stand listening to it, anymore. It was ripping me apart. So I took Dave's dog for a walk. Just to get away from the yelling."

Alicia pulled out some clean tissues, wiped her eyes, and blew her nose. Jane opened up the plastic grocery sack that she used as a trash bag, and Alicia deposited her soggy tissues.

"Are you going to tell the police about their argument?" Jane asked.

"I don't know," Alicia said. "Isn't there some law about how a wife doesn't have to testify against her husband? Anyway, the police are already interviewing Teddy, so they must know he was there. They must have found his fingerprints or something. Or maybe Sheryl told them."

"Sheryl?" Jane asked.

"She was there, too, in the barn. Probably stopped by to see Dave. She wasn't too pleased when she found me there, of course. She didn't approve of our relationship, Dave and me. She made that crystal clear. But Dave adored her, so I just ignored her remarks. Dave says he never would have made it through school without Sheryl." Alicia took a deep breath. "That's part of why I decided to leave. I figured she'd put a stop to it if the argument got physical."

"So Sheryl was at the barn when Dave and Teddy were fighting," Jane said. She began piecing together the answers to the questions that she'd written on her notes. Is that when Sheryl picked up Maggie's helmet and gloves? Was Sheryl in the shadows behind the barn when they were giving CPR to Dave? Was the argument the reason that Sheryl wanted to talk with the police? Jane felt a needle jab into her thoughts: What did Sheryl witness? Is that the reason Sheryl was killed?

"So you heard Teddy and Dave arguing?" Jane asked. "But they weren't arguing about Lancelot's overdose? They were arguing about your relationship?"

Alicia shrugged. "Well, it started out with the horse. You know how those things go. First, Teddy accused Dave of being careless with Lance. He got into a screaming fit. Said Dave must have been drunk. That he wasn't careful about keeping track of when he dosed the horses. Dave denied it, of course. Denied everything." Alicia looked at Jane. "Dave never drank when he was working. Those horses were his life.

"Then Teddy started in about Dave about being too lax," Alicia continued. "Letting other people have access to the horses. But that's nonsense. Nobody got near the horses unless Dave was with them."

"If nobody got near the horses unless Dave was with them," Jane said, "then who overdosed Lance? Who else would have had access to him? Besides his owners?"

Alicia bit her lip. She looked down at her hands, which she was kneading together.

"I think Lancelot was bred at your stables?" Jane said. "Before Walter and Arthur bought him?"

"They bought the major shares," Alicia said, "but we're still part owners." Tears erupted from her eyes, popped off her lashes, and inched down her cheeks. "I begged Teddy not to sell him. Lance was the sweetest foal we've ever had. Affectionate, almost like a big puppy. He didn't have the fire to be a racehorse. Or the stamina. His legs were terrible. But Teddy insisted. We need the money, that's what he said. Unless they kept Lance racing, he was worthless. A money drain. None of them cared about how much pain he was in."

"Alicia, in the greenhouse, you said Dave couldn't possibly have overdosed Lancelot." Jane looked her. "How can you be so certain of that?"

When Alicia looked up, her eyes liquid with tears, Jane felt like she was looking directly into the woman's heart. No need for words - the answer to Jane's question was obvious.

CHAPTER SIXTEEN

Jane set her alarm for five-thirty to accompany Pam on her morning dog walk. The sun was just beginning to break through the tree tops as they left the lobby. Jane's head was still swimming from hearing Alicia admit to overdosing her own beloved horse, so she was eager to talk with Pam about it. To try to make sense of the details.

As soon as they were outdoors, Jane related her conversation with Alicia.

"I don't get it," Pam said. "Why would Alicia overdose Lance? I thought you said she hated to use drugs on her horses. Did she mean to kill him? Maybe she wanted to put him out of his misery because he was in so much pain?"

Pam let Tillie off her leash. This early, they weren't likely to encounter anybody in the gardens. Tillie bounded along ahead of them, her fur waving like black grains of wheat. She sniffed the roots of tree trunks, chased leaves, then doubled back to run circles around the women's legs.

Patches of light dappled the path in front of them, and a hint of a breeze ruffled Jane's hair. During the night, it had rained - just a sprinkling - and the freshly-bathed gardens sparkled with glints of light, like a Mediterranean sea. Tinged with soft perfumes from the flowers, the air felt invigorating, enticing.

"I'm sure Alicia didn't mean to kill Lance," Jane said. "She thought his leg was doing better, and she wanted to get him out of his stall for a while. Figured it would boost his spirit. Help him heal."

"But if she was riding him," Pam said, "wouldn't it make his leg worse? Putting her weight on him?"

Jane shook her head. "She wasn't riding him. She was walking him on a lead. Alicia said they were near the reflecting pool when he went lame. I guess it happened fast. He started limping - severely limping - and Alicia was afraid he was going to topple over. Break his leg."

"Why didn't she call...." Before Pam could finish her question, Tillie jumped, her paws on Pam's chest. "Tillie, you lummox, get down!" Pam pushed the dog down. Tillie dodged sideways and stuck her nose in Jane's crotch.

"Tillie, quit it!" Pam grabbed Tillie's collar, then apologized in the time-honored tone of an exasperated mom. "I'm so sorry, Jane. Now where was I?"

Jane laughed. "I think you were going to ask me why Alicia didn't call for help as soon as Lance went lame. To Alicia, Lance was like her baby. He was born in her stable, and she'd cared for him when he was a little foal. She thought she knew what to do for him, what was best for him. They had a special bond." Jane raised her eyebrows. "Like you and Tillie."

"Okay, I get that." Pam giggled and tousled the fur on top of Tillie's big square head. "But if they were out walking, where'd Alicia get the painkiller?"

"She had a fentanyl patch in her bag. She'd brought it along just in case. But she'd misread the time on the medication log. She thought Lance was due for his next dose and that's why he'd gone lame. Dave kept the log hanging on a clipboard in his office, and it was handwritten, so I guess it was hard to read," Jane said. "Anyway, Alicia led Lance over to the pool for a drink, and she applied the patch. Lance immediately reared up and started punching the air. Then he faltered, stumbled on the cement side of the pool, and went crashing into the water."

"Why didn't she rip off the patch?" Pam asked. "Or go get Dave?"

"At first, she was confused about the way Lance was acting. Big animal like that, and his body was thrashing all over the place. Her first thought was to grab Lance s head and keep it above the water so he wouldn t drown, but he was flailing around so much, she had a hard time. As soon as she realized that she'd overdosed him, she did rip off the patch. But it was too late," Jane said. "His breathing had gotten labored. Alicia groped for her phone and dialed Dave's cell, but the horse was dead when Dave arrived."

"Wow, that was quick!" Pam said. "Who would have thought such an enormous animal would go down that fast?"

"I know," Jane said. "Alicia said she fell apart. She loved that horse. It's ironic, isn't it? She was the one who was always objecting to giving him drugs to keep him racing. And she's the one who killed him with drugs."

"So she just left the horse there? In the water?"

"What choice did she have? He weighed too much for her to drag him out, even with Dave's help," Jane said. "Plus, she was hysterical. She said she was shaking all over. Dave coaxed her back to the stables, and they were trying to figure out what to do. That's when we came along and found Lance. Then it was out of their hands."

"Why didn't Alicia explain what happened? It wasn't like she did it on purpose. Anyway, Lance still belonged to her, didn t he? Didn't you say that she and Teddy still owned the horse?"

"They only partly owned him," Jane said. "The Stauntons and Arthur had bought most of the shares. And since Alicia was a part-owner, it made the whole situation worse - her killing him. The insurance would never cover the loss if the horse's owner killed him."

Jane and Pam had reached an 8-foot brick wall that enclosed one side of the gardens. They could hear the morning traffic on the other side. Ahead, the path curved away from the wall. Suddenly, Tillie dashed out of sight.

"Tillie!" Pam called. "Here, Girl!"

The dog came charging back along the path, but she didn't slow down when she reached them. Instead, she cannonballed into Pam, who slipped and stumbled. Jane reached out a hand to steady her friend. Taking advantage of the confusion, Tillie swooped and swabbed Pam's mouth with her tongue.

"Ugh, Tillie, stop that!" Turning to Jane, Pam said, "When is this dog going to stop acting like a puppy? I mean, she weighs more than I do."

Jane was tempted to say that Tillie wasn't going to stop acting like a puppy until Pam stopped treating her like one. But she decided she'd better keep that opinion to herself. Being a cat-person, Jane understood how attached a person could get to a pet. But Tillie s slobbering, boisterous, tail-wagging affection was very different than a cat's elegant, aloof tolerance of a human. Jane wondered about an owner's relationship with a horse. Was it more like having a cat? The human sets out food and drink and then awaits the cat's permission to touch or cuddle? Or was it more like Tillie, more of a physical relationship involving gobs of enthusiastic, large motor responses? Since a person rides a horse, Jane mused, the horse and human would have to share long periods of body-to-body contact. Maybe that made the bond between a person and a horse especially close, almost like a human mom who holds her infant close to her chest for long periods each day.

Jane's thoughts were interrupted by the sound of women's voices. As they rounded the curve, they saw the two schoolteachers, Amanda and Rachel.

"Well, hey, you two!" Pam called out. "I forgot to ask you last night if you were waking up early to go for a walk. So I dragged this one out of bed to help me walk Tillie." Pam pointed her thumb at Jane.

"We knew you were out here. Tillie's already come and told us," Amanda said. She laughed, displaying her Shirley Temple dimples.

"It's lovely out here in the early morning," Jane said. "I can see why you're willing to drag yourselves out of bed for this. I mean, that hotel bed is luxury personified, but a bed's just a bed. These gardens are majestic. Definitely worth waking up for."

Amanda grinned. "It is beautiful out here, you're right. And I can't ever sleep late, anyway. I'm just too used to waking up for school. It's like I've got an internal alarm clock, and it's always set."

"That is SO not my problem," Rachel said. "Most mornings when my alarm goes off, Larry has to shut it off and shake me to get me up. Sometimes, he has to dash out of the shower to shut my alarm so it won't wake up the kids. And I sleep with my head practically touching the alarm!"

"I guess you aren't sleeping well here because you're in a strange bed?" Pam said.

Rachel shook her head. "Usually, that's not a problem for me," she said. "It's this place. I've been on edge ever since we arrived. The stables, the museum - all this horse stuff. It's like we're in a shrine to horse racing."

"I think everybody is feeling a little nervous," Pam said. She gave Rachel a sympathetic smile. "Especially after one of our own - Sheryl - was killed. That's why I brought Jane along on my walk this morning. I didn't want to be walking around alone. I know I've got this big oaf of a dog with me, but can you just imagine what Tillie would do if we ever come face to face with an attacker? She'd probably slobber all over him and try to get him to play fetch."

"Now watch your assumptions," Jane said, her eyebrows raised. "You just called the attacker "him," but how can you be sure it was a man?" Jane turned to the schoolteachers and said, "What do y'all think? Do you think the person who attacked Dave and Sheryl is one of the painters in our retreat?"

Amanda wrinkled up her nose and mouth. "I can't imagine who it could be," she said. "I mean, who'd want to murder an older woman who paints watercolors? I tell my students that art is important, yes. Maybe even life-changing. But to murder for?"

Jane shrugged. "How do you know the attacks had anything to do with art? There's a lot of money involved with horses. Especially race horses. And like Rachel said, this place is full of horses. And horse owners."

Rachel frowned. "Tell me about it. The whole horse scene makes me want to puke. I despise horse racing. If you ask me, it ought to be outlawed - like cock fighting."

"Because of the sport's cruelty to animals?" Jane asked.

"Because of the sport's cruelty to humans," Rachel said. "Horse racing practically destroyed my family."

"Really?" Pam said. She placed a motherly hand on Rachel's shoulder. "How so? Your husband's not a gambler, is he?"

"Oh no, Larry doesn't gamble. He won't even play poker for pennies. No, my father gambled. Loved betting on the horses. He ended up in jail, and my mom finally divorced him, but not before he'd thrown away every cent we had. Mom had to work her fingers to the bone to raise us kids. She's from Brazil, you know - never got a chance for an education. She cleaned houses to support us, and it wasn't easy, not with five of us kids. It was so bad - one winter, we actually spent almost three months living in our car."

"Oh, how awful!" Jane said. She studied Rachel's expression. The woman's perfect little features had hardened into the face of a stone warrior; a petite statue of Joan of Arc. Her expression captured the frenzied determination of the legendary saint charging off to battle injustice. "I guess your dad had what they call a gambling addiction?"

Rachel nodded, her mouth a thin hard line. "Yup. And I've heard of lots of people who have gambling addictions. Oh, I could tell you stories," she said. "If I had my way, I'd burn down every race track. Then I'd neuter every thoroughbred stallion."

"My! That sounds pretty drastic," Jane said.

"There are laws against dog fighting in this country, aren't there?" Rachel stormed. "I bet that horse racing has destroyed lots more lives than dog fighting. Or cock fighting. Make no mistake: Horse racing isn't a sport, it's a vice, and that's how it should be treated. What's so sporty about watching animals run until their legs break? There's nothing athletic about it. Even the jockeys do nothing but sit there while the horses run. It's not like kicking a ball or doing gymnastics. Unless you count finger dexterity, I guess."

"Finger dexterity? You mean holding the reins?" Jane asked.

"No. Flexing your fingers to crack open your wallet - otherwise known as betting," Rachel said. "And, like you said, horse racing is cruel to the horses, too. They're abused. Literally run into the ground. They're bred with twiggy legs that can't support their weight, just so they can run faster. They live short, miserable lives. They're in so much pain they have to be drugged before every race. The whole business is riddled with scandal and corruption."

"You have a point," Jane said. "I was just reading how much money is spent every year on gambling revenues. It's mind boggling. Plus, gambling is associated with mob activity - drugs, prostitution, violence. That's why a lot of places outlaw it."

"Exactly!" Rachel said. "Horse racing would be against the law if there weren't so many rich, powerful people who get their thrills from it."

After Rachel's impassioned speech, there was an awkward pause in the conversation. Jane glanced at her phone and said to Pam, "We need to start heading back. You've got to drop Tillie off at the kennel, and I need to shower. What time did we tell Donna and Grace that we'd meet for breakfast?"

"We need to get going, too," Amanda said. She turned and started walking toward the hotel. "Rachel, are you going to work out before breakfast?"

"Work out before breakfast?" Pam said to Rachel. "After taking a walk? My goodness. Well, I guess that's why you're so trim and fit. And I'm not!"

Rachel smiled, the sun obliterating the angry clouds that had gathered across her features when she talked about horse racing. "That's me - too much nervous energy, I guess. Larry says I have ants in my pants. The only time I can stay still is when I'm sleeping," she said.

As they neared the hotel, Jane and Pam said goodbye to the teachers and headed to the dog kennel. After they deposited Tillie in "doggie prison," they went through the automatic doors into the lobby. Riding upstairs in the elevator, Pam bit her lip. "You're right, you know."

"Right about what?" Jane asked.

"I shouldn't make assumptions," Pam said.

"Huh?"

"About the murderer being a man."

Jane squinted at Pam. "Are you saying you think it's Rachel?"

"Love, money, revenge," Pam recited. "Aren't those the motives for murder? When you think about it, Rachel has all three. She despises horse racing because of what it did to her family - that's love and revenge. And what it did to her family was all about money."

Jane's eyebrows raised. "But Rachel is so petite. She's probably the smallest person at the retreat," Jane said. "Dave seems like a fit, strong guy. I know Sheryl was older than Dave, but still - she kept herself in good shape. She swam laps."

"Rachel may be petite, but she said herself that she's full of energy. And did you see how passionate she got when she went into that tirade about horse racing? People can summon a lot of strength when they're emotionally involved."

"Maybe we should go to the workout room tomorrow morning?" Jane suggested. "After we walk Tillie."

"You want to see what Rachel's workout routine looks like?" Pam asked.

Jane grinned. "You know me so well."

CHAPTER SEVENTEEN

Alec stood in a shaft of sunlight, paintbrush in hand, facing one of the garden's larger-than-life bronze horse statues. This morning, the class topic was using highlights and shadows to "model" a round surface. He'd taped a large sheet of watercolor paper to a foam board to give it a sturdy backing, then propped it against an easel he'd borrowed from one of the students. On the paper, Alec had pencil-sketched a section of the statue. His sketch filled the paper so all the students could see it.

Their class had started right after breakfast, but the sun had already burned through the morning clouds. Jane was glad she'd remembered to wear a sunhat. The air was still steamy from the night's rain, and the gardens smelled of wet soil and mown grass. It was going to be a hot, muggy day.

Jane listened closely, eager to master this lesson on round objects. Every introductory watercolor course seemed to include a session on painting pears, with the same goal: teaching students to make a two-dimensional painting look like it contained three-dimensional objects. Although every painter studied this technique, Jane knew it was difficult. Rounded surfaces come in soft and hard substances, and light plays differently on each surface. Jane always found the hard surfaces much more difficult to capture. Since the bronze statue was a manmade object, its shiny surface would reflect light in sparks and glints.

Grace raised her hand. "Alec, I wondered how this interacts with composition."

Alec looked up. "What do you mean? Are you referring to focal point? Usually a painting's focal point will be its brightest area."

Grace frowned. "Yes, but the bronze is shiny. It's a hard surface so it will have distinct highlights. Won't the viewer always be drawn to it, even if it's supposed to be in the background and not the main focus of the painting? If I wanted to make, say, a patch of flowers the focus of my painting but I wanted to paint the bronze statue in the background, how would I do that? The highlights on the flowers would be soft. Subtle. With blurry edges. Wouldn't the viewer automatically be drawn away from the flowers to the bright, distinct highlights on the metallic statue?"

"I see what you're saying." Alec began to explain how to deemphasize one part of a painting. "Sometimes, you can direct the viewer's eye with detail. In addition to light, detail captures attention. Think of the way a photographer uses the camera settings to make the focal point more crisp, while the backdrop is fuzzier. Generally, anything in the backdrop grays out, and even the metallic surface of the...."

Jane's concentration was broken by the appearance of the two plainclothes police officers, Goode and Kennedy, who were approaching their painting group.

The policemen reached the outskirts of the cluster of students and stopped a few feet to the left of Jane. Goode signaled to Alec with a wave of his arm. "Excuse me," he said. "Sorry to interrupt. I need to speak to Mr. Pickridge."

Teddy and Alicia both turned.

"Mr. Pickridge, I need you to come with us," Goode said, his voice calm but firm. "Now."

"Am I under arrest?" Teddy weaved through the knot of painters to face the policemen. His face and neck, already pink in the heat, had turned an angry reddish color, like a wound. Alicia, looking pale and upset, followed Teddy.

"Not at this time," Goode said. "But we want to take you down to the station for questioning. And we'd like to inspect your car while we're here. I assume it's in the hotel parking lot? You have the right to refuse access, of course. In that case, we will be forced to get a warrant. But understand that such a refusal would be considered part of the evidence against you, should this come to trial."

"I'd like to call my lawyer," Teddy said.

Goode shrugged. "As you wish."

As Teddy walked off with both policemen flanking him, Arthur edged through the painters. He put his hand on Alicia's back. "Are they arresting him?" he asked her.

"No. Not now, anyway," Alicia said. "But they're taking him to the station. Teddy asked for his lawyer."

"Smart man," Arthur said. "I assume you want to join him down at the station? I'll call Walter and have him meet us. I can give you a ride if you don't feel like driving."

"No, that's okay," Alicia said. "I already asked Jane. She'll drive me downtown."

Jane was startled by this announcement but she tried not to show her surprise. "You and Walter must have things to discuss," she told Arthur. "Alicia said you were Lancelot's owners. I don't mind giving Alicia a ride downtown. I'm ready to get out of the sun. Never been much for the heat."

Arthur hurried back through the painters to gather up his easel and painting supplies. He put his hand on Grace's arm and leaned close to her to say a few words. Then, nodding goodbye to Alicia, he headed off toward the hotel.

Alicia waited until he was out of earshot to turn to Jane. "Thanks for covering for me."

Jane gave her a faint smile. "I've never been good at doing a poker face. I hope I didn't look too surprised."

Alicia grinned. "You were terrific. A for acting."

"Sounds like the police are going to be searching your car. I guess you didn't want to have to depend on Arthur for a ride?"

"Yeah. And I have another stop that I want to make," Alicia said. "I didn't want Arthur coming with me. Do you mind missing the rest of this session? I don't want to impose. I guess I could call a taxi."

Jane hesitated. She looked at Alec, who was talking as he wet his drawing of the statue. When it was shiny with water, he dabbed in yellow then red and let the pigments swirl together on the paper. Jane had been looking forward to this demonstration. But her curiosity was also piqued. Were the police going to arrest Teddy for the attack on Dave? What did the police know? If they were searching his car, did they suspect him of Sheryl's murder, too? Jane was also curious about the other stop that Alicia said she wanted to make. Pam, Grace, and Donna could fill her in about whatever she'd miss from Alec's lesson. But if she missed this chance to accompany Alicia, she'd probably never learn the outcome of the case.

"Let me just tell my friends where I'm going," Jane said. "And I want to drop off my easel. I'll meet you in the lobby in, say, ten minutes?"

"You're a lifesaver," Alicia said.

As Jane walked back to the hotel, she reflected on what Alicia had called her: A lifesaver. Surely she didn't mean that. Did she? Not literally? Given this was a murder investigation, a common expression like "lifesaver" took on a charged meaning. Then Jane had a chilling thought: Was Alicia in danger? Could Jane be putting herself in danger by driving Alicia downtown? Jane wondered if she should return and ask one of her Atkinsville friends to come along with them. There was safety in numbers. But then, Alicia might not feel as free to discuss the situation if someone else was along. In the end, Jane's curiosity got the better of her caution. The common expression, "curiosity killed the cat" sprang to mind as she pushed the elevator button in the lobby. When the elevator doors opened with a clang, Jane felt an electric jolt of fear. She forced herself to ignore it. After all, she told herself as she rode up to her floor, there was that other common expression, "a cat has nine lives." And she'd always considered herself a cat person.

After they were settled in Jane's car, Alicia said, "I'd like to stop off at the hospital before we go to the station, if that's okay with you. It won't take long."

Jane glanced at Alicia. "The hospital?"

"Yes. I spoke to one of Dave's nurses this morning. She said it would be okay for me to see him. As long as I limit my visit to a half-hour or so." Alicia bit her lip. "I've made a decision. And I think Dave has the right to know. First. Before I tell anybody else."

Alicia lapsed into silence. Jane wanted to ask her to explain but decided it was wiser to let her volunteer information, rather than press her with questions.

Jane looked for a shady parking spot in the hospital lot. She ended up in front of the stairs that led down to the lake, the same stairs that Sheryl must have descended before she was murdered. Another jolt of fear ran up

Jane's back. "I'll go inside with you," Jane said. "It's too hot to wait out here. I can read a magazine or something in the lobby."

"You're welcome to come up with me," Alicia said. "Actually, I'd rather if you'd come along. I always lose my nerve when I'm face to face with someone. And I need to get this said. It's been on my mind for a while."

They got in the elevator, and Alicia pushed the button. "Dave was transferred to a regular room this morning," Alicia said. "He's on the eighth floor."

"I'm glad to hear that," Jane said. "If they've let him out of Intensive Care, he must be doing well. Sounds like they managed to stop the brain bleed, and the swelling must have gone down."

They checked at the nurses' station for directions. When they located Dave's room, the door was closed. Alicia knocked. A female voice called, "Just a minute, please."

They waited outside until a nurse opened the door. "You can come in now," she said. "I was changing his dressings."

Dave was propped up on white pillows in a white bed. Clean white bandages surrounded the top of his head. Although his complexion was paler now than it was on the afternoon when Jane had first met him on the patio, he was pinker than his backdrop, and he looked alert. He grinned when he saw Alicia. He squinted as Jane approached, as if he was curious about what she was doing there.

"This is Jane," Alicia said. "Remember her? From the painting class? She gave me a ride over. I didn't think you'd mind if she came with me. The police are searching Teddy s car so I couldn't drive myself over."

Dave smiled at Jane. "I hear that I owe you my thanks. If you hadn't pulled me out of that trough, I would have drowned. And the police said you were the one who started CPR. You're a lifesaver."

There was that word, lifesaver, again. "I didn't realize the police knew which of us had started CPR," Jane said. "It all happened so fast, I can hardly remember who did what. But I guess every little detail matters in a murder investigation."

Dave's smile vanished. He shut his eyes for several seconds and took a deep breath. When he opened his eyes, tears had beaded along his lower lids. "I can't believe she's dead. When the police told me, I .... I've known her since I was a little boy, I met her in kindergarten. In all these years, she's never given up on me, no matter what. When I was a kid and things were rough at home," Dave's voice cracked, "I couldn't wait to get to school. I couldn't wait to go see Miss Sheryl. She always seemed to know what to say to make me feel better. Without her, I don't ...."

"It's not your fault, Dave," Alicia said. "You know that, don't you? There was nothing you could have done to protect her."

"She was the one who broke up the fight," Dave said, looking at Alicia. "That evening, when Teddy and I started throwing punches at each other." Dave looked down at his fingers, which were twisting the bed covers. "Sheryl came charging out of the barn and let us have it. Can you imagine? A slim, elderly woman like her. She used her schoolteacher's voice to break us up, like we were two little kids brawling on the playground." He gave a nervous, tinny-sounding giggle.

"Teddy wasn't the one who came at you. With the shovel? Was he?" Alicia asked.

Dave shook his head and then winced. "Yow! I keep forgetting how much it hurts when I move my head." He looked at Alicia. "I never saw the person who hit me with the shovel. I don't remember that at all. I remember the argument with Teddy. We were both shouting, then one of us pushed the other. I don't even remember which one of us started the physical stuff. All I know is Sheryl came rushing out of the barn and put a stop to it. I remember the two of us - Teddy and me - we were still breathing hard, like bulls in the arena, when Walter and Arthur showed up."

Jane raised her eyebrows. Had Arthur mentioned that he'd been to the stables earlier that evening? Or that Walter had been there with him?

"All three of them were furious," Dave continued. "Screaming at me. Accusing me of negligence. Said the insurance wouldn't pay for Lance, and it was all my fault. Walter demanded to see the log of Lance's meds. I kept it hanging outside my office door, and I always wrote in pencil. You've seen it, Alicia. They claimed I changed the times after Lance died. There was no way to prove that I didn't."

"Why didn't you tell them that it was my fault?" Alicia said.

"What good would that do?" Dave said. "You were part owner, so the insurance wouldn't cover the loss if it was your fault, either. And they'd make your life miserable. They'd never let you live it down. They already treat you like you're some dimwitted hippie, not a grown woman who actually has some principles, some compassion."

Tears streamed down Alicia's face. "I can't believe what a mess I've made of everything." She looked out the window. "I really don't think Teddy hit you with that shovel and stuffed you in the trough to drown, Dave. He's just not capable of that. He's never been a violent man. Somebody like Walter, yes, I'd believe it. He's so repulsive. A snob. A total sneak. No decency whatsoever. The only thing he's ever cared about are his pants."

Jane turned to Alicia, a puzzled look on her face.

A hint of a smile washed across Alicia's face when she saw Jane's expression. "I meant what's inside his pants," she explained. "His wallet and his dick, to be specific. Walter's been cheating on Saundra as long as I've known him. Not that I'm one to talk."

She looked at Dave. "I don't know if this is the right time to say this. But I've got to start sometime. I've been doing a lot of thinking since all this began. It's time for me to get my life together, Dave. Either I stand beside Teddy now, when he needs me the most, or I walk out the door and make a clean break. As much as I resent him for some things - his parents, but I guess that's not his fault. How much he worries about appearances. All his hang-ups about material things. Still, none of that is an excuse. Teddy has never been anything but fair and decent with me. More than fair. And the kids. I just can't.... What I'm saying is I think it's time to...."

Dave and Alicia locked eyes. One single teardrop popped off his eyelid and rolled slowly down his cheek. "I understand," he said. "I don't know how many times Sheryl has said the same thing to me. It isn't right, it was never right. We both knew that. You're a married woman. But I couldn't...." He swallowed. "I knew this was coming. I've always known."

Alicia stood. "Look, I don't want you to feel like I'm abandoning you. What's between us, it's always been about respect. Admiration. Friendship. And it always will be. You're a good man, a really good man. And a good friend. I'll always consider you my friend. If you need help - you know, financially.... If they say you need to spend some time in physical therapy. Or maybe there'll be other medical problems from the coma. Anything.... I'll take care of the money."

Dave started to speak.

"Please," Alicia said. "It's the least I can do." She turned and headed for the door as if she was determined to move forward, rather than dwell anymore on the uncomfortable conversation. "Look, I'm going to go now. I need time, we both need time, to think about everything. But I meant what I said. All of it. Just don't hesitate - okay, promise me. Don't hesitate to call me if you need something." Alicia took a deep breath and walked out of the room without looking back.

Jane stood. She had no idea what she should say to Dave before she left the room. Wish him a speedy recovery? Tell him to have a nice afternoon? What do you say to a man who has just heard life-changing news? A man who is lying in his hospital bed after a close shave with death? In the end, Jane simply nodded in his direction. She hoped her face showed ample sympathy for all he'd been through. Then she hurried out the door.

She caught up to Alicia, who was dabbing at her eyes with her fingertips, in the hall. "I'm sorry," Jane said.

"What are you sorry for?"

"I don't know. Listening, I guess," Jane said. "That should have been a private conversation. I thought about tiptoeing out, but I figured if I got up, it would just interrupt everything. Remind you that I was in the room and make things even more awkward."

Alicia exhaled and shook her head. "No, I'm glad you were there. I don't think I'd have had the courage to say all that if you hadn't been there. It needed to be said. This has been eating at me - for months really. It came to a head when Dave was attacked, but I'd been mulling it around, putting it off, just letting everything go on."

The elevator discharged them at the hospital lobby, and they walked slowly to Jane's car. "Dave's a wonderful person," Alicia continued. "He really is. He's the kind of guy that I should've married. But I didn't. I married Teddy, I vowed to stand by him. And that's what I need to do.

"I've always thought of myself as an honorable person," Alicia continued. "Someone you could depend on. And I hated myself for what I'd become. I've been a cheat, a sneak. As much of a cheat as Walter Staunton. Carrying on an affair that I knew was hurting my husband, humiliating him. What would I say to my kids if they found out? That Mommy was hurting Daddy every single day - on purpose - but she kept doing it anyway?"

Alicia began crying, but Jane didn't know what words to offer in comfort. Instead, she tried to make their surroundings comfortable by turning on the engine, increasing the fan speed, lowering the air conditioner setting. She handed Alicia the box of tissues.

After several minutes, Alicia's crying subsided. "I must look a mess," she said. She pulled down the visor and popped the mirror open.

Jane shrugged. "You certainly look like you've been crying."

Alicia smiled. "I guess it's alright if I show up to the police station looking like I've been crying. What woman wouldn't be crying if her husband was accused of attacking her lover?"

"What about Sheryl?" Jane asked. She looked at the staircase leading down to the lake. "You said you don't think Teddy is capable of murder. But the police are surely going to ask where he was when she was killed."

"I know. I've been thinking about that." Alicia paused. "Trying to decide what I should say."

Jane raised her eyebrows. "What do you mean? He wasn't with you?"

"No. We weren't even on speaking terms Tuesday. He left the room in a huff after class. He didn't tell me where he was going, and I didn't ask. I assumed he was going to go have a drink with Walter. Or Arthur. I didn't see him when I went down to supper. But he showed up after a while. He came into the dining room with Alec."

"So he could have been having a drink with Alec?"

Alicia shrugged. "I guess."

"Well, that should be easy enough for the police to check," Jane said.

"So you think I should tell the police the truth?" Alicia said. "Or should I try and cover for him?"

Jane frowned. She didn't think it was her place to tell Alicia what to do. But she didn't want to encourage her to lie. This wasn't like telling a little white lie - this was a murder investigation, and truth was crucial.

"I don't know," Jane said. "I think it'd probably be better to tell the truth, rather than be caught up in a lie. If the truth comes out later, it'll look worse for Teddy - like he asked you to lie for him. It would make him look guilty." Jane looked at Alicia. "On the other hand, I guess you're going to feel terrible if your testimony ends up putting your husband in jail for murder."

"I already feel terrible," Alicia said. "Nothing like overdosing a million dollar horse. Not to mention cheating on my husband with the stable boy. And I've probably ruined poor Dave's reputation forever with any future employers since the horse set knows all about our affair. Now my husband is facing an accusation of murder, all because of what I did. That's pretty terrible, don't you think?"

Again, Jane found herself without adequate words. Again, Alicia retreated into her thoughts. Jane waited for Alicia to indicate that she was ready to face the ordeal of the police station. She adjusted the vent so cool air would blow around the car's interior. As Jane waited, she reflected on the conversation with Dave.

"Alicia, do you remember what Dave said just now?" Jane asked. "About Walter and Arthur being at the stable? That the three of them were angry? Accusing him of negligence?"

Alicia nodded.

"Do you think Dave told the police that all three were there?" Jane asked. "Because any of them could have been the person who attacked Dave with the shovel and left him for dead. Any of them could have murdered Sheryl to keep her from telling the police what she'd seen or heard at the stable."

Suddenly, a chilling possibility erupted in Jane's brain: It could have been all three of them who tried to murder Dave. All three of the "Mischief-eers" could have decided to silence Sheryl. Together.

CHAPTER EIGHTEEN

The police station was on the same city block as the hospital. As Jane pulled up in front, she offered to wait. "In case you need a ride back to the gardens," she told Alicia.

"No, that's okay," Alicia said. "I've already used up enough of your day. I appreciate it, I really do. You've been like a mom to me. Actually, better than a mom. No judgements, no telling me what to do. Just a sympathetic ear and level-headed advice. I wish my real mom would act like that."

"It's easier for me," Jane said. "Your real mom probably feels like what you do reflects on her, on how she raised you. She's probably worried that your marriage might break up, and that would be tough for your kids. They're her grandkids, too. Unlike a real mom, I don't have any personal investment. You're not my daughter - or my little sister."

Alicia's mouth flew open. "Oh, I'm sorry. I didn't mean to imply that you're an old lady - comparing you with my mom, like that. What I meant is that you've been motherly to me. In a good way. Understanding. Helpful."

Jane smiled. "Don't worry, I'm not insulted. I ve never been the least bit embarrassed about admitting my age. And I probably am around the same age as your mom." Jane patted Alicia's arm. "I don't have kids, so I don't have much practice at acting motherly. But my own mom was as good as they get. I'm honored if you think I'm anything like her."

"Some moms are treasures, aren't they? And some aren't," Alicia added. "Sheryl Calhoun, for instance. She might have acted like the mom that Dave sorely needed when he was in grade school. But she was a royal pain when she found out about Dave and me. I know I shouldn't speak ill of the dead, but you wouldn't believe the things she said to me. In front of Teddy. Even in front of my kids. Honestly, I wanted to kill that woman." Alicia thanked Jane again and got out of the car.

Stunned by Alicia's last sentence, Jane sat still for a minute. Her brain was caroming around the inside of her skull - like the shiny little ball in a pinball machine. That last statement - had Alicia just confessed that she'd killed Sheryl? Surely not! What Alicia said about wanting to kill Sheryl was just a common expression. Just a way of saying that Sheryl had annoyed her. An expression, not an admission. Or was it?

Glancing at the clock in the car's dashboard, Jane realized it was time for the painters to assemble on the hotel patio for lunch. But she didn't feel ready to blend back into watercolor, not yet. She felt unsettled, distracted. She needed some time alone to process everything she'd heard and observed this morning. What she really needed was to make sense of the new information by recording it in her notepad.

She decided to pick up a sandwich and eat it in the cool solitude of her hotel room. She remembered seeing a sign for a sandwich shop in the little strip mall where The Cheese Board was located, so she headed over there.

After a calm lunch sitting at the carved wooden desk in her room, Jane felt much better. She'd written several pages of notes and organized them under headings, like: "Who Was At the Stable Before Dave's Attack?" And "People With Motives/Opportunity For Killing Dave." People With Motives/Opportunity For Killing Sheryl." "Who Can Be Eliminated As Suspects?"

The Suspect Elimination page had two columns: One for Dave, the other for Sheryl. Under Sheryl's column, Jane wrote Arthur King as well as Walter and Saundra Staunton, since all three had been at Arthur's supper. She wrote Catherine Manfred in the same column, since Catherine was still in the hospital at the time of Sheryl's death.

But then again ..... What was that ABC mnemonic that the detective always repeated in her favorite mystery series? "Assume nothing. Believe nobody. Check everything." Hospital patients are allowed, even encouraged to take walks in the halls, aren't they? Although Catherine had what seemed like the perfect alibi, she actually had the perfect opportunity to kill Sheryl. If, for instance, Catherine had gone for a walk in the hallway, then slipped downstairs, she could have intercepted Sheryl in the hospital parking lot and suggested they take a walk around the lake. But why would Catherine want to kill her friend? Jane reminded herself to assume nothing. In a long acquaintanceship, there would have been many opportunities for disagreements, tensions, even hate between the two women. Catherine seemed like a sensible, level-headed woman, but how could Jane know what jealousies the woman might have been harboring? Jane crossed Catherine's name off the Suspect Elimination list.

Absorbed in these disturbing thoughts, Jane nearly leaped out of her chair when she heard a sudden knock on the heavy door.

"You in there, Jane?" Pam called from the hall. "You missed lunch."

Jane got up and opened her door. Pam, Donna, and Grace faced her in the hallway.

Pam was holding a styrofoam plate covered with another upturned plate. "I didn't want you to go hungry," Pam said, "so I brought you lunch. It was delicious, of course. Lettuce wraps, Asian style. With these crispy little potato pancake-y things that came with a spicy sauce. And itty-bitty cream cakes in different flavors for dessert. I didn't know what you'd like, so I brought you some of everything."

"And here's some iced tea," Donna said, as she marched into the room with a tall paper cup. She glanced in the trash can beside the desk. "Uh oh, looks like you already ate. Well, maybe you can put this stuff in the refrigerator and have a midnight snack tonight." After plunking down the cup on the desk, Donna plunked herself down on Jane's bed. "I hope we're not intruding."

Before Jane could answer, Pam plopped herself down in the elegant wing chair in the corner by the side of the desk. "I'm dying to know what happened," she said. "Did you go into the police station with Alicia? What happened? Did they arrest Teddy?"

"Maybe this isn't a good time?" Grace said. She was standing in the open doorway as if hesitant to barge in. "Did you want some time alone? If Alicia asked you not to repeat what happened, that's fine. We wouldn't want to pester you."

"Hell, yes we would!" Pam said. "Come on, Grace, get in here and shut the door. Now, Jane, tell us what happened. Every juicy detail."

When Grace didn't move, Pam glared in her direction. "Come on, Grace, you know you're curious, too. Stop being so polite. Get in here."

"Yes, and, by the way, Grace, you have some catching up to do, too," Donna said as Grace shut the door behind herself. "It feels like it's been months since we've laid eyes on you. What's happening with Sir Galahad?"

"Sir Galahad?" Jane said. "Do you mean King Arthur?"

Donna shrugged. "Sir Galahad, King Arthur, whatever. You know who I'm talking about. The knight from that Round Table story - Mr. Camelot."

"Alright, I say we focus on one piece of gossip at a time," Pam said. "First, Jane. What happened with Alicia? I see you've been writing notes." Pam picked up Jane's notepad and thumbed through the pages. Her eyebrows shot up. "Look at all these notes! Have you decided to write your own whodunnit? I had no idea you were recording all this. Your fingers must be numb."

"I'm just trying to make sense of all of it," Jane said. "There are so many people involved. And each one seems to have a complicated relationship with everyone else. It's hard to keep track of who said what and who went where. The only people that I'm sure I can trust at this retreat are us."

"What makes you think you can trust us?" Donna said. "For all you know, Grace could have been lying about posing for Arthur when she was actually running around and killing the competition." She looked at Grace. "You've always wanted to become the wife of a snobby estate-owner, haven't you? Marry into billions? Have your own cook? Bonsai collection?"

Grace exhaled as if exasperated. "I really don't think Arthur has billions," she said. She sat side-saddle on the edge of the bed. "And, by the way, I wouldn't have called Arthur snobby. He's been very down-to-earth with us. And I think he's been awfully kind, too."

"That's what I was afraid of," Donna said. "The whole time we thought you were posing for a portrait, Arthur was getting you down to earth. Never trust an artist. Especially a rich, snobby artist."

Grace was about to object, but Pam held out her hand as a stop sign.

"Girls, girls," Pam said. "Restrain yourselves. We haven't heard the dirt about Alicia yet. Remember, one piece of gossip at a time. Come on, Jane, spill it."

Jane giggled. Her friends' antics were a welcome relief after the tense conversations with Alicia. "Alright, let me think where to start." She told them about the morning visit to Dave at the hospital and about how Alicia had broken off her affair with him. "Man, was that ever awkward! I was sitting there the whole time. Through the entire conversation. They were both crying. I couldn't figure out how I could slip out of the room without making the situation even more uncomfortable."

"I guess they ignored you, like you were a fly on the wall," Grace said. "But it sounds like your presence gave Alicia the courage to say what she needed to say. I bet you gave her emotional support, too."

"I guess so," Jane said. "But it sure made me squirm."

"And what happened with Teddy?" Pam asked. "Did they decide to arrest him?"

"I didn't go into the police station," Jane said. "Alicia told me she didn't need me. She did ask me for some advice, though." Jane hesitated. "She didn't tell me it was confidential, but I don't want to betray any secrets in a murder investigation. Promise me you won't repeat this."

They all nodded, and Jane told them what Alicia had said about Teddy's whereabouts on the evening when Sheryl was murdered. She also told them about Alicia asking Jane's advice about whether to lie and invent an alibi for her husband. And how much Alicia had resented Sheryl for various remarks about the affair with Dave. "Alicia actually said she wanted to kill Sheryl!"

"Well, those are pretty strong words," Donna said. "Especially considering the fact that somebody did kill Sheryl. It's a good thing Alicia chose you to be her sounding board - not me."

"Why? Would you have told the police?" Jane asked. "Alicia said I was acting motherly. You have more experience with mothering than I do."

"But I pass out whenever there's a murder involved," Donna said. "So I probably would have been out cold for most of the conversation."

Pam had been thumbing through Jane's notes as they talked. "I really don't think Alicia's the one who killed Sheryl. And, anyway, why would she want to attack Dave?"

Then Pam began to read Jane's Suspect Elimination list aloud. That started the four Atkinsville painters on a vigorous analysis of who might have been the culprit in Sheryl's death and whether that murder was related to the attack on Dave. Each of them had a pet theory.

Pam was pushing the possibility that Rachel, the schoolteacher, was the culprit. "The culprit is always the one who is totally unlikely to commit a murder," Pam said.

"That's in a TV show," Jane said. "I don't know if it works when it's the real thing."

"If you ask me, I think it's Alec," Donna said. "Do you remember how mad he got when Sheryl told him about Catherine dropping out of the retreat? With a temper like that, who knows what he'd do if somebody crossed him. I bet he'd explode. Go crazy."

Pam pulled in her lips and wrinkled up her chin. "That doesn't make sense. Wouldn't Alec have murdered Catherine, not Sheryl? Catherine's the one who dropped out of the retreat. Besides, what would be his motive for attacking Dave?"

Donna shrugged. "How do I know? Maybe Alec paints horse pictures, and he was painting Lancelot for some wealthy collector. But the portrait was going to be worthless after the horse died."

"Why would that make his portrait worthless?" Pam asked. "And that seems kind of far-fetched. I didn't see any horse portraits on his website."

"Well, none of this is logical," Donna said. "First, someone kills a horse. Then...."

"The horse was an accident," Jane pointed out. "And Alicia has already admitted to that. I don't think it has any bearing on the other attacks."

"I don't know," Pam said. She wrinkled up her chin again. "Lancelot's owners thought the overdose was Dave's fault. That's a powerful motive. Aren't the classical motives love, money, and revenge? That horse was worth a fortune, so there's money AND revenge."

"Now you're getting me all mixed up, Pam. I thought you decided Rachel did it," Donna said.

Several other suspects were suggested but each was eliminated for lack of motive or opportunity. The more the four of them talked, the more confused they got.

"You know," Grace said. "This is like a painting."

"What do you mean?" Jane said.

"Well, everything in a painting seems to change," Grace said, "depending on the lighting. Instead of a fishing boat on a calm blue ocean, the same scene can look like a menacing storm or a romantic sunset."

"That's very philosophical," Donna said. "I never thought of it that way. But now that you say it, it makes sense. Except I don't know how it helps us find the killer."

"Speaking of sunset," Pam said, "did you hear about the schedule today, Jane? We're going to paint sunsets. Alec arranged for us to have an early dinner, at six. Then we're gathering in the lobby at seven-fifteen for our class. He's going to show us a spot with an excellent view, and we'll paint as the sun goes down. Sunset is at eight-twenty."

"So that means we have the afternoon off," Grace explained. "We can rest or explore the gardens, go back to the thoroughbred museum - whatever we feel like doing. Alec said he'll be on the patio, and he'll critique our work if we want him to."

"So what do you want to do?" Jane said. "I'd be up for painting on the patio."

"I thought I'd take Tillie for a walk," Pam said. "Anybody want to come? I don't suppose I need a bodyguard if Tillie's with me. But I'd enjoy the human company."

"I need to call Bill," Donna said. "He'll be glad to hear that nobody died today. Then I was thinking about a nap."

"I can walk with you, if you like," Grace said to Pam.

"Uh, uh, not so fast," Donna said. "You can't leave yet, Grace. Not until you tell us the news about Mr. Camelot."

Grace's face turned pink. "Oh, there's really nothing to tell," she said.

"Oh, come on. All that time you've been spending with him? He hasn't proposed that you share his throne?" Pam's mouth turned up at the corners into a smile as broad as a slice of cantaloupe. "Or maybe he's hinted at a future art retreat? One on one - ahem! - at his majesty's castle?"

"No, but he did make a really wonderful portrait of me yesterday," Grace said. I was impressed by how accurate the likeness was."

"Do you have it?" Jane asked. "I'd like to see it."

"No, he said he wanted to get it framed before he gave it to me."

"Aha! Then he is planning to see you when this retreat is over," Donna said.

"Well, yes," Grace said. "I guess that does imply that I'll see him afterwards."

"And how do you feel about that?" Jane asked.

"Well, I'm not sure." Grace paused, as if to choose her words carefully, "I guess I feel complimented. All the attention. And he is so charming. Impeccable manners. Almost like he's a gentleman from an earlier century. But there's something about him. Well, it's just happening so fast, I guess. And what with everything else, it's a bit overwhelming."

"You don't have to make any decisions now," Jane said. "Once you're back home, you'll have plenty of time to think through everything. You can decide then if you want to continue seeing him."

"You're right," Grace said. She grinned at Jane. "Always the logical, organized one. See, Alicia was right: You're a good sounding board. Arthur did say that he wants us to come to his house again."

"Oh. When? The retreat is over tomorrow at noon," Jane said. "On our schedule, it says the hotel will provide a to-go lunch. So we can all get on the road and drive home in the daylight."

"Arthur was saying that he wanted us to come to his home for lunch tomorrow before we leave," Grace said. "Nan, his cook, would serve us a meal. We could keep our to-go boxes for a quick supper on the road." She looked at Pam. "He thought you might like to let Tillie run around his yard before being cooped up in the car. And he mentioned that you were interested in seeing the bonsai specimens that Henry - his gardener - has trained."

Grace paused before adding, "I told him I didn't know if you'd want to do that or not. It's a long ride. We'll barely get home before dark, even if we don't stop at Arthur's for lunch."

Donna frowned. "Yeah, it'll be awfully late when we get home. I told Bill I'd be home in time for supper. But I guess I could call him."

Jane looked around. "Do we have to decide now?" she asked. "Maybe we could think about it and let Arthur know tonight? Or tomorrow at breakfast? It's sweet of him to offer, but it may not be the best timing. On the other hand, we have two cars. So we could split up. One car could go straight home, and the other could go to Arthur's for lunch. I'm fine, either way."

"Well, if anybody's going to go to Arthur's, count me in," Pam said. "This may be our last chance to 'do lunch' at Downton Abbey without the price of a plane trip. And, besides, it would give us another chance for some snooping." She flashed a naughty grin. "Oops, did I say snooping? Sorry, slip of the tongue - I meant sleuthing. Who knows? We just might find a dead body or two scattered around the bonsai trunks. Or floating in his bathtub."

"Then I'd better not go to lunch," Donna said. "W B O."

"Huh?" Pam said. "W B O? What does that mean? Did you just make that up or is it a real expression?"

"Let me guess," Jane said, laughing. "Water. Body. Out. It's Donna's theme."

Donna laughed. The funny little heh heh sound of her peculiar laugh started all of them laughing. Looking around the room, Jane reflected that laughter had been sorely lacking since they'd arrived at this art retreat.

"I don't know about the rest of you," Jane said. "But this has been an awfully intense week. I admit that I've learned a lot, and not just about art. I'm looking forward to getting back home."

Pam picked up Jane's notebook and waved it at her. "But if I know you," she said, "you can't stand to leave before figuring out whodunnit."

CHAPTER NINETEEN

A few minutes later, Jane, Grace, and Pam went downstairs. Jane asked the lobby clerk if she'd store their easels and painting supplies behind the desk for an hour. Then she and Grace waited outside while Pam signed Tillie out of the kennel.

Tillie, exuberant about an afternoon outing with her humans, charged out of the building. As soon as she spotted Jane on the patio, Tillie leaped. With her front paws on Jane's chest, the dog nuzzled neck and licked ears. Jane struggled to push Tillie off while holding fast to her now-slimy earrings. Pam finally managed to pull Tillie off Jane, but the dog immediately turned and jumped onto Grace's delicate peach-colored top.

"Honestly! You'd think she hadn't seen a living soul in months," Pam panted as she reined in her dog. "What's it been? Maybe five, six hours since our morning walk? Tillie, you are such a lummox!"

Grace gave a strained smile as she dusted off the debris that Tillie had deposited on her blouse. "She does make one feel loved and appreciated, I suppose."

Jane giggled. "Yup, I expect that's the reason why people love dogs. My cats certainly never show this wild enthusiasm. Or any enthusiasm, actually. I could go away for a month, and as long as someone was feeding them, they'd barely notice my absence."

They began to stroll along the dappled path, the same path they'd taken on Sunday evening, when Jane, Grace, and Donna first arrived at Gardens and Horses. Tillie fell into step beside them, and Pam unfastened the leash to give the dog a chance to work off her kennel confinement.

"To think we've been here less than a week," Grace said. She sighed. "It seems like a lot longer, doesn't it?"

"Nothing like death to make time feel eternal," Jane said.

As they approached the reflecting pool, they saw Margaret and Maggie with their easels set up side by side. Unfortunately, Tillie saw them, too. Before Pam could grab the dog, Tillie sprinted.

"Nooooo!" yelled Pam.

Too late. Tillie stuck her snout in the plastic bowl of paint water beside Maggie's feet and promptly knocked it over.

Laughing, Maggie called, "It's alright." She crouched on her knees and rubbed Tillie's ears. As the dog licked the teen's eyes and nose, Maggie said, "What's her name?"

"Tillie," Pam said.

"Tillie. Silly Tillie. What a friendly girl you are," Maggie said.

As if to answer, Tillie rolled over and wriggled on the ground to invite Maggie to rub her belly. With her mouth open and tongue dangling, Tillie looked like a zany toddler.

"I think you've made a friend," Pam said as she moved closer to them. Before Tillie could wiggle herself over to Margaret's easel, Pam grabbed her collar.

"This place certainly looks a lot prettier without yellow crime scene tape," Jane said.

Margaret pursed her lips. "It is a relief to be able to put that unfortunate incident behind us."

Maggie stood up and dusted off her shorts. "Poor Mrs. Pickridge. She must feel awful about what happened to Lance. I know she really loved that horse."

"It's a good lesson," Margaret said. "If you are giving a horse medications - or for that matter, giving medications to anyone - it's important to check and recheck dosage and time of administration. The slightest mistake can have serious consequences."

Maggie began to refill her paint bowl with her water bottle. Tillie pulled away from Pam's grasp and slurped up the contents before Maggie could finish pouring. Giggling, Maggie patted the dog's head. "Well, aren't you a thirsty girl, silly Tillie."

Grace stood beside Margaret and looked at her sketch of the reflecting pool, with trees arching overhead. "I like your composition," Grace said. "Do you paint many water scenes?"

"Gram's done a whole series of seascapes," Maggie said. She beamed at her grandmother. "She won second prize at the South Carolina Watercolor Show for one of her paintings."

"Well, how wonderful! Congratulations," Grace said. "Did somebody buy the winning painting? Or don't you sell your work? I keep reading that seascapes are the subjects that sell the best."

"Gram gave that painting to Miss Sheryl," Maggie said. "Miss Sheryl always loved the ocean."

"Oh," said Grace. "That was very generous of you."

After the mention of Sheryl, there was an awkward pause. Since the conversation was already strained, Jane decided to take advantage of the moment to do some probing.

"Did you know that Sheryl broke up a fight between Dave and Teddy Pickridge at the stable on the evening when Dave was attacked?" Jane said to Margaret. "A physical fight. I think that's why the police brought Teddy in for questioning."

"No, I didn't know that," Margaret said. "But I'm not surprised. Sheryl has been protecting Dave ever since he was a small boy. Even when he became a wild teenager and everybody else gave up on him. Even after she'd gotten him the job here and he promptly began carrying on with a married woman."

"You mean his affair with Alicia?" Jane said. "I guess that was the best-known secret in town."

Margaret glanced sideways at Maggie, then looked at Jane. Her mouth was a tight, straight line. "Yes, it was."

"On a related subject," Jane continued, "did you know that Arthur and Walter joined Teddy at the stables? And all three of them got in a shouting match with Dave about overdosing Lancelot?"

Margaret's eyes opened wide and she tilted her head as she glanced at Jane. "But Arthur was with us at the stable when we found Dave in the trough. You say he was there earlier?"

"Apparently," Jane said. "Did Arthur say anything about that after we left? After the ambulances came and picked up Dave and Donna?"

"No," Margaret said, "but as you can imagine, it was awfully hectic. The police were taking statements from us. And Rupert kept interrupting. Poor man was a nervous wreck. Asking what he should do about the horses while the police kept the area cordoned off. I guess Arthur could have said something and I missed it."

"How about you, Maggie?" Jane asked.

The teen shook her head. "No, I don't remember Mr. King saying anything. But everything was crazy, like Gram said. And I was so upset about Dave, I wasn't really paying attention to what everybody was saying."

"Do you know if Arthur or Walter had anything against Sheryl?" Jane asked.

"Not that I know of." Margaret shrugged. "Catherine - you know, Sheryl's friend - worked for the Stauntons. She had to quit; it was because of her asthma. But as far as I know, Catherine was still on good terms with Walter. And neither Walter nor Arthur would've had any reason to dislike Sheryl."

Margaret frowned as if concentrating, then continued: "You don't think that Sheryl might have seen something, do you?" she asked Jane. "At the stables. Maybe Sheryl saw the person who attacked Dave?"

"That's what I'm wondering," Jane said.

Margaret pursed her lips. "But that wouldn't make sense," she said. "When we got to the stables, Dave was lying in the trough. If Sheryl had been there .... well, she wouldn't have left him in the water - he could have drowned."

Maggie looked at her grandmother. "But Miss Sheryl couldn't have gotten him out by herself. Remember what a hard time we had pulling him out? She would have had to go for help."

"If Sheryl knew who attacked Dave," Margaret said, "why didn't she go to the police?"

"I'm wondering if she was on her way," Jane said, "when she was killed."

Margaret's eyebrows shot up. "So you think both attacks were done by the same person. Have you told the police about your theory?"

Jane shook her head. "No. But I'm pretty sure the police are thinking on the same lines. I'm assuming that's the reason they pulled Teddy in for questioning this morning. And searched his car."

Margaret frowned again. "But if Sheryl came back to the stables to get Dave out of the trough, we would have seen her."

"I thought I saw someone in the shadows behind the barn," Jane said, "when we were doing CPR. I couldn't be sure, though. There was no time to stop and investigate."

"And you think that was Sheryl?" Pam asked. "You never told us that."

"I'm still not sure," Jane said. "But I believe that we arrived at the stable shortly after Sheryl found Dave. She tried to pull him out. That's why there was blood on the lip of the trough. But she couldn't, so she ran off to get help. You remember there's no cell phone service at the stables."

"And you think she heard us and turned back?" Margaret said. "But why would she stay in the shadows? Why wouldn't she come out to lend a hand?"

"That's what I've been wondering," Jane said.

Margaret squinted at Jane. "So you're saying one of those three men attacked Dave in a fit of rage? And then left him to drown?"

Jane shrugged. "It's one possibility."

Maggie's mouth formed a perfect letter O. "You think one of those men killed Miss Sheryl? But they all knew her! I can't believe anybody who knew her could do such a thing. Miss Sheryl was such a good, kind person. And those men - Mr. Pickridge and Mr. Staunton and Mr. King - they wouldn't ... they aren't.... I mean, they don't seem like murderers."

Margaret's nostrils flared. "There are evil people in this world, Maggie. It's a hard lesson to learn, but it's part of growing up. There are people who seem nice but do unspeakable deeds for selfish reasons."

Suddenly, Tillie stirred. She dashed along the path that led to the museum. Pam hurried after her, yelling behind her, "Gotta run. Literally! See y'all later."

Looking at Margaret and Maggie, Grace smiled. "Well, I guess it's time for us to move on. See you this evening. Enjoy your painting time."

"Have a nice afternoon," Jane said to Margaret and Maggie. Margaret nodded. Maggie smiled and waggled her fingers to wave goodbye.

When Jane and Grace caught up with Pam, they found her standing behind the schoolteachers. Amanda and Rachel were sitting on a bench, watercolor pads on their laps, sketching. Pam was clutching Tillie's collar.

"Look who I found!" Pam called. "Actually - to be accurate - Tillie found."

"I never expected I'd find you here during our free painting session," Jane said to Rachel. "You're painting the thoroughbred museum? I thought you hated everything about horse racing."

"I do," Rachel said. "But I love buildings, and this one is so attractive - perfectly situated in its garden surroundings. I actually started out with a major in architecture. I still love to study buildings. They're so peaceful. Orderly, predictable. Straight lines. Planned walkways. Maybe it was a mistake to switch into the ed school."

Pam giggled. "Buildings are everything that school kids aren't, huh?"

Rachel nodded. Amanda grinned, showing her Shirley Temple dimples.

"I never thought of it like that," Amanda said. "But you're right on. Kids are the exact opposite of peaceful, orderly and predictable. How in the world did you ever decide on education after architecture, Rachel?"

While the humans chattered, Tillie settled down on the grass beside Pam's shoes. When a flying insect swooped out of the bushes, Tillie sprang to her feet, jumped, and executed a half-turn in the air. With a clomp, the dog's jaws snapped open and shut. Swallowing noisily, Tillie licked her lips and settled back down on the grass. All five women giggled as they watched the dog's performance.

"Buildings are definitely more peaceful than dogs," Pam said. "Or at least this dog." She reached down and tousled Tillie's ears.

Grace watched Rachel sketch. "Very nice. You know, it does look a lot like an architect's rendering. It's so detailed. And accurate. I can see ...."

Suddenly, a woman's scream split the afternoon like a jagged burst of lightning. All five women tensed. Tillie stood and began barking - furious, insistent barking. Pam quickly grabbed the dog's collar as she reached into her pocket to snap on Tillie's leash.

"I think that came from the direction of the stables," Jane said.

"You don't think it's another....?" Amanda asked.

"I don't know," Jane said as she started to move. "It sounded like a woman - a woman who needs help!"

Tillie, her body stiff and her eyes focused, tugged at Pam. Then the dog took off, towing her owner behind her like a sled. Amanda and Rachel tossed their sketch pads onto the bench as they jogged to catch up.

"I'm calling the hotel," Grace shouted after them. She took out her cell phone and plugged in the hotel's number to request help. Then she hurried off toward the stables.

Jane's mind was racing even faster than her legs. A scream in broad daylight? Surely, this wasn't another attack? When she finally reached an unobstructed view of the clearing in front of the stable and barn, she stopped. Gulping air, she realized she'd been holding her breath ever since she heard the scream.

Standing just outside the wooden fence were the two SCAD sisters, Dee Dee and Harry. Two easels were set up on the grass, and painters' bags were open beside each easel. But neither of the women were painting. They were doubled over, their hands clutching their middles. And they seemed to be laughing.

Pam and Tillie reached them first. "Are you alright?" Pam called, breathless from her rendition of the Iditarod. "You scared us to death!"

Dee Dee started to speak, but she was laughing too hard to form distinct words. "A snake!" she finally managed to spray out. "Harry... Harry is scared to death of snakes."

After several more seconds of struggling to regain speech, Dee Dee continued. "A black snake. Just a harmless little black ...."

"It was NOT little!" Harry sputtered. "It was four feet long. Maybe five." She stretched out her arms to demonstrate.

Dee Dee straightened up and wiped the tears from her eyes with the back of her hand. "It was not. Maybe two feet." She held out her own arms to show the length.

"Three feet," Harry said, grabbing her sister's arms and stretching them farther apart. "At least three feet."

Dee Dee rolled her eyes. "You're such a drama queen," she said. She turned to the crowd of women gathered in front of them. "It was just a harmless little black snake. That's all."

"It touched me," Harry yelped. "You saw it. It slithered right up to me. It was going to bite me."

"No it wasn't," Dee Dee said. "Why would it bite you? A snake that size is too small to eat you. Why would it bite you?"

"How do I know?" Harry exclaimed. "It's a snake. How do I know what a snake thinks? Maybe my foot looked like another snake. It was fighting over its territory. Or it wanted to mate."

At this, both sisters burst into laughter again. Jane shook her head. She could see that the sisters were past the point of logic. Any word, any sound would spark a fit of uncontrolled laughter.

"Well, I'm glad to see you're alright," Jane said.

"Everything alright, ladies?"

They all turned to see a uniformed policeman approaching them at a jog. Beside him was Arthur. Both men looked worried. Arthur immediately went to Grace and put his hand on her shoulder.

"I'm the one who phoned for help. We were over by the museum," Grace said. "I didn't know if we'd have cell service when we reached the person who was screaming. I'm so sorry for alarming everybody."

"False alarm, that's all," Jane said to the policeman. "We heard a scream. A woman's scream. We didn't know if it was serious."

"No problem, ma'am," the policeman said. "Better safe than sorry. He scanned the women's faces. Um, what was the reason for the screaming?"

Dee Dee and Harry, who had managed to stifle their laughter, both blurted out, "Snake!" at the same time. This simultaneous response apparently struck both of them as hilarious, because they dissolved into another fit of laughter.

"A snake crawled by them," Jane explained. "Evidently, a little black sna..."

"It was NOT little!" Harry roared, prompting more uncontrolled laughter.

"I think everything's fine, now," Jane explained to the policeman. She tried to position herself in front of the sisters to divert the policeman's view of their antics. "Thanks for coming to check."

The policeman's mouth formed a thin smile, but the rest of his face did not look amused. "If you need any more help, just let me know," he said and turned to return to the hotel.

Arthur shot Dee Dee and Harry a stern glance.

The sisters, who had finally managed to squelch their laughter, both gave him a dirty look. When he turned away from them, Harry stuck out her tongue. That sent both of the sisters into yet another gale of laughter.

Arthur turned to Grace, his expression solicitous. "I guess you've had quite the scare out here," he said. He gently brushed a clump of hair off her sweaty forehead.

Jane found herself studying Arthur's face. She was fascinated by the rapid mood transformations portrayed by his features. But she had to stifle her grin when Tillie, who had been straining on the leash, managed to get close enough to sniff his pant legs. Evidently, Pam had relaxed her grip on the leash, because the dog lunged forward and jammed her face into Arthur's crotch. Jane pretended to cover a cough so she wouldn't laugh out loud when the man's formerly tender countenance switched to anger.

Rachel, who was wearing the patient look of the long-suffering teacher, said, "Glad everything turned out okay." She and Amanda waved and began walking back toward the museum.

"Are you heading back to the hotel now?" Arthur asked Grace.

Grace nodded. "I guess so. We were just taking Tillie for a walk."

"I saw your painting supplies behind the desk in the lobby. I was wondering where you'd gone," Arthur said. "I have something I want to show you."

"Oh?" said Grace.

As they began walking toward the hotel, Arthur placed a hand between Grace's shoulder blades.

"Your portrait," he said. "I stopped by the frame shop. I think I've found the perfect frame. But I didn't want to get it - not yet. Not until you took a look to see if it would match the decor in your house. Do you have time to take a ride?"

"Yes, I think that would be okay." Grace looked at Jane and Pam. "You don't mind going on without me, do you? I'll be back before supper."

"Um, maybe not," Arthur said. "There's this terrific Italian place near the frame shop. Very authentic. A charming couple run it. They moved here from Naples."

"I was looking forward to the twilight paint-out tonight," Grace said.

"So am I," Arthur said. "That's why I thought an early dinner. This place is really wonderful. I'd hate for you to miss the chance to try it. While you're here."

Grace hesitated. Then she smiled at Arthur before turning to Jane and Pam. "I guess I'll see you after dinner," she said. "You don't mind asking the front desk to hold my painting supplies until a quarter to seven, do you?"

"No problem," Jane said. "Have fun, you two!"

Arthur and Grace left the path and cut across the lawn that led to the hotel parking lot.

"Whew, that was something!" Pam said, as she and Jane headed back to the hotel. "I don't know about you, but when I heard that scream, my heart started beating like a bongo on steroids."

Jane laughed. "Thank goodness this time it was a case of hilarity - not homicide." Jane let out a sigh. "Those sisters are quite the pair, aren't they?"

"At least they're not on your list of suspects," Pam said. "Are they?"

"I haven't discovered any motive for them," Jane said. "Saundra called them man-eaters. Particularly the red-headed one - Harry. But that doesn't give them a reason to kill Dave. Or Sheryl."

"Well, if Arthur survives the retreat, I guess you can add the sisters to your Suspect Elimination list," Pam said.

They had reached the door to the hotel lobby, and Jane stopped walking so they wouldn't be overheard inside. "Arthur? He's in danger? What do you mean?"

"Did you see the look they gave him?" Jane said. "I mean, what's that expression? If looks could kill...."

CHAPTER TWENTY

Arthur pulled over two chairs so he and Grace could join the Atkinsville painters around their dinner table in the hotel's restaurant.

"Well?" Pam said. "Was the Italian restaurant worth missing this?" She gestured at her plate.

Jane followed Grace's eyes as she surveyed their plates. The evening's entree was beef stroganoff, which looked every bit as rich and heady as it smelled. A golden mound of potatoes au gratin and thick spears of green asparagus balanced the composition. If this meal was a watercolor, Jane would title it "A Portrait of Delicious."

"That certainly does look yummy," Grace said. She beamed at Arthur. "But the Italian restaurant really was charming. And the food definitely lived up to its recommendations."

"Are you going to have dessert here?" Pam asked. "The chef made a rum cake for our last dinner. With chocolate shavings. It looks scrumptious."

"Oh, no, not me," Grace said. "Arthur ordered the restaurant's homemade tiramisu for us to share."

"If all you've had is a few crumbs of tiramisu, then you really ought to get yourself a piece of the rum cake," Pam said. "Alec told us it's the chef's specialty."

"After all," Donna said, "people can't live on love alone."

Grace blushed. "Rum cake does sound wonderful, but I don't think I have room for another bite. It was a very generous serving of tiramisu." She looked at Arthur and added, "Although I think I could do with a glass of wine."

Arthur flashed a gallant smile as he stood up. "Let me get you a glass. I assume you want a red? Anybody else?"

All of them gave him their wine orders. After Arthur left, Jane asked, "What happened with the portrait? Did you find a frame?"

"Yes, I think so," Grace said. "But I need to measure my wall when I get home. The frame is kind of wide. I told Arthur that I'd call and let him know. The frame shop said they wouldn't charge extra to send it."

"Too bad," Donna said.

Grace looked at her, puzzled.

"I was expecting Mr. Camelot to deliver the painting in person," Donna said. "I pictured him galloping across the countryside on his white steed, portrait under his arm and a red rose between his red lips."

Grace shot Donna a pouty frown. Jane and Pat tried to stifle their giggles.

When Arthur returned with a tray full of wine glasses, Donna announced that she'd talked with her husband. "Bill encouraged me to stay and have lunch at your place tomorrow, Arthur. He said it was safer for us to drive both cars home together as a caravan - not split up. And he's been a bachelor all week - he's sure he can manage for a few extra hours without me."

"Wonderful!" Arthur exclaimed. "I'll text Nan - my cook - right now." He looked at Pam. "I know Henry will be excited about showing off his bonsai collection to another garden enthusiast."

As soon as they finished dinner, the painters gathered up their supplies and easels. They met Alec on the patio and then fanned out across the far end of the lawn. With their backs to the hotel, they had a spectacular view of the evening sky over the trees. Jane felt like she was walking into Van Gogh's "Starry Night."

"This is all about light," Alec said as they set up their easels. He encouraged them to complete their rough sketches as quickly as possible. "And it's going to fade fast. So don't waste your time sketching little details. Just lay in the bare minimum with a few pencil strokes - the tree line, the sun, maybe some clouds. When you begin to paint, I suggest you work wet on wet, and let the colors blend on the paper. Be generous with your pigment; don't expect to work in layers. There won't be time for the paper to dry between applications. If your paper gets too wet and forms plumes - so be it. Just go with the flow. Overworking is the only mistake in this kind of painting. Everything else is a pleasant surprise."

Since they were working under time pressure, none of the painters chatted. Like the others, Jane found herself totally absorbed in the drama of light piercing through reddish-pink clouds above the darkening mounds of trees.

"There you go," Alec announced as the last light faded from purple to charcoal. "The magic moment is past. Put the finishing touches on your painting, and let's lift a glass to the glory of watercolor."

As they walked back across the lawn toward the hotel, the gaslights at the corners of the patio lit up, as if on cue. The painters set their easels around the edges of the patio to let their paintings dry. While the group settled onto chairs, waiters joined them in what seemed like an orchestrated dance. Delicate fluted glasses on trays were offered, then the waiters opened bottles of champagne. Together with the sound of corks popping, the liquid flumes spraying into the air created a gala atmosphere.

Alec delivered the first toast: "To the sunset - the glorious sunset. A painter's delight!"

Then Saundra raised her glass toward Alec and called out, "To the man who gives art a good name, Alexander Robert Treville!"

Everybody took a sip and then clapped. Alec bowed. Somebody shouted, "Speech," and a few others echoed the shout.

Alec held up his hands. "No speech tonight," he said. "I've been doing most of the talking all week. All I have left to say is thank you." He bowed again. "You've displayed both talent and tact under difficult circumstances. I applaud and appreciate you."

Teddy and Alicia Pickridge - who had missed both supper and the sunset painting session - came through the patio doors while Alec was speaking. They were holding hands. A waiter handed them glasses of champagne. Alicia looked at Jane and smiled. Jane thought Alicia looked lovely - youthful, contented, almost serene. Like a college coed holding the hand of the beau who had just proposed marriage.

"To friendships - both new and everlasting!" Amanda said as she stood and clinked her flute against Rachel's. She turned toward the Atkinsville group and saluted.

Smiling, Pam touched her hand to her lips and blew a kiss in Amanda's direction. Then she raised her glass and clinked it against the glasses of the other Atkinsville painters.

"Here's to each of us," Harry hollered out. "The brave survivors of the retreat to die for!"

Dee Dee laughed, and Jane heard a few nervous snickers around the patio. But Saundra, who was sitting at the table beside the Atkinsville group, spoke in a voice loud enough to be heard by everyone: "Of course, SHE would have to splash mud over a delicate moment."

"To farewells," said Harry, baring her teeth in a vengeful smile. Waltzing toward the nearest waiter, she waved her flute under the bottle of champagne. As soon as the waiter refilled her glass, she continued, "Farewells. Some sweet sorrowful and others...." Harry looked directly at Saundra. "Hmm. What's that other adjective that starts with s? Sour?"

Alec cleared his throat. "Perhaps this is a good time for me to announce tomorrow morning's schedule. We'll start at ten. That will give you an extra hour in the morning to pack. Some of you might want to check out of your rooms so you'll be ready to get on the road as soon as our last session is over.

"We'll meet in the conference room. Please bring your easel and the two paintings that you consider your best work from the retreat. We're going to have a general critique session. Some of you have been asking me about opportunities for displaying and selling your work. We'll go over some of these options, too.

"Again, I want to tell you how much I've enjoyed meeting each of you. And I've admired your spirit under what can only be described as extraordinary circumstances." He smiled and winked at Grace. "Actually, I was about to say you have displayed, 'grace under fire.' But given the week's events - not to mention the name of one of our painters - I will forego that metaphor.

"The hotel has graciously supplied us with several complimentary bottles of house wine for our last evening." Alec waved his hand in the direction of one of the tables, which had been set up with bottles of wine, silver ice buckets, stemmed glasses, and crystal bowls of nuts and pretzels. "Please enjoy."

Jane circulated around the patio to say her goodbyes to each of the painters. While she chatted, several people refreshed her stem with the hotel's excellent wine. At about midnight, she realized that her rosy glow had turned into an unsteady reel. Time to head for her room while she could manage the journey on her own two feet!

That night, Jane slept the dreamless sleep of the innocent and the drunken. Awakening at six to her alarm, she found herself greeted by a cheery sun. That's when she noticed that she hadn't gotten around to closing her drapes. Glancing at the floor beside her bed, she discovered her outfit in a tangled heap, together with her shoes and painting supplies. She sat up and tried to employ her head in a review of what she'd said and to whom at the end of last night's wine party. But the only clear thought that she could muster was an ache. Seems I overdid the wine, she thought. She forced herself to get up and head for the bathroom. Before she ran a shower, she fished around her cosmetics bag for an aspirin.

As soon as she dressed, Jane packed her suitcase. Then she spread out all of her paintings on the bed. Which did she consider her two best? She really liked the way the sunset painting had turned out. It looked spontaneous, as if colors had splashed onto the paper and shape-shifted to suggest trees and clouds and a setting sun. The painting had that mesmerizing quality - as if inviting an onlooker to find pictures emerging from patterns in wood grain or in the swirls of a puddle. But she felt like the painting's success was almost accidental - displaying not so much skill as luck.

She compared the two paintings that she'd done of the patio - the chairs with their thin, angular shadows crisscrossing over a sunny floor. The second painting was more orderly, more controlled. The chair legs were straight, and the thicknesses of the shadows were accurate. But her first attempt had more of that loose, casual look that she considered desirable in a watercolor. Somehow, she'd lost that when she'd made the second attempt. She'd always wanted to try her hand at this type of composition, and she was reasonably pleased with her success. But she wasn't sure if these paintings represented her best work or just the mastery of a long-desired skill.

In the end, Jane decided that her best painting was the one of the irises in the foreground with the brick wall behind them. Everything about that painting pleased her - the delicate irises washed in the pink-y light that had resulted from Tillie's muddy paw print, the suggestion of the rough brick wall, the contrast of textures natural and man-made. Although the painting looked controlled rather than flowing, Jane found it satisfying. It looked finished, a complete presentation.

For her other choice, Jane chose the painting that she'd done at the reflecting pool. She liked the way the water seemed to draw the eye down to its depth, to dark and glimmering secrets lurking below the surface. Jane decided that this painting represented her experience at this retreat. There were mysteries within mysteries, secrets layered upon secrets. Some were disturbing. Others were murky. Still others sparked the imagination. But overall, the retreat - like the painting - was both illuminating and intoxicating, an altogether unforgettable experience.

Jane placed the two paintings beside her easel by the door, ready for the morning's critique session. She packed up the others with her art supplies before she phoned the front desk to request her bill. Then she sat down with her pen and notepad. She wanted to be sure that all her notes were legible and her thoughts were clear before she dropped off the last pages at the police station today.

At last, Jane closed her notepad and tucked it into her pocketbook. On an impulse, she called the station to inquire about whether Officer Goode would be on duty today. The clerk said he'd be in at nine. There were a few points that Jane really wanted to discuss with him in person. Although she'd been glad - for Alicia's sake - that Teddy Pickridge showed up for the farewell party last night, Jane assumed his presence meant the police did not consider him a serious suspect. Or maybe they didn't have enough evidence to hold him in custody? Jane hated to leave Garden and Horses before the murders had been solved. It was frustrating. Like working a complicated crossword puzzle but leaving one clue unsolved. She knew that the outcome of a murder case was strictly police business. But she couldn't help but wonder.... How would Goode respond, she mused, if she asked him to inform her when a suspect was finally apprehended? Would that seem too nosy?

After breakfast, the painters filed into the conference room and took seats around the table. Their easels, each displaying two paintings, encircled the walls. Jane marveled at the exhibit. Of course, each painter had chosen only their best two paintings. But still. In Jane's opinion, the paintings rivaled any juried show for mastery of technique and variety of approaches. As she looked around the room, Jane chose her favorites. In her opinion, Saundra's vivid painting of the greenhouse was the most striking painting in the group. Arthur's paintings were the most clever. He had a way of revealing the quirky, the surprising in a commonplace scene. Alicia's work was rich in detail, as were Rachel's architectural subjects. Although Jane admired loose brushwork, she couldn't help but admire the precision displayed in their pinpoint renderings of building cornices and formal urns. Taken as a group, the work of the Atkinsville paintings were neither the best nor the worst of the paintings - Jane was proud that their work displayed a solid knowledge of composition as well as technical competence with the medium.

Following a rushed but insightful critique session, Alec talked briefly about sales opportunities. At twelve-fifteen, he closed the session. He thanked the painters again for their dedication, and he handed out certificates that could be used as coupons for a discount on another of his classes. By then, everyone seemed eager to get on the road, so goodbyes were brief.

"I'm texting Nan," Arthur said to the Atkinsville group, "to let her know that we're done now and we'll be heading over to the house. How long do you think it will take you to pack the cars and check out?"

"I packed my suitcase and art bag in my car before breakfast. And I've already checked out of my room," Jane said.

"Of course you did," Pam said. "Did you even need to tell us that, Miss Organized? Well, Donna and I put our stuff in my car. But I still need to settle up with the hotel. And I have to spring Tillie out of doggie jail. I'd better take her for a quick walk before we leave. Just ten minutes or so. To be sure she's on her best behavior when we get to Arthur's."

"I can help you carry your suitcases down, if you like," Arthur said to Grace.

"That's sweet of you, but I'm okay," Grace said. "I always need a minute to think about how to organize everything. And there s not much to carry."

"Okay, then I'll see you in what? Forty-five minutes? An hour?" Arthur said. He waved as he walked out the lobby door to the parking lot.

The Atkinsville group stopped by the front desk to pick up their bagged lunches, which they planned to keep in the cars for a picnic supper on the road. In the elevator going up to their rooms, they decided that Grace would pack her belongings in Jane's car for the trip home. That way, each car would hold two of the painters' suitcases and art supplies. Grace would ride with Jane for the first leg of their journey.

"We can always swap riders part way home," Grace said. She looked at Pam. "I suppose it's only fair to split Tillie's enthusiasm between both cars."

"Now, now," Pam said. "Tillie is much better in a car than on a leash. Really, she is. She devotes the first hour to sticking her nose out the window. Then she curls up and goes to sleep. Besides, there's no mud in the car for her to smear on your blouse, Grace."

"As long as she doesn't want to sleep on my lap, I don't mind sharing the car with the dog," Donna said. "I'm a farm girl, remember?"

"I have an errand to do before I go over to Arthur's," Jane said. "So can you all pile into Pam's car over to his house?"

"An errand?" Pam said.

"Yes, I need to stop by the police station," Jane said. "I want to give the last few pages of my notes to that policeman, Goode. Who knows? Maybe something I wrote will mesh with something that he observed. Or shed light on something that someone mentioned to him. I think that solving a crime is often about fitting together tiny details."

"You can't stand leaving this retreat without figuring out whodunnit, can you?" Pam said. "It's just so unfinished. Sloppy. So disorganized."

Jane laughed. "You know me too well," she said. "By the way, did you go down to the exercise room this morning when Amanda and Rachel were working out? I forgot all about it."

"I did," said Pam. "Then the schoolteachers took a walk with me and Tillie. Those two girls are in better shape than I am, that's for sure. But I really don't think either of them is strong enough to whomp Dave on the head with a shovel or drag Sheryl into a lake."

"Oh, surely you don't suspect them? They seem like such sweethearts," Grace said.

"It's always the one you least suspect," Pam said.

"Honestly, I think you've been reading too many murder mysteries," Grace said. "I can't believe that anyone from our retreat had anything to do with the attacks. It had to be one of the workers at the hotel. Or maybe someone from the outside. Anyone can get into the gardens by hopping over the brick wall. Or driving in through that road to the stables. And besides, Sheryl was attacked downtown."

Donna shook her head. "Murder mysteries are definitely not your forte," she said.

Grace opened her lips to respond.

But Donna added, "Nope. You're the romance type."

Grace rolled her eyes. Then she turned to Jane. "I don't mind stopping with you at the police station on the way to Arthur's. If you'd like a companion."

"No, I think I'd rather go alone. I'm hoping to talk to Goode in person, and I don't think he'll be as straightforward with me if there are two of us." Jane gave Grace a mischievous grin. "Besides, we're going to be driving home in separate cars, so Donna won't have any chance to tease you for the rest of the day. You've just about perfected your eyeball-roll during this retreat, Grace, and I wouldn't want you to deprive you of your last opportunities to practice your new skill."

Grace smirked. "Oh, I have a feeling that Donna will give me plenty of opportunities once we're back in Atkinsville."

CHAPTER TWENTY-ONE

Jane gave her room one final check before leaving the key and a twenty-dollar tip for the maid on the desk. She clicked the door shut behind herself.

At the police station, Jane spotted Officer Goode talking with the uniformed policewoman who was sitting behind the glass-fronted entrance counter. Jane took her notepad out of her purse and held it up for Goode to see.

Goode nodded. Walking to a locked door to the left of the window, he opened it and beckoned her inside. "Mind if I have the clerk make a copy?"

Jane opened her notepad. "I dog-eared the page where the new notes start."

He nodded, took the notepad and handed it to the clerk, then ushered Jane into his office.

"I guess the retreat's over," Goode said.

"Yes," Jane said with a smile. "I survived it."

"Glad to hear it," Goode said, returning her smile. "I appreciate you bringing your notes by. I've found your observations very helpful. You keep an open mind. And you have a good eye for detail. I noticed that you copied out the detective's ABC's in the margin of one page: 'Assume nothing, Believe Nobody, Check Everything.' I got a kick out of that."

Blushing, Jane said, "You're thinking that I read too many murder mysteries? I guess I'm guilty as charged."

"I read them, too," Goode said. "Keeps the mind sharp. Of course, most of the time, real-life murders aren't as interesting as the novels. And most killers aren't nearly as smart as the ones in crime fiction." He laughed. "Then again, most cops aren't as clever - or as handsome - as the characters in the mysteries."

"I don't know about that," Jane said. She thought Goode looked a little embarrassed by her response so she removed her eyes from his face and glanced around his office. "So this is what a real-life detective's office looks like. Desk, chairs, filing cabinet. Cream-colored walls, vinyl floor. Nothing to make it stand out from any other office."

"Yup, pretty dull," Goode said. "Nothing that would inspire a novelist. Or a painter, for that matter." He pushed back his chair. "Well, thanks again."

Jane slid the strap of her pocketbook over her shoulder, but hesitated before standing. "I know it's none of my business. But I can't help but feel ... I don't know ... unsatisfied. Between finding the dead horse in the reflecting pool and then helping to pull Dave out of the trough, I got so wrapped up in this whole thing. I hate to be leaving without knowing how it turns out. Since I don't live in this area, I probably won't see anything about it in the news. Is it possible.... I mean, I know the details of an investigation have to be kept secret. But when you finally arrest someone, could you possibly let me know?"

Goode paused. "I think I could do that," he said. "It's routine to let the next of kin know how a murder investigation is proceeding. Although you're not related to Ms. Calhoun, you're certainly a concerned party. And your notes have been very helpful. We like to reward people for offering important information.

"I won't be able to share all the details with you, of course," he added. "There are always things that the police hold back until the trial. But I can let you know when an arrest is made."

"I understand," Jane said. "I wouldn't want to put you in any position that would compromise the investigation."

"I will tell you that we're planning to release the time of Ms. Calhoun's death to the media tomorrow," Goode said. "We decided it might encourage people to come forward if they noticed anything at the lake or in the area around the hospital parking lot around that time."

"Oh," Jane said. "How did you determine when she was killed?"

Goode shrugged. "Nothing fancy. She was wearing an old-fashioned watch," he said. "The kind with moving dials. It wasn't waterproof. It stopped as soon as water got in it. At six-thirty Tuesday night."

Jane cocked her head. "So what you're telling me isn't actually the time of death," she said. "It's the time her wrist was immersed in water."

Goode chuckled. "Like I said, you have a good eye for detail."

As he escorted her out, Goode picked up her notepad from the clerk's desk and handed it to Jane. "So you'll be heading home now?" He asked as he held the front door open.

"Actually, I'm going to Arthur King's house," Jane said. "The other painters in my group are already over there. He invited us for lunch."

Goode cocked an eyebrow.

"There's a bit of a romance going on between one of the painters in my group - Grace Tanner - and Arthur. I think he wants to prolong our stay as long as possible. So he asked his cook to prepare lunch for us before we head out."

Goode nodded. "I remember you mentioning in your notes that he has a private cook. I guess he has quite the estate."

"Yes. Have you ever been there? I've never seen anything like it."

"Never had the pleasure," Goode said, grinning. "I'm not part of the local estate set. If anything interesting turns up during your lunch, you'll be sure to let me know, won't you? Shoot me a text. Or give me a call."

"I will. Promise." Jane said and trotted down the station-house stairs.

As she opened her car door, Jane glanced around the downtown's central square: The red-bricked hospital where Donna, Dave, and Catherine Manfred had been cared for. The neatly-landscaped lake where Sheryl Calhoun had been killed. The upscale shopping strip where they'd purchased wine for the supper at Arthur's house. All these - like the gardens - had become prominent elements in a real-life game of Clue.

Actually, Jane thought, maybe she ought to stop by that little shop and get something to bring to Arthur's. Maybe another bottle of wine? As she pulled into the drive running in front of the shop, she looked for a place where she could park and run inside. All the spaces in front of the shop were full. Remembering that Arthur had said there were more spaces in back, she followed the circle around to the rear of the shop. Across the parking lot, she spotted a grocery called Locavore Gourmet. I bet they'd have a nice selection of cheeses, she thought. Or perhaps she could find some homemade pastries in there.

Jane pulled up in front of the grocery. The cheese and savory section was extensive. Next to a glass display cases of cheese wheels, there were bowls containing store-prepared entrees, like chicken salads and stuffed olives. And beyond that were the luxurious desserts - fruit tarts and chocolate confections. Jane was tempted to choose one of the desserts, but she didn't want to compete with whatever Nan was planning to serve. In the end, she decided to get a few packages of fancy cheeses and some crackers. If Nan had already prepared a cheese plate, this cheese could always be stored for another meal. In a waist-high refrigerator case, Jane found pre-packaged varieties of the store-brand cheeses. She grabbed a Brie, a Camembert, and an Edam, as well as a box of Locavore Gourmet specialty crackers. On the way to the checkout counter, she passed a display of glorious cut tulips. Jane paused. Maybe flowers would be a better house gift?

Jane glanced at the time on her phone. She was running late. She shrugged. No guest gets chastised for being too generous, she figured. She picked out a bunch of multicolored tulips and headed for the checkout counter.

In the car, she peeled the price stickers off the flowers and cheese wrappers. Then she set her GPS for Arthur's house.

Nan greeted her at the door and ushered her inside.

"Here you go," Jane said, handing over the bag and the tulips. "I went by that little grocery downtown - Locavore Gourmet. I ran in and got some cheese and crackers. They had a spectacular display of tulips - I couldn't resist."

Nan took the bag and the flowers. "Oh, these are something," she said as she looked at the tulips. "Wait 'till Henry sees them. I'll find a vase."

Nan led Jane down the hall and through the enormous dining room to the glass doors that led to the patio. The doors were open. "Your friends are outside," Nan said, pointing at one of the buildings. "I think they're all in the greenhouse. Henry was so tickled when Mr. Arthur said that y'all wanted to see his bonsai collection."

Jane thanked her and headed toward the greenhouse. She hadn't walked ten feet before two dogs streaked across the garden toward her. Jane stopped, ready to fend off Tillie's usual overenthusiastic greeting. But Tillie was so preoccupied by her new doggy friend that she didn't even bother to nuzzle Jane's hand as she ran by. The two furry giants dashed off, alternating between playing the chaser and the chased. As Jane watched them, she wondered how many of Henry's carefully-nurtured irises they'd already trampled.

In the greenhouse, Jane found Henry and Pam standing in front of a workbench. Jane saw bags of soil, a stack of pots, handheld spades, tweezers, scissors, and a small stash of rocks.

"You've got to think of the rocks as a permanent part of the display," Henry was saying, "because the tree roots grow into them. They have wee tiny rootlets, hair-like strands, that fasten into cracks and crannies in the rocks. Once the tree is firmly established, you'd have to cut off the roots to remove the rock." Henry was obviously proud of his knowledge about bonsai.

Henry continued: "Mr. Walter - you know, the fellow you had dinner with the other night, Walter Staunton? - he taught me how to choose the right rock for each display. Color and texture, them's the two keys. A rock has got to flatter its tree. It's the foreground, so to speak. And you mustn't just think of how it's going to look under the trunk and leaves. The tree is going to blossom, and when it does, the rock's got to show off the flowers."

Henry picked up a handful of the rocks and showed them to Pam. "Artful rocks, that's what Mr. Walter calls them when they have unusual shapes and colors. He brought these over the other day - when y'all came for dinner."

"Does Walter grow bonsai trees, too?" Pam asked.

"Oh, yes, he's a real connoisseur, that he is," Henry said. "Inherited most of his collection from his own father. In fact, Mr. Walter's the one who got our Mr. Arthur started with bonsai," Henry said. "I always ask Mr. Walter to help me when I'm transplanting a valuable tree. He's a genuine expert."

Jane perked up and looked at Henry. "You said Walter brought those rocks when he came over to dinner on Tuesday night?"

Henry nodded and grinned, his mustache twitching with merriment. "Actually, he was here all afternoon." Henry chuckled. "You know the old saying, 'When the cat's away, the mice will play'? Well, Miss Saundra was at her art retreat all afternoon. So Mr. Walter said he might as well fiddle around with some 'nature paintings' of his own. That's what he calls the bonsai trees. 'Nature paintings.'"

"How long was Walter here?" Jane asked.

"Oh, I don't know," Henry shrugged. "Guess he got here around four." His mustache twitched again. "We might have had a nip or two of whiskey after we got this here tree fixed up." With the tenderness of a new mother, Henry lifted an impossibly shallow pot holding a five-inch tree.

The mini tree had a distorted, asymmetrical trunk which grew in a vertical direction for only about an inch and a half before it bent nearly sideways and extended its branches beyond one edge of the pot. Without the puckered gray and pink rock on the opposite end of the pot to balance the tree's weight, the whole arrangement would have capsized.

To Jane, this bonsai resembled an illustration of a phantasmagorical tree - perhaps an illustration from a rare, antique book. Although she didn't know anything about bonsai, she would have guessed the tree was very old.

Mirroring her thought, Henry said, "Guess how old this here tree is."

"I have no clue," Jane said. "Seventy-five years?"

"Over 150 years old," Henry said, with awe in his voice. "Imagine! This tree has seen two of a man's lifetimes, and it's still as healthy as a colt. Mr. Arthur got it at an estate auction in Charlotte. I hear he paid the pretty penny for it. But its pot was broken. Had to be replaced. I'd been putting the task off. Afraid the tap root had grown into the pot and it'd snap right off when I tried to get the tree out. So Mr. Walter, he volunteered to help." He held up the tree in its new pot. "Exquisite, isn't it?"

"Fascinating," Jane said. "So you're saying that Walter spent the afternoon here on Tuesday? He didn't leave to pick up Saundra and come back?"

Henry shook his head. "Didn't have to. Miss Saundra drove her own car from the gardens," Henry said. "She left it here overnight, you might recall, because she'd had a might too much wine. Mr. Walter dropped her off Wednesday morning and she picked up her car to go back to the art class."

"I remember she was pretty tipsy that night," Pam said.

Henry raised his eyebrows and gave a knowing smile. "Some things never change, do they?"

Jane wandered away from Henry and Pam and caught up with the others, who were touring the shelves of bonsai along the glassed sides of the greenhouse. Arthur was telling Grace and Donna about the origin of each little tree.

The trees seemed to be growing in different environments, some resembling forests with mossy ground cover. Others looked like they were struggling for life on the sides of rocky cliffs. Most were a few feet tall. But Jane was captivated by the smallest of the trees, which would have looked perfect beside a child's dollhouse. After what Henry had said about choosing rocks, Jane paid attention to the way the trees were planted. Some of them were planted in handsome Asian-inspired pots. A few of the tiny trees looked like their bare roots were tiptoeing across shallow trays.

Strolling along beside the group, Jane nodded as if she was listening, and she took care to smile whenever Grace or Donna laughed. But her mind had traveled far beyond this avenue of miniature trees and entered the dark forest of crime. I've ignored what Officer Goode called the ABC's of detective work, she realized. 'Assume nothing, Believe nobody, Check everything.' On her Suspect Elimination list, she had written everybody at the Tuesday night dinner, assuming the dinner gave all of them an alibi for the murder of Sheryl Calhoun. But Jane realized this was an incorrect assumption. Walter Staunton had an alibi for both the afternoon and the evening when Sheryl Calhoun was killed. He'd been here, with Henry, working on the bonsai collection. But what about the others? Could someone have killed Sheryl and still attended their dinner? A sizzle ran down Jane's spine when she remembered that Arthur's car had pulled up behind hers as they arrived. What time, exactly, had they arrived? She remembered that Bill had called Donna just as they pulled into the avenue of trees at the entrance of Arthur's estate. So Donna would have this information on her phone.

Officer Goode had said the police would release the time of Sheryl's murder tomorrow. Jane decided she should text Officer Goode and inform him of Walter's - and, for that matter, Henry's - alibi. Immediately.

Excusing herself, Jane left the greenhouse and followed one of the garden's meandering paths to a black wrought-iron bench. After texting Goode, she sat and mused about the implications of her discovery.

"No! Put that down!"

Jane looked up to see Nan running out the open door from the kitchen in pursuit of the two dogs. Nan's voice had the unmistakable tone of a person reacting to Tillie's mischief. Tillie dove into the bushes, and Jane could see that she had something in her mouth. Some sort of wrapper. Arthur's dog, Malory, caught up and pounced on Tillie, then both dogs tumbled and rolled all over the mulch that tucked around some seedlings. Suddenly, Malory lunged, grabbing a corner of Tillie's prize. Growling, both dogs pulled at the wrapper in a spirited tug of war. The wrapper tore as Nan caught up with them. She tried to grab the ragged scraps, but the dogs were too nimble and dashed out of her reach.

Jane hurried over to help. "Here, Tillie," she called, "come here, girl." Reaching for the scrap, Jane spoke in her most convincing voice of authority, "Drop it, Tillie!" To Jane's amazement, Tillie did just that. Jane looked at the shredded and soggy waxy paper in her hand. The label was still readable. It was the wrapper from Locavore Gourmet's pre-packaged cheese.

Panting, Nan caught up to Malory. "Bad dog!" she yelled and yanked the other piece of wrapper out of the dog's mouth. Nan shook her head and exhaled with exasperation. "They've ripped open a whole plastic bag full of garbage. Spread it all over the kitchen. You never saw such a mess! Oh, here, I'll take that," she said as she held out her hand to Jane. "I swan, I've never seen Malory behave like this."

Jane giggled. "It's probably Tillie's fault. She's always getting into something. Let me help you pick up the trashcan they overturned in the kitchen."

"It wasn't the trashcan. At least they left that be." Nan held up the wrapper. "This is old garbage. From the bags piled up in the pantry," Nan said. "See, Henry had took the barrels down to the shed to wash them out. So I've been bagging up the week's garbage. I've got it all piled in plastic bags in the pantry."

"But this is the wrapper from the cheese I brought today," Jane said. "From Locavore Gourmet."

Nan reached for the shred of wrapper in Jane's hand. "No, that's from the cheese that Mr. Arthur got for our dinner on Tuesday. Ooh, does it stink! I'm so sorry. Come inside with me and wash your hands."

"But this wrapper says Locavore Gourmet," Jane insisted. "Arthur told me he got the cheese from that little shop. I think it's called The Cheese Board."

Nan shook her head. "That shop's where he usually goes. He always says he likes to give the little shop the business. But he said they were already closed when he got there, so he went over to that grocery instead."

"Are you sure?" Jane asked. "We got the wine from The Cheese Board, and Arthur said we'd just missed each other. That he'd parked around the back, and that's why we didn't see his car."

Nan shrugged. "Well, you can see for yourself. This here wrapper says Locavore Gourmet. And it was in the bagged trash so it must have been from the cheese plate that I made up Tuesday night."

Nan turned toward the house. "Come on with me. I've got some soap in the kitchen that's good for getting them kitchen odors off your hands." As they walked, Nan muttered, "I've never seen Malory behave like that. When he's around Mr. Arthur, that dog minds his p's and q's." She hesitated, then lowered her voice. "I don't know if I'm going to mention anything to Mr. Arthur about this." Nan shook her head. "Not that it's for the likes of me to question what Mr. Arthur does. He's as smart a man as they come, he is. And I'm probably too tenderhearted, anyway. But I do hate to hear it when he gets after Malory. The way the dog hollers! Almost sounds like a woman screaming."

Jane followed Nan through the open kitchen door. "I guess Arthur can't afford to put up with any nonsense from Malory. You can't let a big dog like that get the better of you."

Nan harrumphed. "Believe me, nothing and nobody gets the better of Mr. Arthur. And if his wife, God rest her soul, was here, she'd say the same thing." As she handed Jane the bottle of lemon-scented kitchen soap, Nan lowered her voice. "Between you and me, Mr. Arthur's got quite the temper. He wants things like he wants them, and he doesn't cotton when things don't go his way. I guess that's how it is with men like him. You know - rich, powerful men."

Jane finished washing her hands and again offered to help pick up the garbage that the dogs had scattered over the tiled floor. But Nan wouldn't hear of it. "No, no," Nan said. "You go sit. Enjoy the garden. You're the guest."

Jane allowed herself to be persuaded. She needed to think about what Nan had just told her. Sitting down on the wrought iron bench, she reviewed her memories of their arrival on Tuesday evening. She was sure that Arthur had said that he'd picked up cheese from The Cheese Board. Why would he lie about such a trivial matter? There was only one reason that made sense, and Jane shuddered when she considered that reason: Arthur had to establish an alibi for the time when Sheryl was murdered. But the police hadn't released that information yet. So the only way he'd know the time was if he....

Jane's breath was racing. When would the garbage service pick up the trash bags? There was crucial evidence in those bags. Goode needed to get over here today; tomorrow might be too late. Jane began typing a text to Goode. She didn't want to seem pushy, but the more she thought about it, the more important it seemed for the policeman to interview Nan before the evidence disappeared. Jane read over what she'd written:

Important evidence here. Come now.

Was that enough information to convince Goode of the importance of coming immediately?

"Grace tells me you just paid a visit to that policeman, Goode," Arthur said, coming up behind Jane. She jumped at the sound of his voice.

"My, my! Nervous?" Arthur said. He glanced at Jane's phone.

The screen was still lit up with the message printed across it! Quickly, Jane pressed send. Had Arthur read the message? Had he seen Goode's name?

"I know you must be anxious to get on the road," Arthur said. "Grace says you're an excellent driver, but it's always best to drive in daylight. I hope you didn't mind our long tour of the bonsai collection. It's become quite the passion for Henry."

Jane forced herself to smile. She hoped that Arthur wouldn't notice how her lip was quivering. She could feel a coating of sweat forming there. "I do prefer daylight driving," she said. Did her voice sound shrill? "But the bonsai display was, well, unforgettable. Actually, everything about you, um, your estate is unforgettable."

"Then I can hope for another visit," Arthur said. He looked at Grace and stroked her cheek as if he was blending the colors in a pastel portrait. "And I hope it will be very soon."

Grace gave a strained smile, then edged over to an azalea bush and cupped one of the cherry-red blossoms in her hand. "I think azaleas should be the official flower of the South," she said. "So vivid."

Pam said, "Well, if Tillie has any say in it, you can bet we'll be back." She pointed at the two dogs, who were digging up some small plants. "You'd think they were two puppies."

The smile on Arthur's smile hardened into a scowl. "Malory, no!" he shouted. "Come here!"

Malory's demeanor immediately changed. The dog straightened up and trotted along the path. As soon as it reached them, it sat with its deep brown eyes fastened on Arthur's face. In a severe voice, Arthur commanded, "Home, Malory. Now."

The dog immediately rose and slunk away, headed for the kitchen door. "Aw, look. You've ruined the romance," Donna said.

Arthur frowned at Donna. "What do you mean?" he snapped.

"Puppy love," Donna said. "Look at poor Tillie. You've sent away her boyfriend. I think you've broken her heart." They all turned to watch Tillie plop onto the ground, crushing three or four seedlings under her. She began to shred one of the little plants between her teeth.

Pam groaned. "Oh, Tillie, you big galoot! Where did I put your leash? Did I leave it in the car?"

Arthur took a deep breath, cleared his throat, and recovered his host-with-the-most manner. "I thought you'd enjoy lunch on the ...."

Arthur stopped mid-sentence when a car's engine sounded in the driveway. They all turned toward the gate. As the car door swung open, Officer Goode nodded at them and strode across the manicured path.

CHAPTER TWENTY-TWO

Jane's tummy grumbled. She peeked at Grace - who was sitting in the passenger seat beside her - to see if she'd noticed. Grace didn't react. In fact, Grace hadn't uttered a single word since they'd gotten into the car and driven out of the King estate.

Although she wanted to allow her friend the privacy she needed to process what had just happened, Jane was brimming with curiosity. After all, a man had just confessed to murder in front of them. A man Grace was dating. Arthur had taken Grace for walks to hidden nooks in the gardens. He had painted her portrait. She'd ridden in his car to the Italian restaurant. In other words, Grace had spent lots of time alone with a murderer. Jane had been unnerved by Arthur's fiery outburst when Goode was questioning him. Surely, Grace must feel shaken to her very core. And betrayed. Grace may have been in love with Arthur, and now she realized that he was capable of murder. She must be heartsick.

Glancing at the clock on her dashboard, Jane realized it was quarter to four. She hadn't had a bite to eat since breakfast. And it had been an early breakfast at that. She thought longingly about the lunches that the hotel had packed for them, which were sitting in bags on the floor behind the front seats. She shot another glance at Grace. Would it be completely insensitive for Jane to mention food?

The phone rang through her car's bluetooth system. Jane punched the button on the side of her steering wheel, and Pam's voice blasted through the speaker system.

"What are you thinking about lunch?" Pam said. "Should we stop somewhere? I'm starved. Or should we break open the lunch bags and eat while we're driving?"

Donna, who was riding in Pam's car, spoke through the bluetooth speaker: "I don't know if I can do that," Donna said.

Jane heard Pam ask, "Why? Do you get carsick?"

"No, I just don't think I have the strength," Donna said.

Jane shot back an urgent question: "You're not feeling faint, are you, Donna?"

"It's Tillie," Donna said.

"Tillie feels faint?" Jane asked. "How can you tell? Is the dog sick?"

Pam's voice came through the bluetooth speaker. "Oh, no! Did Tillie throw up on the back seat?" she asked Donna. "I don't smell anything."

"No, Tillie's fine," Donna said. "She didn't faint. Didn't throw up." Donna began to chuckle. "What I mean is, I don't think I have the strength to hold off Tillie if we open up our lunches in the car."

The sound of Donna's husky 'heh, heh' magnified by the speaker system struck Jane's funny bone. Maybe she was getting light-headed from lack of food? Or maybe she was becoming slap-happy after the intense scene at Arthur's estate? For whatever reason, Jane couldn't stop herself, and her giggles came bubbling out in spite of her efforts to suppress them.

Glancing over at Grace again, Jane felt guilty. Grace was not laughing, and she didn't look the least bit amused. Jane bit her lip to control her silliness. Poor Grace must be devastated. And here Jane was - sitting right beside her - tittering like a silly schoolgirl. Some friend, she was.

"What do you think, Grace?" Jane said, trying to keep her voice steady. "Do you want to stop and eat?"

"I thought you'd never ask," Grace said. "My stomach's been rumbling ever since we got in the car."

They agreed to pull over at the next convenience store. "Just stay behind me and watch my blinker," Jane said to Pam through the car's speaker system. "As soon as I see a place, I'll pull over."

"Sounds good," Pam said.

In another few miles, Jane spotted a service area and pulled off the ramp. She turned into a truck stop with rows of gas pumps and a spacious parking area. Attached to the gas station was a convenience store, a fast-food burger restaurant, and a donut shop.

"This okay?" Jane said to Grace as she pulled the car into a parking spot facing a grubby picnic table.

"Suits me," Grace said. "I'm going inside to get something to drink. Do you want anything?"

"I could use a cup of coffee," Jane said. "The donut place probably has decent coffee. What are you going to get?"

"They probably don't have what I need," Grace said. "Which is a shot of whiskey. Or actually a whole bottle. But maybe the convenience store has some wine in their cooler."

Pam parked in a nearby space and took Tillie for a walk on the little plot of dirt beside the convenience store. Donna went inside to the ladies' room. Then they all convened around the picnic table, a splintery wooden table with attached benches. Nearby, a black trash barrel overflowed with the remains of former lunches. A garbage odor wafted around the picnic area, but Jane didn't see another option for an outdoor lunch.

Pam tied Tillie's leash around one of the metal pipes that joined the table to its benches. "There, you go," she said to the dog, "just in case you were planning to go pawing through the stinky garbage."

Jane removed the little bottle of water, a foil-wrapped turkey sandwich, chips, and a bag of chocolate chip cookies from the lunch bag packed by the hotel. Grace handed her a styrofoam cup of coffee, then unscrewed the cap on her wine bottle and offered to pour some into the disposable glasses that she'd bought.

Pam refused. "I'd better not," she said. "I'm driving."

"Me, neither," Jane said, "although I'd sure love a glass. My nerves are a wreck."

"I'll take some," Donna said and held out a glass. "How're you feeling, Grace? Heartbroken?"

Grace snorted. "More like heartburn. I'm so angry at myself, I could spit. I can't believe I trusted that horrible man. What was I thinking? I put our lives in danger, all of us."

"Don't be too hard on yourself," Jane said. "Arthur King is a charmer. Handsome as they come. Manners like a butler on Masterpiece Theatre. It's

196 A BRUSH WITH MURDER

perfectly understandable that you - or any woman, for that matter - would fall for his attentions."

"Not to mention that estate of his!" Pam said. She shrugged. "Anyway, I think it was worth the flirtation with him just to get us a tour of that bonsai collection. Speaking of which, I wonder who will get all those bonsai when he's in prison?"

"I don't think he has children," Jane said. "I guess Henry and Nan will stay on as caretakers until somebody figures out what to do with his estate."

"It belonged to his wife," Pam said. "Remember? He said she was from a rich family. The Parkhursts. Arthur came into all that wealth by merit."

"What do you mean? Merit?" Grace asked. She scowled, finished the wine in her cup, and poured herself more. Jane noticed that Grace hadn't even opened her lunch bag.

"Well, from what Saundra said, he was the poor scholarship kid at a fancy school," Pam said. "Smart enough to get himself in with rich boys. He made Walter Staunton and Teddy Pickridge his best buds. Then he managed to charm the heiress to the Parkhurst fortune and get her to marry him. Arthur got his wealth through merit. He used his brains, his looks, and his social savvy to get what he wanted."

"Yup, I think you're right," Donna said. "I wouldn't worry about his estate. His wife probably had nieces or nephews. Rich families always seem to have lots of relatives. They'll inherit his property."

"Lucky them," Jane said. "That place has got to be worth a fortune."

"And lucky you," Donna said to Grace.

Grace frowned. "Me? Why am I lucky? I'm certainly not going to get anything out of this. Except maybe a reputation as a foolish old woman."

"You never know," Donna said. "There's that portrait Arthur did of you."

Grace looked confused. "Huh?"

"You know how they always say that paintings sell for more after the artist dies?" Donna explained. "Well, Arthur killed Sheryl and practically killed that stable fellow, so he may get the death penalty. Even if they just send him to prison - I bet paintings go way up in price if the painter is convicted of murder."

"I never want to see that painting, again," Grace wailed. "I want to forget that I had anything to do with that man."

"Don't beat yourself up," Jane said. "Nobody knew what he was like underneath that polished exterior."

"Actually, I think you should feel flattered," Pam said. "Arthur King is a man who appreciates the finer things. You're a fine-looking woman. The kind of woman that he was proud to show off."

"Did you ever mention your husband's company to him?" Donna asked. "That probably would have caught his attention, too. I wouldn't be surprised if he did some checking around and discovered that Mickey made a bundle on that corn harvesting gizmo that he invented. As soon as Arthur realized you had a substantial bank account, he turned up the charm volume."

"Judging by his estate," Pam said, "there's no reason to think that Arthur King needed money."

"Oh, he's got to need money," Donna said. "The horses alone must cost him a fortune. Not to mention live-in servants. Maintenance on that fancy property. And all the rest of it."

A tear popped out of Grace's left eye and rolled down her cheek. "I can't believe I encouraged him," she said. "It's just that he's the first man who seemed the least bit interesting since .... Oh, I feel like such an idiot!"

Jane patted Grace s hand. "Nobody could have suspected that he'd turn out to be so despicable," Jane said. "Look - we were at a painting retreat at an upscale garden resort. How safe can a place get? Who would have predicted that a murderer was enrolled in our class?"

"I wonder if he'd ever murdered somebody before," Pam said. "I think he said his wife died of cancer. But who really knows? He definitely showed his true colors today when that policeman started pressuring him. Did you see how he looked at you, Jane, when you led us into the kitchen and had Nan open the garbage bags with the cheese wrappers in them? If looks could kill...."

"I don't understand how the cheese wrappers proved Arthur was the killer," Donna said. "What's the difference if he bought the cheeses from that little shop or a grocery store?"

"Timing," Jane said. "When I brought my notes to the police station today, Goode told me that they were planning to release Sheryl's time of death to the news media tomorrow. He went ahead and told me that her body was put in the lake at 6:30 on Tuesday evening. But that information has been a secret. Except for the police, the only person who knew the time of death is the killer."

"How'd the police determine the time?" Pam asked.

"She was wearing an old-fashioned watch," Jane said. "It wasn't waterproof. The watch stopped when water got in it."

"I still don't get it," Donna said. "How does the time of death prove that Arthur was the murderer?"

"Remember that his car pulled up just after we did on Tuesday evening? Well, we arrived about quarter past seven," Jane explained. "That's why I asked you to check your cell phone - to see what time it was when Bill called you. You got that call as we entered that long drive leading up to the King estate. The GPS shows that it takes about forty minutes to drive to the estate from that cheese shop. We were probably driving slower than Arthur, since he knows the way."

Donna looked puzzled. "So Sheryl was drowned at 6:30, and he got home at quarter past seven. How does that prove Arthur killed her? And what's the cheese got to do with it?"

"When we handed Arthur the bottle of wine, he said he'd just bought cheese from the same shop, The Cheese Board," Jane said. "But he didn't. Those wrappers that the dogs pulled out of the garbage were from Locavore Gourmet. That's the little grocery where I got the cheese and flowers today. You remember that I remarked about how we didn't see his car in the lot near The Cheese Board? And he said he'd parked around back. That was a lie. I couldn't understand why Arthur would lie about which place he'd gotten the cheese from. It didn't make any sense. Then I realized that he had a reason why he wanted to establish where he was at 6:30. The cheese shop was his alibi."

"I thought the supper at his house was his alibi," Pam said. "But you're saying that while we were trying to pick out a fancy bottle of wine, he was killing Sheryl. Then he hurried to the grocery, grabbed some cheese, and sped home?"

"Well, why didn't he go to The Cheese Board after he killed Sheryl?" Donna asked.

Jane shook her head. "He couldn't. Because The Cheese Board closes at 6:30."

"That's right," Pam said, nodding. "I remember the woman was starting to close up when we went in to get the wine."

Donna shrugged. "Well, he could have bought the cheese before he killed Sheryl," she said.

"I suppose he could have," Jane said. "But why would he lie about where he was at 6:30? Unless he wanted to cover up something. He'd shopped at The Cheese Board many times, and he knew it closes at 6:30. He knew it would give him an alibi for where he was at 6:30."

"But wasn't that kind of risky? If the police checked with the shopkeeper, she could have told them that he wasn't there on Tuesday," Pam said.

Jane shrugged. "He probably figured that she wouldn't remember. So many people come in and out of a shop, and he was a frequent customer."

"I still don't understand why he murdered Sheryl," Grace said. "Do you think she saw him attack Dave?"

"We know Sheryl broke up the fight between Dave and Teddy Pickridge," Jane explained. "Then Arthur and Walter arrived and all three of them got into a shouting match with Dave. Sheryl probably waited around until she heard the men leave. Then she started walking back to the hotel. But she must have heard something that made her return to the stable."

"That would have been Arthur returning to attack Dave," Pam said. "Right? That's when he hit Dave with the shovel."

Jane nodded. "So Sheryl hurried back to the stable and found Dave's body in the trough. He was unconscious, and she wasn't strong enough to pull him out by herself. Sheryl was able to hold up his head so he wouldn't drown, but she had to get help. So she wedged him up as best she could, then she cut across the pasture - running to the hotel. That's when she heard us coming up the road."

"I remember you said you saw someone in the shadows behind the barn when you were doing CPR," Pam said.

"I wasn't sure if there was someone back there," Jane said. "But I think that was Sheryl."

"I don't understand why she didn't come out and help," Pam said.

"No need to. We had enough people," Jane said. "We got Dave out of the water and we started CPR while Maggie ran to get help. I think Sheryl stayed behind the barn until the ambulances arrived. I'm guessing that she was trying to sort out what she'd seen and heard. She wanted to think it through before going to the police and making accusations."

"That's basically what Arthur said today," Donna said. "Actually, his words were more colorful: 'Damn meddlesome woman. Always poking her nose into other people's business.'"

"So Arthur caught up with Sheryl in the hospital parking lot on Tuesday night," Pam said, "when she was on her way to deliver Catherine's suitcase. We know Sheryl hadn't gone up to Catherine's room yet, because the suitcase was still in her car after she was killed."

"That's right," Jane said. "Arthur must have convinced Sheryl to take a short walk. The lake was right at the foot of the stairs from the hospital parking lot. He wanted to find out what she'd seen or heard at the stables. Maybe turn on his charm, convince her not to go to the police. But I don't think Sheryl had much patience for Arthur. He was part of the wealthy horse set - practically an aristocrat - and she was just a secretary at the local public school."

"When you introduced me to Sheryl out on the patio," Pam said, "the day I arrived, I remember she seemed to dislike Arthur."

Jane looked at Donna. "Remember when we visited Catherine at the hospital? She talked about how Sheryl and Margaret bought coats and shoes for the needy kids at Gilbertville Elementary. Sheryl had always taken a special interest in Dave. She was his champion. Stuck up for him even after he got into drugs in high school. Got him his job at the Gardens and Horses stable.

"So I think Sheryl stood her ground with Arthur," Jane continued. "She insisted she was going to the police. She might have even told Arthur that she suspected he was the person who attacked Dave. Sheryl seemed like the kind of person who didn't mince words. And she wasn't afraid of anybody. Dave said that when she broke up the fist fight between him and Teddy Pickridge, she stepped right in as if they were kids tussling on the playground. I think Arthur lost his temper when he was talking with Sheryl. Just like he did when he attacked Dave with the shovel."

"Just like he did today when Goode was pressing him about his alibi," Pam said.

"That's right," Jane said. "Arthur picked up a rock and hit Sheryl on the head. Then he shoved her body into the lake."

"Same modus operandi as the attack on Dave," Pam said. "Hit 'em on the head, then push the body into the water. I wonder why the police didn't look for fingerprints on the shovel? Or the rock?"

"They probably did," Jane said. "But the shovel was at the stables. Arthur kept horses there. All kinds of people used that shovel - Dave, all the interns, anybody who had horses there, including Arthur. As for the rock, Arthur probably tossed it into the lake."

Suddenly, Grace gasped. "Arthur called and invited me for a glass of wine after he attacked Dave!" she exclaimed. "Remember? He called my room Monday after class and invited me to join him in the lobby before we went to tour the stables." She looked up, and tears spilled over her the rims of her eyes. "That bastard was using me as his alibi. He left poor Dave for dead at the stable, then sat on the sofa and sipped wine with me!"

"You know," Pam said. "If it wasn't for his temper tantrum today, he probably could have gotten away with it. Both the attack on Dave and Sheryl's murder. There was no hard evidence that he attacked Dave. And there really wasn't much evidence that he killed Sheryl. Just some cheese wrappers. With a good lawyer - not to mention that charm of his - he probably could have convinced a jury that he was innocent."

"His temper was his downfall," Jane said. "Arthur King wasn't a cold-blooded murderer. Not the kind of assassin who plots to kill somebody for money or revenge. I think he was a man who couldn't rein in his temper. If things didn't go his way, he lost it. Nan told me today that he goes into a rage when the dog disobeys. She said she always felt sorry for Malory - hearing the dog's screams - when Arthur punished him. Apparently, he used to unleash his temper on his wife, too."

"I guess he charmed his way through life," Pam said. "And when that didn't work, he exploded. That's the reason he attacked Dave. That's why he killed Sheryl."

"That certainly was some explosion when Goode drilled him about the cheese wrappers," Donna said. "Did you see his face? He turned blood red. Like Mount Vesuvius erupting. The way he roared!"

"I bet Nan - and Henry - were scared to cross him, too," Grace said. She shut her eyes. "To think what might have happened if .... You know, I was actually starting to muse about whether I might want to marry again. He was so polite, attentive. Always offering to help. And then, today, the way he started screaming at that policeman! The fury in his eyes - they looked almost, I don't know, demonic. I don't think I'll ever get that image out of my mind. To think I allowed that monster to touch me. It makes my skin crawl, thinking about it."

Pam nodded. "He was a true-life villain, for sure," she said. "But he did have a great house. And an incredible bonsai collection."

Donna scrunched up her wrapper. She took the last sip of her wine, then stuffed the paper waste into the disposable cup. Tillie sat up, hopeful, at the sound of the crinkling paper. "Oops, sorry, Tillie," Donna said. "I was too hungry to save you anything."

Standing, Donna stretched her arms and massaged her back. She looked around the group. "Well, it's too bad what happened to Sheryl. She was a nice lady. And I'm glad you won't have anything else to do with Arthur King, Grace, since he turned out to be such a horrible man. Although I'm not sure that you ought to forget that portrait." She shrugged. "Who knows? It might pay for another retreat. But now we know whodunnit, I'm ready to head for home. How about you, ladies?"

Back in the car, Jane pulled onto the highway and turned on cruise control. After a few miles, she snuck a sideways glance at Grace. She was relieved when Grace returned her glance with a subdued smile.

"If you want to stop somewhere to pick up some food," Jane said, "just say the word. You didn't eat much of your lunch."

"I had a sour taste in my mouth. But I did save my sandwich for the road." Grace held up her lunch bag. "It was good we stopped, though. I needed to talk through it. I'm ready to erase this painting class from my memory. But I won't let myself forget the Arthur King lesson."

"Which is?" Jane asked.

"'You can't judge a person by his manners. Or his estate,'" Grace said. She bit off a corner of her sandwich and chewed thoughtfully. "What about you, Jane? If you ever turn your notes into a book, what would you say was the moral of this retreat?"

"Hmm, let me think," Jane said. Some advice from the very first art course that she'd ever taken - an art appreciation course in her freshman year - popped into her head. On the first day, her instructor had told them:

'Never judge the value of a painting by the gold in its frame.' Jane repeated that wisdom to Grace.

"Good advice," Grace said. "I'll certainly keep it in mind if we ever go to another art retreat."

Grace finished her lunch, then leaned back on the headrest and closed her eyes. When Jane glanced over at her, Grace had dozed off. The last rays of the afternoon sun slanted across her face. In spite of the day's turbulent events, Grace looked peaceful. Composed. She looks like a painting, Jane thought: The Portrait of an Elegant Woman After a Brush with Murder.

Book Club Discussion Suggestions for

A Brush with Murder

Plot

—Mysteries always include misleading clues and "red herrings." What were the false clues in this story? Did you guess whodunnit before the end? How did you figure it out?

—How did the author's research into horse-racing help her develop the plot?

—How did the author's experience as a painter contribute to the story?

Characters

—Which of the characters did you relate to? If you had to pick someone to go on a retreat with, who would you choose? Who was your favorite character, and why?

—Jane said that taking notes helps to calm her. What helps to calm you in stressful situations?

—Jane and her three friends belong to a painting group that meets weekly. Do you belong to any groups that meet regularly? Do the interactions between Jane, Grace, Donna, and Pam remind you of interactions between members of your group?

—How did the author use the painters' styles to reveal details about their personalities? Did their painting styles match their approaches to solving the mystery?

—Although this book featured female characters, several males were pivotal to the story: Which did you admire? dislike?

Setting

—Have you ever stayed at an inn/resort like Gardens and Horses? How did the setting affect your conference/vacation?

—Have you ever joined a group for a retreat or tour? What was memorable about your experience? What did you learn about yourself from interacting with new acquaintances?

—If you could go anywhere to learn to paint, where would it be?

ACKNOWLEDGEMENTS

I owe this book to good luck and to bad luck.

The Pandemic provided the bad luck - and plenty of it for people around the world, millions suffering mightily and dying lonely. I was one of the lucky few who experienced a silver lining. Forced to shelter in place with idle fingers, I embarked upon this novel. Although I'm the ghostwriter of a memoir - as well as the author of many novels and picture books for kids - I've always enjoyed cozy mysteries, and I wanted to try writing one.

The good luck is an amazing local art center, the Oconee Cultural Arts Foundation, where I connect weekly with a group of writers and a group of watercolor painters. Although we were forced to go virtual during the Pandemic, we kept connecting, and I gleaned the encouragement to write this book. Thanks for inspiring me, Patricia A. Adams, Loretta Hammer, Debra Harden, Diane Norman Powelson, Muriel Pritchett, Janet Rodekohr, Barbara Schell, Susan Vizurraga, and Mia York.

Of course, I have others to thank, notably my husband Chester Karwoski, my constant companion who sits patiently by my side as I immerse myself in my new genre. And my daughters, Leslie Anderson and Geneva Karwoski, who are my cheerleaders no matter what crazy new notion their mom entertains.

Can't get enough mysteries?
Here's a preview of the next
Watercolor Mystery by Gail Langer Karwoski:

SKELETON IN THE ART CLOSET

CHAPTER ONE

While ladling ice from the punch bowl into a glass cup, Jane Roland heard the first scream.

She froze. A scream? Surely her ears had misinterpreted the sound.

Her nerves thawing, Jane picked up the ladle and splashed spiked cider over the ice in the cup. The second scream stopped her mid-splash. This scream was louder and more piercing than the first. Jane put down the cup, lest she drop it.

The third - louder still - was followed by a crescendo of insistent screams which seemed to gain intensity with repetition. The screams were coming from the direction of the Central Gallery.

All of the ordinary noises of an opening night reception at an art gallery - people greeting, laughing, feet shuffling, fabric swishing, glasses tinkling - disappeared. The crowd, with Jane among them, moved as if compelled by a magnetic force. They pushed through the doorway that led out of the Small Gallery toward the source of the screams.

In the larger gallery, the sound was panic personified. Horrifying screams bounced off the brick walls, the plaster ceiling, the polished wood floors. Terror penetrated deep inside Jane's brain and electrified her every nerve, forehead to toes. She stood on tiptoe and strained to locate the source of the sound, but she was a petite woman in a bulging crowd. Grey hairs and balding heads, dangly earrings, sport-coated shoulders, and silken scarves blocked her view.

At last, the screaming dissolved into weeping. Great gasping sobs. And a woman's soothing voice: "No, no, it's not real, Noah. Just a decoration. Because it's Halloween. That's all."

Another scream, this one assuming the shape of words. A child's trembling voice. "Yes, yes, it is. Look. See inside the bones. That grey bumpy stuff. That's marrow inside the bones. So, it IS real. It's from a dead body!"

Jane forced herself, wriggling and pushing, through the mass of bodies and into the eye of the storm. "It's not real," she announced to the small blonde boy gaping at the skeleton that dangled from the ceiling. Jane guessed he was about 6 years old. "I promise you, it's not real. I hung it up yesterday when we were decorating the gallery for the show. It's just a decoration." Turning to the woman kneeling beside the boy, Jane added. "I'm so sorry this scared him."

Jane stood on tiptoe and reached up to touch one of the skeleton's foot bones. She twisted the foot up and down, then looked at the child. "See how light the bones are? They're plastic. There's no marrow inside - just rough plastic with some dirt on it. Do you want me to pick you up so you can touch the bones?" Looking at the woman, Jane said, "His name is Noah? You're his mom?"

The mother nodded.

"It's a pretend skeleton, Noah," Jane continued her explanation, her voice high and shrill with tension. "I found it in the drawing classroom. Artists use this to sketch from. The bones are wired together. See? So the artists can pose the body and draw people in different positions; sitting down, reaching out, stepping forward."

As she babbled, Jane felt a hand on her shoulder. She was relieved to see Ruth Alice Morton, the Director of the art center.

"I had no idea something like this would happen," Jane said to Ruth Alice. "When I saw the skeleton in the drawing classroom, I thought it would be a nice touch. You know, Halloween theme, and this reception on Halloween weekend." Jane grimaced. "It just seemed like a good idea. To me, at least. I admit Chandler was hesitant." Chandler was the show curator. "But he humored me since it was my first time hanging a show. Maybe we should take it down? I don't want it scaring anybody else."

Ruth Alice smiled; a large, sunny smile that came from her whole body and communicated happiness. When Ruth Alice smiled, her brown cheeks, her round shoulders, even her purple-spotted eyeglasses seemed to radiate love and joy. It was one of the reasons - one of the many reasons - that both the artists and the volunteers at the Atkinsville Art Center (the AAC or "Ack" as everyone pronounced the acronym) adored this new director. Of course, part of Ruth Alice's appeal came from following a bad act. The last director had practically eviscerated the center. The treasury had dwindled to practically nothing, not to mention membership and attendance. And, as if that wasn't bad enough, the former director had just taken off. One fine day, he disappeared - into thin air.

"If you want to make AAC inviting for children, this is not the way to do it," said Noah's mother as she stood and dusted off the back of her dress.

Ruth Alice got down on one knee in front of the child so she could talk with him, eye to eye. Do you think we should take down the skeleton, Noah?"

Noah nodded between sniffles.

"Okay, that's what we'll do. First thing tomorrow. Thank you for helping us decide which decorations to use, Noah. We have several schools scheduled to come see this show, and we wouldn't want to frighten any of the kids coming through the gallery, would we?"

Noah nodded again, still sniffling.

Ruth Alice gently took one of Noah's hands. "Art is for everybody, Noah. It makes the world a happier place. Nobody meant to scare you. Jane, here, she was kind enough to help Chandler hang the show. It took them days and days to get all these beautiful pictures hung on the walls. They weren't thinking the skeleton might be scary. Sometimes even grownups make mistakes. And mistakes are how we learn. You know?"

Noah nodded again. This time, he forced a tiny smile. His mother mouthed "thank you" to Ruth Alice and guided the boy away from the skeleton.

"We have some chocolate chip cookies on the refreshment table. Homemade," Ruth Alice called after them. Noah's mother smiled back.

"Well, that was a bit alarming," Ruth Alice said. She exhaled. "Never a dull moment."

"I'm sorry," Jane said. "It never even crossed my mind that the skeleton would scare someone. They're so common this time of year. Do you want me to come and take it down in the morning? I don't think I should bring in the ladder now, with everybody here."

"Don't worry about it," Ruth Alice said. "Chandler is working tomorrow afternoon. I'll get him to help me take it down."

"I don't want you and Chandler to waste your time taking it down. I feel like this is all my fault," Jane said. "It was my idea. Chandler told me he was afraid the skeleton would distract from the art."

"You should have listened to Chandler," a woman said. "Those screams were quite the distraction. I almost passed out."

Two members of Jane's Tuesday watercolor group, Donna Norton and Pam Gerald, had joined them. They stood, punch glasses in hands and smirks on lips.

Donna, her white hair topped with a black and orange beret, began to chuckle. Donna was the oldest member of their group, and she experienced fainting spells because of her high blood pressure. Jane usually found Donna's gruff, "heh, heh, heh," amusing. But right now, she was too tense to laugh.

"You know how I generally pass out whenever I see a dead body?" Donna added, looking at Ruth Alice, Jane, and Pam.

Pam grinned, "Nah, I wasn't worried. If I recall, you only pass out when the dead body is floating in water."

Donna and Pam were referring to their spring adventure at an art retreat, where four members of their group had gotten immersed in a real-life murder mystery involving dead bodies and bodies of water. Jane - as well as Pam's dog - had been instrumental in solving that mystery. When they came home from the retreat, they told the story to everyone who would listen. By fall, everybody at the art center had heard it. Their adventure had even earned itself a title. Pam, who was the poet of their painting group, had dubbed it, "A Brush with Murder." She kept urging Jane to write a whodunnit about their experience.

"I'll come first thing in the morning and get the skeleton down, Ruth Alice," Jane said. "I don't know why I didn't listen to Chandler. He's the one with expertise at hanging a show."

"It's okay," Ruth Alice said. "All's well that ends well. I'll see you in the morning. Right now, I'm going to head over to the office. Who knows?

Maybe those moments of panic will produce a rush in sales."

"I think that only works with gun sales," Donna said. "Not paintings."

"Thank goodness we don't sell guns at the Art Center!" Pam blurted. Her silk scarf slipped off her shoulder, and she grabbed a corner to toss it back into place. Somehow, she managed to dunk it in her glass of cider. "Hmnn, seems I have a wardrobe malfunction," she said. "I'm off to the little ladies room to rinse off this mess. But I'll be glad to relieve you at the punchbowl, Jane, if you feel like you need some down time after all the excitement."

"I'm okay," Jane said. She checked her phone. "My shift is over in about fifteen minutes, anyway."

Jane waved goodbye to her friends and headed back to the smaller gallery, where she was in charge of the table with the adult refreshments. As soon as she got to the punch bowl, she poured herself a full serving of spiked cider, gulped it down, then refilled the cup. What I really need is some spike without the cider, she thought. But I'm driving myself home, so I better go easy.

Of all the members of their painting group, Jane was considered the level-headed one. A short, trim woman, she'd never married, and she had only herself to arrange all the details of everyday living. Now that she was retired, she arranged her days into an orderly routine of painting, singing in choirs, and embroidery - all activities that she dearly loved. Volunteering at the art center was her way of saying thank you for the wonderful life she lived. As she ladled cider into cups, she felt her back muscles begin to relax. Now that she had something to do with her hands, a job to do, Jane's breathing slowed.

"I saw you talking to that little boy. Is he feeling better?"

Jane looked up at Grace Tanner, an attractive woman with lustrous, platinum hair. She was wearing an airy lilac and pink dress that seemed to float around her body. Standing beside Grace was Betsy Winkle. Both were members of Jane's watercolor painting group, a group of six women that met on Tuesdays in the AAC kitchen. Grace had also been part of their now-famous retreat, "A Brush with Murder."

"That dress looks great on you," Jane said as she refilled Grace's cup. "I don't think I've seen you wear it since the retreat. I thought maybe you'd purged it from your wardrobe because it brought back unpleasant memories?"

"You've got a good memory. This is the first time I've worn it since then," Grace said. "But I do like it. And it's not the dress's fault that I let myself get bamboozled by that terrible man."

"Well, I certainly don't think you should let a man get between you and a fabulous dress," Betsy winked, grinning at her mildly ribald remark. "Hey, what was that screaming business about, anyway? The kid just got spooked by the skeleton?"

Jane nodded and sighed. "Yeah, it was really dumb of me to hang that up. I should have known it would scare kids."

Betsy frowned. "Don't beat yourself up," she said. "At Halloween, there are more skeletons scattered around than candy corn. I think that kid was overly sensitive."

Betsy had ear-length brown hair, sensible shoes, and a straightforward, practical view of the world. With a background in occupational therapy, she was generous with her advice and confident about her opinions. Always eager to patch wounds, both medical and emotional, Betsy jumped into every situation with the energy of the Eveready Bunny.

"Dear Jane," Grace said as she reached out to pat Jane's hand. "Anybody who knows you would realize that you never intended to scare anybody. That wouldn't be like you at all."

"You know," Betsy said, as she turned to Grace, "Donna is so right about you."

Grace, clearly puzzled, looked at Betsy. "What do you mean?"

"Whenever Donna tells the story of that retreat, she talks about how you fit your name. Grace. You're so ... well, gracious. All the time. How did your mother know that? To name you."

Grace sighed. "Oh, will you stop that!"

Jane giggled. "Where are your menfolk, you two? Didn't you tell me you were bringing a date tonight, Grace?"

"We left them over there," Betsy said. She pointed at two men - Betsy's husband Jim and Grace's date, a tall attorney named Edward Walker. The men were talking with Maisie O'Rourke and her husband, Win. Maisie was the sixth member of their watercolor group.

"So, what are you going to do?" Betsy asked. "Take down the skeleton?"

Jane nodded. "Tomorrow morning. I don't want to bring in the ladder tonight."

"That big old ladder behind the stage? I better come and help you,"

Betsy volunteered. "You shouldn't be lugging around that heavy thing by yourself. And you certainly shouldn't be climbing a ladder without a spotter. That's the classic recipe for broken bones in older people."

"You're right," Jane said. "Ruth Alice offered to help, but I hate to take her away from her desk. She has so much going on, between coordinating this show and getting ready for all the holiday events." Jane looked around the room. "You know, I'm really glad that so many people came out for this reception. But I hate that everybody will remember it as The Night of the Screaming Child."

"Now that'd be a pretty good title for a whodunnit," Betsy said. "Except it needs a real dead body - not just a plastic skeleton - if anybody's going to read it."

Jane groaned. "Please. Do me a favor and don't go there. The last thing we need after all that screaming is a real skeleton in the art closet."

Betsy burst out laughing, spraying out cider in the process. Jane handed her a napkin. As she mopped her chin, Betsy said, "There, that's your title. Skeleton in the Art Closet."

CHAPTER TWO

The Atkinsville Art Center opened at ten AM on Saturdays. At quarter 'til, Jane sat on the metal bench outside the Gallery Building's front entrance, gazing at the dandelions going to seed around the edges of the bushes. Jane decided the weeds were symbolic: Under the former director, the center had started to go to seed. Thank goodness Ruth Alice was running the center now. Under her skilled and generous leadership, the arts were beginning to flourish again. It was time to weed this area, Jane thought.

The Gallery Building had originally been a school, a red brick building that housed elementary through high school students. As the town's population grew, a second building was added, which was now called the Studio Annex. Together with a freestanding gymnasium, where longtime residents remembered playing basketball and dancing at proms, the three buildings had been the rural town's entire school system. Eventually they were replaced by schools located closer to burgeoning subdivisions. These old buildings had stood, unused and neglected, until a group of artists and art-lovers bought them for a ceremonial dollar. Volunteers had transformed the complex, using donated supplies and sweat equity, into a modern gallery space, classrooms, and an event venue.

As she waited, Jane relived last night's reception in her head. Thankfully, she hadn't gone to bed dwelling on the scene. She'd been able to shut off her brain - probably thanks to the spike in the cider - and get a decent night's sleep. But now, as she stared at the weeds dotting the cement walkway, she felt totally responsible and very guilty about hanging the stupid skeleton. What was I thinking? Maybe I should come in Monday and do some weeding. She was feeling like she ought to pay penance for messing up the opening of the show.

Betsy parked her car and joined Jane on the bench. When Ruth Alice arrived promptly at ten, Jane stood up. "Betsy volunteered to come and help me get the skeleton down," Jane told her. "So you won't have to eat up your morning."

Ruth Alice let them all into the building and turned on the lights. "Oh, you know I don't mind helping," she said. "I'm always glad to support our volunteers. But if you ladies can handle it by yourselves, I'll get busy making out the bank deposit. We really did have a sales rush last night. We sold twenty-nine pieces, and two people said they were going to come by this morning to purchase. It's probably the best opening night we've ever had."

"Way to go!" Betsy said and slapped the flat of her hand against Ruth Alice's palm. "See, Jane, that skeleton was worth its weight in gold. Maybe you should leave it up? That little boy probably won't be back."

"No, but his mother has a piece in the show," Jane said. "So, she'll probably be back, and we told her we were taking it down."

"Besides," Ruth Alice said, "school groups are coming to see the show. Other kids might get spooked, too." Ruth Alice glanced at the clock mounted above the doorway of her office. "Speaking of kids - two Girl Scout troops are coming this morning. So, I better get moving." Ruth Alice scurried off toward her desk, which was piled with papers and brochures.

Jane and Betsy found the ladder propped against the back wall of the dusty storage area behind the stage. The ladder was as heavy as it was awkward, and Jane was grateful that Betsy had volunteered to help. Of all the painters in their watercolor group, Betsy was probably the strongest. Jane always pictured her marching through life with the hardy, no-nonsense attitude of a character in a PBS show about the Scottish Highlands.

They managed to get the ladder down the creaky steps and into the back door of the Central Gallery. After they'd set it up beside the skeleton, Jane climbed up, while Betsy held onto the legs. The ladder swayed and groaned with Jane's every step.

"I wonder how old this ladder is," Betsy said. "The wood looks really old. I bet it's been here as long as the building. This place was built when? In the 1930s? How long does wood last, anyway?"

"Let's talk about that later, shall we?" Jane said. She reached up to pull the skeleton's neck out of the rope that held it. Then, holding the skull, she lowered it into Betsy's arms. Betsy gathered up the wired-together bones and lowered the skeleton to the floor.

Jane reached up again to flip the rope off the hook attached to the ceiling. "I don't think I can reach the hook to unscrew it," she said. "Chandler screwed it in for me, and he's taller than either of us. You think it would be okay to leave it there?"

"Sure, if anybody notices it, they'll think it's left over from a hanging plant."

"Hmm," Jane said. "Not a bad idea. Maybe we should go get a plant and hang it up?"

"With a Halloween theme?" Barb said. "Maybe poison ivy?"

Jane giggled. "Don't make me laugh when I'm up here," she said. "Every time this ladder creaks, I'm thinking, 'It's probably not going to break today. But it's probably been here for nearly a century. So then again, it might.'"

After folding the ladder and storing it behind the stage, Jane and Betsy went back to the Central Gallery to retrieve the skeleton and the rope.

"Where should we put this stuff?" Betsy held up the rope.

"Here, I'll take that," Jane said. "There's a box of rope in that closet behind the door to the tunnel - where all the tools are."

When Jane came back into the gallery, she found Betsy waltzing around the room, holding the skeleton like her dance partner. "We did the mash," she sang as she twirled, "the monster mash." Betsy grinned. "Alas, there's only one of you, Yorick. So poor Janie will have to dance by herself."

The sound of the front door opening interrupted Betsy's song and dance. Jane peeked into the hall and announced, "The Girl Scouts are here. Let's go through the tunnel so the kids don't see the skeleton. I want to put Yorick back where I found him."

Jane and Betsy carried the skeleton down the narrow steps to a damp storage room that smelled like clay and mold. From there, they entered the earthen tunnel that connected each of the buildings in the old school complex. At the door that led up to the Studio Annex, Betsy grabbed the doorknob. "It's locked," she said to Jane.

"I know the combination," Jane said. "Chandler told me. So I could get in when we were getting supplies to set up the show."

"You've been in this tunnel by yourself?" Betsy said. She wrinkled up her nose.

"It's the quickest way to get to the Studio Annex," Jane said.

"But it's kinda creepy. Don't you think? Especially when you pass that locked room off to the side."

"You mean the old bomb shelter? Yeah, I guess it is kinda creepy. It smells downs here, and there are always noises - probably from critters that live in the walls." Jane shrugged. "But I live alone. If I let myself get creeped out by stuff like that, I'd be hiding under my covers every night."

Betsy held Yorick so Jane could punch in the combination to the lock. They went up the wooden steps and entered the spacious atrium of the Studio Annex. Jane noticed that the door to the drawing classroom was ajar. That's odd, she thought. She was sure she'd closed the door on Friday, after she'd gotten the skeleton. There weren't any classes scheduled in that room after lunch on Friday afternoons. Maybe one of the instructors had come in to get something?

"Remind me to tell Ruth Alice that somebody keeps leaving that door open," Jane said. "It's a waste of money and electricity." In this building, the studios and classrooms were heated and air conditioned, but the big atrium wasn't.

There was no need to turn on the light in the drawing classroom because morning sun from ceiling-high windows bathed the room. All the easels were folded and stored against the side wall, just as they'd been when Jane had come in yesterday to get the skeleton. To the right of the easels, the back wall was covered by a wide chalk board. It was clean - erased and washed - just like it was when Jane had last seen it. Along the wall to their right was a narrow walk-in closet where art supplies were stored.

"It's blacker than sin in here," Betsy said as Jane opened the closet door. "Is there a light somewhere?"

"Yeah, wait a minute while I feel for it," Jane said. She stuck her hand into a recess in the shelf on the right and fumbled around until she finally managed to locate the light switch. "Whoever designed this art supply closet didn't make it easy to turn on the light."

"Shall I tuck Yorick in beside his friend?" Betsy asked.

"Huh?"

"Over there. On the shelf," Betsy said. "Where the other skeleton is."

Jane blinked. Sure enough, there was another skeleton lying across the shelf at the back of the closet. The thing was on its back, lying on a woolen blanket. Its skull was looking up, and its arms were crossed across its chest, in the classic skeletal pose.

Jane swallowed. "Um. There wasn't another skeleton when I was here yesterday," Jane looked at Betsy. "And I'm sure I locked this building behind me."

Betsy shrugged. "Well, someone must have brought it in later," she said. "Maybe they let the students take home the skeletons? You know, like a classroom lending library? Kinda gruesome. But the students need models to draw from. And modeling rates for a skeleton are probably dirt cheap. Get it? Dirt. As in, buried six feet under."

Jane's frown did not loosen. "A lending library for bones? I've never taken a drawing class here, but I kind of doubt it." She pushed the blanket to slide the new skeleton farther back on the shelf so there'd be room for Yorick. But the bones weren't wired together. They jiggled and fell apart. "You know, this skeleton doesn't feel like it's made of the same material," Jane said. "And the bones aren't wired together. They're just lying here on the blanket."

Betsy draped Yorick over her shoulder so she could pick up one of the loose bones. Some flecks of dirt fell off the bone. "This isn't the same material," she said.

Even in the dim light of the ceiling fixture, Jane could see that Betsy's face had gone ashen.

"I'm pretty sure these bones are made of bone," Betsy said. "As in: The kind you get from a dead body!"

ABOUT THE AUTHOR

Gail Langer Karwoski is the author of *The Wedding Heard 'Round the World;*
America's First Gay Marriage, as well as fourteen books for young readers. Her
award-winning juvenile novels include *Seaman, the Dog Who Explored the West*
with Lewis and Clark and *Quake! Disaster in San Francisco, 1906.* Gail also wrote
the acclaimed bedtime story, *Waterbeds, Sleeping in the Ocean.* When Gail isn't at
her keyboard, you can find her painting with watercolors. Or reading cozy
mysteries.

NOTE FROM THE AUTHOR

Word-of-mouth is crucial for any author to succeed. If you enjoyed *A Brush with Murder*, please leave a review online—anywhere you are able. Even if it's just a sentence or two. It would make all the difference and would be very much appreciated.

Thanks!
Gail Langer Karwoski

We hope you enjoyed reading this title from:

BLACK ROSE
writing™

www.blackrosewriting.com

Subscribe to our mailing list – *The Rosevine* – and receive **FREE** books, daily
deals, and stay current with news about upcoming
releases and our hottest authors.
Scan the QR code below to sign up.

Already a subscriber? Please accept a sincere thank you for being a fan of
Black Rose Writing authors.

View other Black Rose Writing titles at
www.blackrosewriting.com/books and use promo code
PRINT to receive a **20% discount** when purchasing.

CPSIA information can be obtained
at www.ICGtesting.com
Printed in the USA
BVHW070918021122
650894BV00004B/23

9 781684 339747